A BLANCO COUNTY MYSTERY

© 2020 by Ben Rehder.

Cover art and interior design © 2020 by Bijou Graphics & Design.

All rights reserved.

This novel is a work of fiction. Names, characters, places, and incidents are either the product of the author's imagination, or, if real, used fictitiously. No part of this book may be reproduced or transmitted in any form or by any electronic or mechanical means, including photocopying, recording, or by any information storage and retrieval system, without the express written permission of the author or publisher, except where permitted by law.

This one is for Bob Daughdril,
my hilltop pal and neighbor.

ACKNOWLEDGMENTS

I'm so grateful to everyone who provided assistance, several of them for the 21st time. Many thanks to Tommy Blackwell, Becky Rehder, Helen Haught Fanick, Mary Summerall, Marsha Moyer, Jo Virgil, Stacia Miller, Jim Lindeman, Martin Grantham, John Strauss, Linda Biel, Leo Bricker, Naomi West, Richie West, Joe Hammer, and Blanco County Sheriff Don Jackson. Any errors are my own.

1

Twenty minutes after sunrise on Wednesday, November 20, the Blanco County Sheriff's Office received a call from a motorist reporting a zebra grazing on the shoulder of Highway 281.

"You sure it's a zebra, sir?" Jean, the dispatcher on duty, asked.

"Well, I ain't no Jack Hanna, but I know a zebra when I see one. The black and white stripes sorta give it away."

"Sir, where exactly are—"

"Oh, hang on a sec."

"Sir?"

Jean could hear the man laughing. "Now there's a dadgum camel. This is crazy. It's standing in the middle part of the highway."

The connection was poor.

"The median?"

"I'm not a comedian. I'm telling the truth."

"I said 'the median.'"

"There is no median. Just a turn lane. Buncha cars are starting to back up. Gonna get messy."

"Where are you located, sir?"

"On Highway 281. Should I stop and try to round up this camel? I wouldn't even know how to do it. Do they bite?"

"Sir, please remain in your vehicle. Where are you on Highway 281?" Jean had a hunch.

"About two miles south of town," the caller said.

"South of Johnson City or Blanco?"

"Blanco."

Exactly where Jean suspected the caller would be located.

"I have a unit en route," Jean said. "What is the camel doing?"

"What's it supposed to be doing? Tap dancing?"

"I mean is it moving or giving any indication it might step into traffic?"

"It's just standing there, but we've got a pretty good traffic jam going on now, so I don't think anybody's gonna hit anything. I'm creeping along in the breakdown lane. Oh, God."

"What's happening, sir?"

"Now I'm seeing one of those other things. I can't remember what it's called."

"An animal?"

"Well, yeah, an animal. The kind that spits at you."

"A llama?"

"Right! It's a dang llama! Oh, Lord, you've got about fifteen or twenty animals loose out here. I don't even know what most of these are. It's like a dang African whatchacallit. Savanna."

"Which side of 281 are you on?"

"Southbound."

"Do you see a tall red fence on your side of the highway? The west side?"

"I do, yeah."

"That's the entrance to—"

"It's a zoo! No wonder!"

It was, in fact, the location of Safari Adventure, a zoo and sanctuary that featured a wide variety of exotic animals from several continents.

"Sir, do you see the front gate?" Jean asked.

"Yep, and the damn thing is wide open. And there's a second gate after that, and it's open, too. You want me to close 'em?"

"I really can't ask you to do that," Jean said. It was against her training.

"But I bet you want them closed, so no more animals can get out, huh?" the caller said.

"Are there any other animals nearby?" Jean asked. She was pretty sure there were no predators at that zoo—if she remembered correctly—but she couldn't ask a civilian to place himself in a dangerous position.

On the other hand, if it was safe, he could help stop a bad situation from getting worse.

"I see a lot of animals behind the fences, but none of 'em are near the gates right now," he said. "Hang on, let me put it in park."

Jean waited. She heard a vehicle door closing.

"I'm seeing all kinds of deer and weird-looking cows and some other things I don't even know what they are," the caller said. "This is a trip. I can't believe I never visited this place. I always drove right past it."

"Are you able to—"

"I'm at the outer gate and I can see that the chain was cut. Got some bolt cutters on the ground and—holy crap!"

"Sir, what's happening?"

"There's a body in here. In the tall grass between the gates. A dead guy."

"Are you sure he—"

"Oh, yeah. No question. This guy is absolutely dead. He's blue and—hang on—he's stiff and he ain't breathing."

"Sir, I need you to exit the property and get back into your vehicle. I have multiple units en route."

"Want me to close this outer gate behind me?"

"No, sir. Don't touch anything. Please just get back into your vehicle and remain on the scene until the units arrive."

"Check it out," Red O'Brien said. "Haven't seen one of them in a long time."

"One of what?" Billy Don Craddock said from the passenger seat. He was too busy looking down at his phone.

They were driving east in Red's old Ford truck. They'd driven south through Blanco just minutes earlier, then turned left on Ranch Road 32, heading for a ranch east of Canyon Lake.

"A hitchhiker," Red said. "If you'd quit screwing around on Facebook for half a second, you might see the world around you."

"Sometimes it ain't worth seeing," Billy Don said, but he looked up anyway, just in time to see the guy as they passed. Young guy in an orange jacket. Blue backpack on his back.

Red could tell from the hitchhiker's general attitude that he didn't expect to actually get a ride. No eye contact at all as he walked backward, right thumb extended. No bounce in his step. He was just going through the motions. And the man was right. Red drove past him without the slightest inclination to stop.

A few seconds later, Billy Don said, "We should turn around and pick him up."

"What?"

"Pick him up."

"Why?"

"Why not?"

"Well, that convinces me," Red said.

"Good."

"I was being sarcastic."

"Oh."

"There's not enough room in here for three of us, especially since you count as two people."

"I'll squoosh over."

Red didn't reply.

Billy Don said, "My grandma used to say it's nice to be nice."

"Well, my grandma used to say it's nice not to be murdered by a drifter."

"Dude, there's two of us," Billy Don said. "Besides, it'd be an adventure."

Red kept driving.

"That guy back there might be one of the best people you'll ever meet," Billy Don said. "Hell, he might have the secret to happiness or a long life."

"Or scabies," Red said. "Or body odor. Or a knife."

"Like I said, there's two of us," Billy Don said. "Besides, we got backup in the glove compartment."

He meant Red's Colt Anaconda. Big old .45 revolver.

"Still no," Red said.

"You 'member that time your truck broke down in August and it was about a hunnert and five degrees out?"

Red turned up the radio on an old song by the Edgar Winter Group.

"And that kid in the Jeep gave you a ride home?"
Red kept driving.
"And he didn't even—"
"All right!" Red said. "Jeez. If it'll shut you up."

2

Blanco County game warden John Marlin was checking hunting licenses on a ranch near Pedernales Falls State Park when he got the call, so it took him more than twenty minutes to reach Safari Adventure.

Driving south on Highway 281, he encountered a line of vehicles backed up at least a quarter-mile from the zoo. Some of the vehicles were making U-turns, heading back to Blanco to find an alternate route. Marlin moved to the shoulder in his state-issued Chevy truck, light bar flashing, and began to ease past the standing vehicles.

As he got closer to the zoo, he saw that several county deputies, Blanco city police units, and a state trooper had already arrived at the scene. All of the vehicles had their emergency lights flashing, but, per the instructions Marlin had given earlier over the radio, none had a siren blaring. Several vehicles were parked in the highway to block traffic in both directions.

Marlin got closer and saw a springbok on the shoulder.

Then a sable.

Then an eland.

And an addix.

Fortunately, this stretch of highway was just two lanes wide. Most of the animals were simply standing, somewhat disoriented, perhaps, but not in a panic. Some of the animals were in the roadway, between vehicles, but most were on the shoulders, grazing, and some had jumped fences onto adjoining ranches.

According to reports over the radio earlier, not a single animal had been hit by a car, which was remarkably lucky. All in all, the scene was less chaotic than Marlin would've expected, and most of the motorists were waiting patiently. Several were taking photos or shooting video.

Now Marlin saw a camel.

And a small herd of fallow deer.

Two llamas.

An ibex.

He parked behind Sheriff Bobby Garza's marked unit, not far from the zoo's front entrance. Marlin could see Garza and Lauren Gilchrist, the chief deputy, about forty feet off the highway, between the zoo's parallel ten-foot security fences, in an area that had been cordoned off with yellow tape. The tall grass between the fences prevented Marlin from seeing the body that had been reported by the 911 caller.

When Marlin first heard about the situation from dispatch, he wondered if one of the zoo employees had been killed by an animal. That seemed possible, but why had the chain been cut on the outer gate? Was the person a trespasser? Had somebody wanted the animals to escape? Maybe the death was something more than a tragic accident. For now, though, that was not Marlin's immediate concern. He needed to round up these animals without herding them through the crime scene.

He jumped out of his truck and quickly filled a bucket with cattle feed from a bag he kept in the bed. Never knew when you might need to coax a stray cow back into a pasture. He also grabbed a pair of bolt cutters, then walked toward the nearest deputy, Ernie Turpin, who was attempting to round up a nilgai—a large Asian antelope that stood about five feet tall at the shoulder and weighed at least five hundred pounds.

"You got it under control, Ernie?" Marlin said.

"Oh, sure. You can tell I know exactly what I'm doing."

Turpin had his arms raised, trying to stop the nilgai from going anywhere, but the antelope was confused, and from the looks of it, so was Ernie. The nilgai was used to seeing trolley-loads of visitors trundling around the zoo grounds with buckets of feed. The animals would approach and be fed by hand. They were essentially tame, although it was always wise to exercise caution around any animal that large.

"You trying to dance with him?" Marlin asked.

"I would if it would work," Turpin said. "Think he two-steps?"

"More like four."

"You got a plan?"

Marlin gave Turpin a gesture that said, *Just a minute*, and keyed the microphone attached to his uniform. "Folks, it's Marlin. Can I make a suggestion here?"

The state trooper—an amiable guy named Max—said, "We've been counting on it."

Marlin said, "I'm fixing to see if I can lure some of these guys back inside the fence. There's a utility gate about fifty yards south, so I'll use that one, for obvious reasons. Just make sure everybody remains in their vehicle. There's a good chance some of the animals on the other side of the highway are gonna come running."

"This should be good," Max said.

They picked the hitchhiker up and learned that his name was Garrett, then silence followed for the first mile. Garrett was sandwiched between Red and Billy Don, who stood six-four and weighed three hundred pounds, or maybe more nowadays.

Red was pleased that he couldn't detect any obvious body odor coming from Garrett. On the other hand, Red had to wonder how long it would take for scabies to spread. He wasn't sure what scabies was—or were—but he knew it—or they— spread easily and made you itch.

Of course, there was always the chance that Garrett might not have scabies. He might have something worse. It wouldn't surprise Red if a hitchhiker was carrying any number of strange diseases or conditions. Scabies was just one example. It must've popped into Red's head simply because the name was so creepy. Scabies. Sort of a combination of *scab* and *rabies*. Yuck.

Garrett, possibly without scabies, was sitting quietly, staring at the road ahead.

"So where ya headed?" Billy Don finally asked.

"I'm not real sure," Garrett said. "How far are you going?"

He had a funny accent. Not like foreign or something weird like that, but from the north somewhere. Or the east. Or the northeast. Not from Texas, that was for sure.

"Know where Purgatory Road is?" Billy Don asked.

"Not really."

"Know where Fischer is?"

"No."

"How about the Little Blanco River?"

"I'm not from around here," Garrett said.

"Okay, well, if we stay on this road, we'll pass the Little Blanco River, and then we'll pass real close to Fischer, but you won't even know, 'cause there ain't much there anyway, and then, maybe ten minutes after that, we'll take a right on Purgatory Road. We're going down that way a couple miles."

Garrett appeared to be in his twenties—just a kid—but it was hard to tell, because his skin was kind of weathered, and he needed a shave. Red figured he was an outdoorsman. Or…Red was starting to wonder if the guy was homeless. He was carrying a backpack, which was now cradled in his lap. Red wondered what was in there. Drugs? Booze? Scabies ointment?

"I guess you can just drop me off at the turn for Purgatory Road," Garrett said.

"That'll be fine," Red said.

"But where're you trying to go?" Billy Don asked.

"I'm not sure yet," Garrett said.

"You don't have any kind of final destitution?" Billy Don asked.

Garrett grinned. "A what?"

"A place where you're wanting to end up."

"I thought I might go to the shore," Garrett said.

"The what?"

"The shore. The beach."

"So you mean the coast?" Billy Don asked.

"Yeah, sorry. The coast."

"Gonna fish?"

"No, just hang out. I've never been there."

"Which part of the coast?" Billy Don asked. "Don't go to Galveston. Maybe Port A or Rockport, or go all the way down to South Padre."

"Quit badgering him," Red said.

Billy Don said, "He needs directions, is why. If you keep going east on 32, you'll hit 12, and if you take a left, you'll end up in Wimberley, which is the wrong direction from the coast. But if you take a right, that'll take you to San Marcos and I-35. But then you'll have to decide where you're gonna go."

Garrett said, "Okay, great."

"You got a phone so you can look at a map?" Billy Don asked.

"We'll just drop him off," Red said, because this wasn't turning into an adventure at all. More like a pain in the ass.

"Anywhere's fine," Garrett said.

"What are you doing on 32 if you're going to the coast?" Billy Don asked.

"Honestly, I just wanted to get off 281, because I saw a traffic jam and a bunch of cop cars," Garrett said. "So I turned around and started walking back toward Blanco, and then I decided to take this road."

"You turned around because of the cops?" Red asked, because now he was wondering if Garrett was a wanted fugitive, on top of having scabies.

"More or less," Garrett said.

"You got warrants?"

"No, I just don't like being hassled. Sometimes they hassle me for hitchhiking, or even when I'm just walking."

"Hassle you how?"

"They stop and ask where I'm going. Sometimes they ask to see my ID, even though I haven't done anything wrong."

"'Cause it ain't a free country no more," Billy Don said. "Man can't even walk down the highway. Me and Red figure it's best to avoid the cops whenever possible, on general principle. Right, Red?"

Red grunted.

"I wonder what all them cops was doing down there," Billy Don said. "How many did you see?"

"At least seven or eight vehicles with their lights flashing," Garrett said. "No sirens, though."

"Was it a wreck?"

"I didn't see one. I saw something that looked like a horse running across the road."

"A horse?"

"Yeah, but I was a couple hundred yards away. I don't think it was a horse, but I don't know what it was. Anyway, I turned around."

"That's a lot of cops for a loose horse," Billy Don said. "Or whatever it was."

"That's what I thought," Garrett said.

"That zoo's down in that direction," Red said.

"That's right," Billy Don said. "They got all kinds of weird animals in there. Maybe one of 'em got loose."

"Hope so," Garrett said.

That was a weird comment. Red waited for Garrett to say more, but he didn't. They rode in silence for a moment.

"Don't your feet get sore?" Billy Don said out of the blue.

"They did at first, but now they're pretty tough. I have calluses."

"What's the most you ever walked in a day?"

"Oh, probably thirty miles."

"Damn. I'd be wore out."

"I'm in pretty good shape now. I don't get tired."

"You just get up in the morning and start walking?"

"Sometimes I walk at night, or real early in the morning. It's nice sometimes, especially if there's a moon. But I have to remember that drivers can't see me, so I have to stay way off the road."

Then Billy Don said, "Hey, if you ain't in a hurry to get to the coast, we could probably use a hand with this job down on Purgatory Road. Wanna earn a few bucks?"

Just great, Red thought. That would mean splitting the money three ways, and probably teaching this guy how to do the job. Maybe he would turn it down.

"That sounds good," Garrett said. "What kind of work?"

3

Ernie Turpin said, "Want some help?"

Marlin handed him the bolt cutters. "Can you go down to that utility gate and cut the lock off, if there is one?"

"You bet," Ernie said.

"And there'll be a second gate in the inner fence," Marlin said. "We'll need that one open, too."

"No problem," Ernie said, and he walked south along the fence line.

Marlin shook the bucket filled with cattle cubes and the nilgai looked at him.

Marlin shook it again and the nilgai took a few slow steps forward, nose low, sniffing the air.

"Attaboy," Marlin said.

Three axis deer nearby were watching intently.

Marlin tossed a couple of cattle cubes on the ground, and the nilgai quickly approached and began to gobble them up. The axis deer trotted toward Marlin.

He raised the bucket high and shook it hard for several seconds, so that any animal within a hundred yards could hear it. Many of them could also see the nilgai eating, and that was a signal in itself. A dozen animals began to walk or trot toward Marlin from all directions. That movement in turn spurred more animals to take notice and begin to hurry toward Marlin. They didn't want to miss out on the food.

"You're a damn genius," one of the Blanco city cops said over the radio. "Why didn't we think of that?"

Marlin walked backward along the grassy shoulder, keeping an eye on all the animals, and tossing a few cubes now and then to prevent any animals from getting too close. Within thirty seconds, he was leading a parade of exotic deer, antelope, goats, sheep, and various other ungulates.

Here came a camel and a pair of llamas and some blackbuck antelopes. By the time Marlin reached the small utility gate, Ernie Turpin had it wide open, and Marlin proceeded through it, and then through the inner utility gate, followed by thirty or forty animals in a surprisingly orderly procession.

Ernie Turpin closed the inner gate behind them.

Now Marlin was in the front portion of the zoo, a fenced area of about one hundred acres, which was essentially an enormous holding pen with suitable ground cover for grazing. Scattered clumps of oak trees provided shade, and the animals had access to several water tanks, or what some folks would call ponds or small lakes. Here, a variety of species mingled together—not unlike the savannas of Africa, but without any predators.

Marlin was elated to see dozens of animals still inside this pen, which meant there were probably very few animals still running loose outside the zoo.

"I guess that's how you do that," a Blanco city cop said on the radio.

Max, the trooper, laughed and said, "The Pied Piper of Blanco County. I hope somebody got that on video."

"See how some of the mortar between the rocks is crumbling?" Billy Don said. "What we're gonna be doing is chiseling some of that out and replacing it with fresh mortar. Depending on how that goes, we might need to replace a couple of the rocks here and there, but we'll try to avoid that if we can."

"Okay, cool," Garrett said.

They were standing in front of a ranch entrance with twin limestone columns on either side of the gate. Nothing too fancy, but it was a nice-looking arrangement. It just needed a little bit of maintenance.

"Ever done this kind of work before?" Red asked. They were all drinking coffee. That's what you did before working at a job site—drink some coffee and shoot the breeze a little. Everybody knew that was an unwritten rule.

"I haven't," Garrett admitted.

"Ain't real difficult," Billy Don said. "Just gotta take it slow and make sure you don't damage the limestone."

"I can do that," Garrett said.

"Not as easy as it looks, in spite of what he says," Red said.

"I'll take it slow," Garrett said.

"It's not like you can just step right up and be a mason," Red said.

"I'm sure it isn't," Garrett said.

"Masonry is a goddamn art form, to be honest," Red said. "Takes a hell of a lot of skill and experience."

"I'll bet it does."

"That's true sometimes," Billy Don said. "But this job right here is pretty simple."

"You've gotta match the new mortar to the old mortar or it looks like crap," Red said. "Billy Don's standards ain't always what they should be."

"How long have you been doing this kind of work?" Garrett asked.

"A long damn time," Billy Don said. "But we haven't been working as much lately."

Here it comes, Red thought. *Billy Don bragging again.*

"Why's that?" Garrett asked.

"We went to Vegas a while back and I won a shitload of money at the blackjack tables," Billy Don said. He sort of tossed it out there casually, like it was no big deal.

"Wow, that's really cool," Garrett said.

Red knew that Billy Don wasn't done yet.

A truck passed on Purgatory Road. Red could hear a dog barking somewhere in the distance.

"Wanna guess how much?" Billy Don asked.

"I don't know. Five thousand?" Garrett said.

"Nearly a hundred and fifty thousand dollars," Billy Don said.

"Apiece."

"Jesus Christ," Garrett said. "Seriously?"

"Yup."

"Damn, man, that's incredible. You won all that just by playing blackjack?"

"Yup."

"You must be pretty good."

"Not to brag—"

"Too late," Red said.

"—but I'm damn good."

"How about you?" Garrett said to Red.

"How about me what?"

"You play blackjack?"

"I ain't got time for card games," Red said. "Reason I got half the winnings is 'cause half the money he started with was mine."

"See, we won fifty grand in a pig-hunting contest," Billy Don explained. "Then we took that to Vegas and used it as our grubstake."

"A pig-hunting contest?" Garrett said, grinning, amused by the idea.

"Well, it was more of a bounty situation," Billy Don said. "This kid died in a motorcycle wreck when he hit a wild pig, so his daddy wanted some of them pigs wiped out. So he caught a pig, tattooed its ear, then turned it loose and said whoever killed it would get fifty grand."

Garrett was nodding. "Jeez, that's brilliant. So everybody was shooting pigs left and right, hoping they'd get the one with the tattoo."

"Damn right they was," Billy Don said. "People were coming from all over for a shot at that pig. Put a serious dent in the pig pop'lation around here."

"So which one of you shot the pig?" Garrett asked.

Which was a whole other story in itself. The truth was, some lowlife East Texas hunters had shot the pig, but they were cheating assholes, so Billy Don stole the pig and Red acted as his getaway driver.

"It was a team effort," Red said.

All this talk about money in front of a stranger was making him nervous. He still had well over $100,000 stashed in an 800-pound gun safe in his closet, and the damn thing was like a miniature Fort Knox—

fireproof, waterproof, and burglar-proof—but you never knew when some scheming hitchhiker might pull a gun and force you to open it.

So Red added, "We took all that money and put it in the stock market."

Good to put that out there before Billy Don could open his fat mouth and reveal that they kept the cash at home. Normally Red would've said they'd stuck it in a bank, but he hated banks, and he couldn't even stand to lie about putting money in a bank. Banks were for suckers who didn't care if they were used as pawns in a system run by rich people. Of course, the stock market wasn't much better, but Red liked the idea of being someone who owned stock. Sounded impressive.

"That's cool," Garrett said. "I've never put any money in the stock market."

Well, that's a big surprise, Red thought. "It can get sort of complicated," he said.

"My dad was a financial adviser, so I learned a little about it," Garrett said. "I just never had any money of my own. What did you invest in?"

"Huh?"

"I was just wondering what you invested in."

"Mostly conglomerations," Red said, using a word he'd heard before. "And acquisitions."

Garrett gave him a funny look. "So did you buy individual stocks or mutual funds?"

"Both of 'em, I think," Red said. "I don't really remember, 'cause I had somebody like your daddy help me out."

"Making any money?"

"Yeah, a little. Not a lot. You know what? We should probably get to work."

By the time Marlin exited through the outer gate, traffic was moving again—slowly, but moving. He walked back to his truck on the highway shoulder and grabbed some binoculars. He climbed into the bed, then stepped on top of the metal toolbox mounted directly behind the cab.

Better view from up here. He raised the binoculars and scanned the horizon in every direction. No more loose animals that he could see, but he would need someone from the zoo to conduct an inventory. Problem was, the zoo was closed on Wednesdays.

But where was the owner, Albert Cortez? He lived in a cabin to the rear of the property. Marlin didn't know the man well, but he knew that Cortez's life revolved around the zoo. Marlin had attended the grand opening thirteen years earlier and Cortez had struck him then, and later, as an intelligent man with a deep passion for animals. As a result, he'd run this place with the welfare of his menagerie as his top priority.

In other words, Albert was a damn good guy. He wasn't in it to get rich, which wasn't likely at $8 a ticket. He was in it to teach people about fauna from around the world. The slogan of the zoo, painted on the sign right out front, was "Bringing the whole wild world to Blanco County."

Unfortunately, Marlin's gut told him Albert wouldn't be making an appearance anytime soon—because he was probably lying in the grass while Henry Jameson, the crime-scene technician, took photos, examined the body for injuries or wounds, collected any available evidence, and tried to establish the victim's identity.

Accident? Natural death? Murder?

Marlin had to set those thoughts aside and focus on the task at hand. His work wasn't done here yet.

4

They were just about to start working when Red received a text from Mandy, his girlfriend. She was a beautiful blonde gal, but not beautiful in a big-city selfie-taking kind of way. More in the way of a woman who turns heads when she struts into a beer joint wearing tight jeans and a low-cut top, halfway soused and looking for trouble. Red's favorite kind of gal.

Mandy's best feature, if you asked Red in polite company, was her gorgeous blue eyes. But if it was just the guys listening, Red would admit it was her amazing body, which was the reason he'd finally broken down and gotten an iPhone. That was because Mandy would occasionally send him a really good photo—the kind of photo you don't share with anyone else—and his old phone, a cheap Korean knockoff, didn't do the photos justice.

Now he walked over to his truck, where he could enjoy the photo, if she'd sent one, without Billy Don trying to peek over his shoulder.

Unfortunately, it was just a bunch of words.

Hear about the crazy stuff at that zoo south of blanco? Mandy asked.

Red used one finger to peck out a reply. *Whats going on?*

He could see that little bubble with three dots in it, which, according to Billy Don, meant she was typing something. A new text popped up a few seconds later.

Bunch of animals got out and were running all over the hiway, and somebody said they found a dead guy.

Red said, *The animals found a dead guy?*

She said, *No the cops did at the zoo and the rumor is somebody killed him.*

Red opened his mouth to call out to Billy Don and Garrett, but then he changed his mind. He wanted to know the full story first.

He sent a reply. *How many annimals.*

Sometimes he forgot proper punctuation or spelled a word wrong, which was okay, because Mandy did, too.

A lot, like a hundred or something, maybe more.

Red mulled that over for a minute. He'd driven past that zoo countless times, and he knew they had two ten-foot fences running around the entire thing. Secure as hell. There might've been one or two animals that could've jumped those fences, but why would they? They had all the food they wanted, and good shelter, and other animals of their kind to get romantic with. Sounded like a damn paradise to Red.

Any idea who it was, he asked.

Nobody knows yet. I heard its someone that works there. Who knows? Lots of gossip flying around.

Then he said, *They think the killer let the animals out on purpose?*

Sure looks that way, Mandy said. *Someone said both gates were open.*

Red thought about the conversation earlier in the truck, when Billy Don had said maybe one of the animals had gotten out, and Garrett had said, "Hope so."

Why would he hope that? Seemed a little weird that a guy would want a wild animal running loose in traffic. There were already enough deer, feral pigs, and other critters creating driving hazards around here without some extras being thrown in from a zoo.

Let me know if you here anything else, Red replied.

K, Mandy said.

And maybe send me a picture if you feel like it, Red said, and he added one of those smiley face emoji thingies.

She replied with an emoji of ruby-red lips, which wasn't nearly as good as the photos she normally sent, but that was okay, as long as it didn't become a habit.

Marlin sat in his truck with his phone at the ready. He needed to contact as many nearby landowners as possible to alert them about the loose exotics. The estray law would apply in this situation, just as if the zoo animals were traditional livestock. Any landowner who shot or stole any of the animals could face a civil suit, and theft of livestock was a state jail felony.

As he dialed the first number—attempting to reach a man who owned three hundred acres just north of the zoo, on the same side of the highway—Marlin spotted a KHIL news van pulling to the shoulder on the other side of 281. Marlin was glad to see it. The media coverage would help spread the word and protect both the public and the animals.

The call he was making went to voicemail.

Hi, it's Kent. Please leave a message and I'll get back to you real soon.

After the beep, Marlin said, "Hello, Mr. Flodin, it's John Marlin. If you haven't heard, a bunch of animals got loose from the zoo next door sometime early this morning. If you see one, please give me a call, will you? And spread the word, if you don't mind. I know we have some hunters in this area, and all of those animals are off limits, legally speaking. Appreciate your help."

Marlin dialed another number, got voicemail again, and as he was leaving the same message, he saw that Kitty Katz, the longtime reporter for KHIL, had emerged from the news van and was waving at him from across the highway. Now she was pointing at a microphone in her hand. Her question was obvious. *Will you do an interview?*

He signaled back through his open window. *Stay there. I'll drive over.*

"Might rain later," Red said.

Garrett glanced at the sky. "Not many clouds."

They'd been working for about thirty minutes, and the truth was,

Garrett was doing a fairly decent job with the chisel. Meanwhile, Red had been trying to think of a way to get information out of the kid. Had to be subtle. Didn't want to make him feel like he was being questioned.

Red hadn't mentioned the dead body at the zoo yet, but it would only be a matter of time before Billy Don heard about it on his phone and blurted it out. No way would he be able to keep something like that to himself.

"Speaking of the weather, we had a terrible drought a few years back," Red said. "I mean, we get droughts all the time, but this one was especially bad. Remember that one, Billy Don?"

"Yep."

"And you asked why it always rains after a drought—and you weren't kidding."

Garrett smiled at that one.

"Whatever," Billy Don said.

"That drought got so bad that everybody was clearing cedar, because they suck up so much water," Red said. "Then that woman came down from Minnesota or somewhere, upset that we were gonna harm some kind of rare bird by chopping down all the cedar trees. Turns out the bird uses the cedar bark to build nests, or some bullshit like that. Remember that, Billy Don?"

"The red-necked sapsucker," Billy Don said.

"That's right," Red said. "That was a strange deal. She was a tall, good-looking, blonde lady, and she had some strange little dude with her. That guy was a major weirdo. I wouldn't have cared why they were here, except this rich old man died and left me his brush-cutting business, which was mostly a bunch of tree-clearing machines—"

"The BrushBuster 3000," Billy Don said. "That's what they was called. Because that's how much pressure the pincher cutting blades could apply—three thousand pounds per square inch."

"You're interrupting my story with useless trivia," Red said. "Anyway, the weird little dude blew up all of my machines—well, all except one, and he tried to kill both of us with it."

Red was wanting to see how Garrett would react to that kind of extreme behavior.

The hitchhiker stopped working for a second. "That's crazy. What happened?"

"Drove it straight into the trailer on the job site. Me and Billy Don were on the front porch, and we had to dive inside."

"So we wouldn't be kilt," Billy Don said.

"And still it was pretty close," Red said.

"Broke my damn arm," Billy Don said.

"I got a big gash on my leg," Red said.

Garrett had a strange expression on his face, and now he was shaking his head. "Between that and your Vegas trip and the pig-hunting contest, you guys lead some interesting lives."

"You got that right," Billy Don said. "That ain't even the half of it. We could tell stories all day. Like the time we trapped what was supposably a chupacabra. Or when Red shot a guy dressed in a deer suit."

"Why was Red dressed in a deer suit?" Garrett asked.

"No, the other guy was."

"What's a deer suit?"

"You know—a suit that's supposed to make you look like a deer. It was dark out, so it kinda worked."

"I was *telling* a story," Red said.

"Whatever," Billy Don said.

"What happened to the weird little dude?" Garrett asked.

"Well," Red said, "as he was coming at us with the tree cutter—"

"The BrushBuster 3000," Billy Don said.

"—I fired a couple shots at him, and then he plowed into the trailer, and he ended up dead. Thought at first I'd killed him, but it turned out he'd broken his neck in the crash."

"That has got to be the wildest shit I've heard in a long time," Garrett said. "And I've heard a lot of wild shit."

For some reason, Red took pride in that.

He said, "He was way out of line, huh? Getting all crazy like that."

"Yeah, I guess," Garrett said.

I guess? Red thought.

"He tried to *kill* us," Red said. "We hadn't done nothing, but he wanted to kill us."

"But you owned the tree-clearing machines," Garrett said.

"So what?"

"I'm not saying he was in the right, but maybe he wasn't really trying to kill you."

"Then what the hell was he doing?"

"Maybe he was just trying to do something, you know, to make a big impression and draw attention to the problem. Maybe he was even willing to die for a cause he believed in. Maybe he knew you were going to shoot at him."

Red had never considered that possibility before. So he considered it now and promptly concluded it was bullshit.

"Maybe that's a lot of maybes," he said. "I'd say the guy was just plain nuts. Who wants to die for some stupid bird?"

"I bet he didn't think it was a stupid bird," Garrett said, "especially if he traveled all the way down here from Minnesota to protect it."

By this point, Red was pretty sure he and Garrett would not get along on a long-term basis.

"Little son of a bitch cared more about birds than people," Red said.

"That kind of thing—taking a stand—changes the world," Garrett said. "Think of the guy in Tiananmen Square."

"Where?" Red asked.

"Or the students at Kent State."

"Never heard of it," Red said.

"Or Nathan Hale," Garrett said.

"The Skipper on *Gilligan's Island*?"

"Or, hey, what about the men at the Alamo?"

Damn it. That was a good point.

5

"Can you tell us what's happening out here today?" Kitty Katz asked, then held the microphone under Marlin's chin.

He had never been enthusiastic about appearing on camera, but it helped to remember that KHIL had a much smaller viewership than the stations out of Austin and San Antonio.

He said, "Quite a few animals were able to get out of the zoo sometime early this morning and we were lucky to get them rounded up before we had any accidents. Thankfully, all of the motorists were patient and cooperative and we got the job done."

"I understand video is already going viral of you leading a parade of animals back into the zoo like a modern-day Pied Piper," Kitty said, smiling. "How did you make them follow you like that?"

"I just used some cattle feed and I guess they were hungry. It worked okay."

They were standing on the east shoulder of the highway, well away from traffic.

"How were the animals able to escape? My understanding is that the zoo has two ten-feet fences encircling it, as well as several other safety measures."

"We're still looking into that," Marlin said, "but both gates were open—I can tell you that much. We have not been able to contact the zoo owner or any employees yet, but the zoo is closed today, so it might be a while before we have any answers."

Before the camera had rolled, Marlin had cautioned Kitty Katz that he would take no questions about the body found on the zoo premises. She would need to speak with Bobby Garza or Lauren Gilchrist about that later, if they were prepared to do an interview. He knew Kitty Katz was a trustworthy reporter and wouldn't ambush him with any unexpected questions.

She said, "Are any animals still loose?"

"We just don't know, but we're hoping people will call the sheriff's office if they see anything out of the ordinary."

"Are any of the animals dangerous?"

"Most of them are tame, but any that are still loose might be hungry or agitated at this point—maybe a little disoriented from being in new surroundings—so if you see one, it would be best not to approach it. Just call it in."

"What kinds of animals might still be loose?" Kitty asked.

"Well, this zoo includes a wide variety of deer and antelope from all over the world, plus camels and zebras and llamas and a lot more. I should point out that it is illegal to shoot any of these animals. That would be no different than shooting a cow that crossed onto your property."

Kitty Katz said, "What is the penalty for—"

The loud crack of a rifle shot stopped Kitty in mid-question.

"Where're you from, anyway?" Billy Don asked. "That accent of yours is just plain weird."

"*My* accent?" Garrett said, laughing.

They were taking a short break for more coffee. Chiseling mortar wasn't a particularly strenuous job, but Red figured sixty straight minutes of work deserved a reward.

"You gotta admit you talk funny," Billy Don said.

"I sound normal where I come from."

"Which is where?"

"Michigan. Born and raised."

"When'd you leave?" Billy Don asked.

"A while back."

"And where'd you go?"

Red couldn't imagine why Billy Don had the slightest interest in any of this.

"California for a while, and then over to Colorado, and then I decided to visit the south."

Red was seated on his tailgate, phone in hand. He sent Mandy a text.

We picked up a hitchhiker earlier.

She didn't answer right away.

So he added: *Guess where.*

"You like it?" Billy Don asked.

"The south?" Garrett said. "The weather is great, except, Jesus, it gets hot in the summer."

Red added: *Not far from the exxotic zoo.*

"How 'bout the people?" Billy Don asked.

"Uh," Garrett said. "Well. Some of them are really nice."

Red sent another text: *He said he hoped some animals got out, what do you make of that?*

"Just some?" Billy Don said. Then he laughed. "Yeah, I guess that's true. We got some good people, and we got some real assholes."

"That's true just about anywhere," Garrett said. "I ran into a real weirdo yesterday. You happen to know a guy named Trevor?"

"Don't think so," Billy Don said.

"He gave me a ride from Marble Falls to Johnson City."

Sure makes you wonder don't it, Red said in another text.

"Why'd you leave Michigan?" Billy Don asked.

"That's a long story," Garrett said.

"But a good one?" Billy Don asked.

"I don't know. I guess."

"Then go on and tell it."

"Maybe later," Garrett said.

Red stepped behind a cedar tree to take a leak, and when he came back, Billy Don had his phone in his hand. "Check this out, Red," he said. "They found a dead guy at that zoo."

"What are you talking about?" Red said, and he stole a glance at Garrett.

The hitchhiker had a look on his face like he'd accidentally drunk from a beer bottle filled with tobacco spit. Red could relate, because he'd done that a couple of times himself. Luckily, it had been his own spit, not somebody else's.

Kitty Katz flinched and blurted out, "Oh, fuck!" and then covered her mouth in embarrassment.

Marlin laughed, which seemed to ease her nerves.

The shot was loud enough that anyone unfamiliar with high-powered rifles might think the shooter was very close by. But Marlin estimated the distance to be more like three or four hundred yards away, probably on the property just south of the zoo.

"I am so glad we aren't live," Kitty said. "What was that? I mean, I know what it was—a shot—but should we be worried about it?"

"I don't think so, but I need to go check it out. You can call me later if you have any more questions."

She thanked him, and as Marlin walked toward his truck, his phone began to ring. Bobby Garza calling.

Marlin answered by saying, "On my way over there now."

The men had known each other for decades and had worked together for many years, so it wasn't unusual for Marlin to be able to anticipate exactly why Garza was calling.

"You get a bead on it?"

"Think it was just south of the zoo."

"You know that landowner?"

"Met him once when he bought the place, which was maybe three or four years ago. I left a voicemail for him fifteen minutes ago, but haven't heard back."

Marlin climbed into his truck and started it up. He was the only law-enforcement officer on the scene who could legally enter private property to investigate the shot. The other officers would not have probable cause. They all knew that the shot was likely unrelated to the body at the zoo, but it could mean someone had just killed one of the exotics. Or it was simply a hunter taking a legal kill—perhaps a white-tailed deer or feral pig. It was, after all, deer hunting season in Texas.

Shots in this area were common. But Marlin had every right as a game warden to enter private property and make sure all hunting laws were being followed.

"Keep me posted," Garza said.

"Will do," Marlin said, pulling onto the highway. "How's it going over there?"

"Got a John Doe and we don't know how he died. Well, we know—it's a deep puncture wound to his neck—but we don't know what caused it yet. If it was a gunshot, there's no exit."

"So it's not Albert Cortez?"

"Nope. Young guy. Dark hair. Average height and build. No wallet and no ID. He had a phone, but it's an obvious throwaway."

"That says a lot right there," Marlin said as he pulled onto Highway 281.

"Yep. We're still trying to find Albert. I sent Ernie to do a welfare check inside the cabin, but Albert wasn't there."

Marlin was wondering if the dead male was one of the zoo employees. Just because the zoo was closed today, that didn't necessarily mean all of the employees were off. Marlin wasn't knowledgeable about the day-to-day workings of a zoo, but obviously the animals would need to be fed, and there were likely some other tasks and chores to be done, such as cleaning pens.

"Any vehicles at the house?" Marlin asked.

"A truck, which comes back to Albert—his only registered vehicle. We'll get search warrants for that and his house later if he doesn't show up soon. Right now we've got a couple of employees heading to the station. We'll see what they can tell us. Lauren is gonna take off now and go interview them."

Lauren was a skilled investigator and interviewer. She also had a self-assured but laidback personality that made people open up. Marlin knew that not just from working with her, but because he and Lauren had dated decades earlier, when they were students at Southwest Texas State University in San Marcos.

When she'd first come to work at the sheriff's office, Marlin had worried that their past relationship might create some awkward moments. Fortunately, after a moderately bumpy start—which included the revelation that Lauren had begun to date Marlin's best friend, Phil Colby—everything had gone just fine.

"Okay, I'll let you know what's going on over here," Marlin said, as he eased his truck onto the shoulder, not far from a modest ranch gate made from horizontal galvanized pipes.

They both hung up and Marlin stepped out of his truck.

The man who owned this property was named Darren Meyer. Marlin had interacted with him exactly one time—right after Meyer had bought the property. Marlin had stopped to say hello when he'd seen Meyer out on the highway, collecting his mail. Quiet guy. Neither friendly nor unfriendly. Said he wasn't a hunter and wasn't planning to let anyone hunt on his place. Gave Marlin his phone number, but Marlin had never had a reason to use it, until today.

Marlin stopped at the gate, saw that it was locked, and called out, "State game warden."

He waited five seconds, then climbed over it, and began walking along the caliche driveway.

This ranch—five hundred acres—was thick with live oaks, cedar trees, and tall grass. No cattle or goats grazing on this place.

Marlin pulled out his phone and opened Google Maps. Went to satellite view. Saw that the house was roughly a mile off the highway. There were no other buildings between the gate and the house.

He kept walking slowly.

After three minutes, he'd covered at least two hundred yards. The person who had fired the shot could be long gone. Or back at the house. Or maybe the shot had come from farther away than Marlin had estimated. The next property to the west? Or to the south? Sound could really carry in these limestone hills. Hard to pinpoint, sometimes.

He kept walking, heading west. Came around a bend and saw a man in a green army jacket holding a scoped lever-action rifle, facing south.

"State game warden," Marlin called out.

The man turned and saw Marlin coming. Forty yards separated them. Even at this distance, Marlin could tell it wasn't Darren Meyer. This man was much younger. Had a scruffy beard. Was several inches taller.

"State game warden," Marlin repeated as he took a few more steps.

The man raised the rifle and pointed it at Marlin.

6

Albert had driven south at first, because that was just the natural way to go. Pull out of the zoo entrance and take a right—south.

Then he realized he needed to think things through. Pick a destination. Come up with a plan. Or should he even bother? It was futile, wasn't it?

He decided there was no harm in taking time to think things through, so when he reached San Antonio, he went west on Interstate 10. Had plenty of time to think.

Zoos are prissons.

That's how it had all started—with that creepy note in the mail. But Albert hadn't seen it for what it really was. Why was he wasting time thinking about that now? It was too late to react differently. Time to focus on the future, such as it may be.

Should he go to El Paso? Was that far enough? Should he keep going? California? The Northwest? If he tried to go to Canada or Mexico, would his name raise a red flag? By now, the cops would be wondering where he was, of course. Asking friends and employees where he might be. Asking when they'd talked to him last. Maybe they'd already identified the body. Maybe they'd already figured out the make, model, and license plate of the rental car Albert was driving.

Wouldn't be long before they put out an APB, or whatever they called it nowadays. Would they monitor the airlines and border crossings? A photo of him could zip from a computer in central Texas to a phone or computer in California in a millisecond.

At 9:38, just west of the town of Junction, he passed a state trooper parked on the shoulder. Same side of the highway as Albert. Running radar, obviously. Albert wasn't speeding. The speed limit on this wide-open stretch of interstate was 80 miles per hour, and Albert had the cruise control pegged at 75. Reasonable. Not so slow as to draw attention.

But the trooper pulled onto the highway and fell in behind him.

Albert was all alone. No other vehicles in sight.

He swallowed hard. His heart was beginning to thump hard in his chest.

The trooper was now fifty yards back, holding a steady speed.

Running his plate? But why? The trooper would have no probable cause to pull Albert over, would he? Or would they say he'd stolen the car? That he was a fugitive? Had the cops in Blanco already pieced it together?

His palms were moist on the steering wheel. Gripping it hard.

He readied himself for the traffic stop. He'd give up, of course, and then keep his mouth shut. Refuse all questions. Hire an attorney. He had plenty of money saved up. The attorney could tell his story for him. Help him obtain a deal. Arrange a new life for him. Start over. Again.

A Corvette in the oncoming eastbound lanes zoomed past at about 100 miles per hour. The trooper braked hard, whipped around, crossed the median, and gave chase.

Albert watched in the rearview mirror for several seconds, just to be sure.

Then he took a deep breath.

Marlin scrambled for the nearest tree—a tall cedar no more than twenty feet away. He had to stand sideways for the trunk to provide full cover.

"State game warden!" Marlin yelled. "Put the rifle down!"

No response.

"You hear me?"

He pulled his .357 from its holster. Not easy to make an accurate shot with a revolver at this distance.

"Put the rifle down!" Marlin yelled again. "Game warden!"

This was not the first time a hunter or landowner had failed to recognize that he was a game warden and had pulled a weapon, thinking he was a trespasser. All game wardens had to deal with that situation from time to time. But it usually happened at night, or when there was a greater distance between them. Or when the subject was drunk or stoned.

By now, Marlin had expected to hear the man shout his apologies—or to at least acknowledge that he had heard what Marlin was saying—but all was silent.

Marlin could either radio for backup or take a quick peek around the tree. Surely this was a misunderstanding. Perhaps the man was deaf or visually impaired? Marlin had to take these possibilities into consideration.

He took a quick peek around the trunk of the tree. The man was nowhere to be seen.

"Thanks for coming in," Lauren Gilchrist said.

"Oh, no problem," the young woman said. "I'll help if I can, but I don't even know what happened out there."

Her name was Tracy Lavelle. Probably 27 or 28. Medium-length brown hair. Tall and slender. Tanned skin. Outdoorsy. She was the assistant zookeeper at Safari Adventure—second in charge after Albert Cortez.

They were seated in one of the interview rooms at the sheriff's office. Lauren had offered coffee or a Coke, but Tracy had declined. Ernie Turpin was conducting an interview in the adjoining room with another zoo employee.

Lauren said, "First question—do you have a list, or some kind of inventory, of every animal in the zoo?"

"Oh, sure. Absolutely. I could list them all by heart. But if you need an actual printed list, I can get it."

"We'll need to determine how many animals are still loose," Lauren said. "Can you help with that?"

"Sure. No problem."

Lauren shifted gears away from public safety concerns and toward the investigation.

"Have you talked to Albert or seen him this morning?" Lauren asked.

"I have not. I was on my way to work when the deputy called."

"When was the last time you talked to him?"

"The deputy?"

"No, Albert."

Tracy laughed. "Oh. Sorry. I talked to him at work yesterday afternoon, when I was leaving. It wasn't Albert, right? I mean the dead person you found?"

"No, it wasn't him, but we're having trouble getting in touch with him."

"So who was it, then?"

"We haven't been able to make an ID yet."

"You think it's one of our zoo employees?"

"We just don't know yet. I'm sorry."

Lauren had asked Deputy Callie Young, a recent hire, to check the zoo's website, Facebook page, and other social media accounts for photos of employees to see if she could make a match with the dead man. Callie had only been here for a month, but she seemed to be a great fit so far—not just in the sheriff's office, but in the community.

"Do you think Albert is okay?" Tracy asked.

"We have no reason to think he isn't, but we'd like to find him, obviously. Did he say anything to you yesterday about any plans for today? Was he planning to go anywhere this morning?"

"He didn't say anything to me," Tracy said. "Normally he'd tell me if he wasn't going to be there. He does tend to run errands on Wednesday, because we're closed, but not always."

"How do you get the gates open when he's gone? You have keys?"

"Yeah, I do, and a couple of the other senior employees."

"How many employees are considered senior?"

"There's me and four tour guides that have been there several years."

"What would their job titles be?"

"To be honest, it's kind of a casual place to work. We don't really have titles or, like, a hierarchy. After Albert and me, everyone is kind of equal, but the newer employees generally take orders and learn the ropes from the ones who've been there longer. Most of them are tour guides, and we all do other things, too, like clean pens or feed the animals or maintain the grounds."

"So you and four other people have a key to the gates?"

"Right."

"How long have you worked there?"

"Nearly six years. I totally love it. Best job I ever had. I worked my way up from being a tour guide. A lot of the employees sort of come and go, or maybe just work summers or weekends, which is cool, but I've stayed there because it's awesome."

Lauren noted that Tracy was wearing blue jeans, work boots, and a faded sweatshirt from the Grand Canyon. That meant zoo employees didn't typically wear their zoo uniforms—a blue polo shirt and khaki shorts or pants—on the day the zoo was closed.

"Is Albert a good boss?"

"The best. Everybody loves him."

"So you and he are close?"

"Well, yeah, as far as a working relationship. He doesn't share much about his personal life."

"So you don't know, for instance, if he's dating anyone?" Lauren said.

"I have no idea. He keeps that kind of thing to himself. I always thought that was kind of sad. I want him to open up more, but that just isn't his style."

"You said all of the employees love him. Literally everybody?"

"Well, I mean, I guess there's always going to be someone who, uh, doesn't fit in perfectly. That's just the way it goes."

"Is there someone like that at the zoo?"

"Kind of, yeah, but I feel bad even bringing it up."

"That's okay," Lauren said. "You can share whatever you like. You never know what might help. I can keep it between us, if you'd like."

"Okay, well, there's a guy named Rory who—let's just say he doesn't get along with everybody there."

"Rory Grafmiller?" Grafmiller was the person Ernie was

interviewing in the next room.

"Right."

"Tell me more about him."

"Well, he's good at giving tours. He can be really funny and charming and he's nice looking. But when he's doing other things—I don't think he even likes animals that much. Why would you work at a zoo if you don't totally love animals? Plus, I hate to say this, but he's kind of a slacker. He runs late a lot, and he's not very good at doing things the way they're supposed to be done. And if you mention something to him, he gets kind of touchy about it."

"Are we talking mildly touchy, or more like full-on arguments?" Lauren asked.

"Sometimes arguments, but not always. He has a temper—that's the problem. I mean, not like anything super ugly, but he sort of gets into a huff and gets all quiet. You can tell he's mad by the way he bangs things around. It's basically a tantrum—slamming gates and things like that. He's kind of immature and spoiled, to be honest. But on the other hand, he can be totally chill and nice. Don't get me wrong. He's not always like that. Most of the time, he's not."

"How long has he worked there?"

"Probably about a year."

"Has he had any arguments or tantrums recently?"

Tracy had a sour expression on her face now. "Yesterday morning."

"Yeah? With whom?"

"Albert."

"What was it about?"

"Rory came to work late again, so Albert got on him about that. Later, I saw Rory kick an antelope that wouldn't move out of his way, so I had no choice but to tell Albert. So then they got into a shouting match and Albert ended up sending Rory home for the day. I was glad, because I thought they were about to get into a fistfight. It was pretty intense."

7

Marlin remained behind the cedar for five minutes, simply watching and listening.

He saw nothing unusual. Heard nothing but birds and traffic on the highway.

So he began to walk slowly to the spot where the man had been standing with the rifle. Unlikely that Marlin would find footprints in the hard caliche soil, but he might spot a path through the grass that would show him where the man had gone.

Instead, he found several drops of fresh blood.

It was possible the man in the army jacket was bleeding, but Marlin figured it was much more likely he'd shot an animal, probably illegally, and that's why he'd pointed the rifle.

Marlin pondered his options for a minute, then thumbed his microphone. "County, be advised that I'm looking for an armed subject that pointed a rifle in my direction. Young white male. Six-three and maybe one-ninety. Short beard, blue hat, sunglasses, and an army jacket." Then he described his location in relation to the ranch gate.

"You want me to send someone over?" Bobby Garza asked.

Marlin didn't want to pull resources away from the investigation at the zoo. Besides, he was used to dealing with armed subjects while working alone.

"Negative," Marlin said. "Not yet. Let me try to make contact again."

"Ten-four."

Marlin studied the blood drops more closely. He could tell by the slant of drops in the grass that the animal had been running to his left, so he walked in the direction with his .357 still in his right hand, keeping an eye out for any movement.

No more than forty yards away, he found a dead axis buck that had been shot behind the shoulder, through both lungs. That was the recommended kill shot for many large game animals, but it didn't necessarily stop a deer like this from dashing fifty or a hundred yards as it used up its remaining oxygen.

Marlin grabbed one of the buck's front hooves and moved it in various directions. Limber. He placed his palm on the animal's neck. Warm. This buck had been killed within the last thirty minutes or so, which would match up with the shot that had been fired during Marlin's interview with Kitty Katz.

Where was the man with the rifle?

Marlin took out his phone and snapped several photos of the buck, then followed the blood trail in the opposite direction, hoping to find the location where it had been shot.

Lauren pulled Ernie out of the interview and they both shared what they had learned so far. Then they both went into the room where Rory Grafmiller was waiting.

Lauren introduced herself, then she and Ernie sat down at the small square table.

Rory Grafmiller was a handsome kid. Short hair. Clean shaven. Maybe six feet tall. Lean. Sparkling blue eyes. Square jaw. He gave Lauren a big smile and she saw that his teeth were perfectly straight and white.

"I hate to make you repeat yourself," Lauren said, "but tell me about your experience working at the zoo. What's it like working there?"

"Sure thing," Rory said. "But I have to admit I'm a little curious as to what's going on."

Earlier, Ernie had told Rory that animals had gotten out of the zoo, but he hadn't informed him that a body had been found. Rory seemed unaware of that fact.

"Hey, we're curious, too," Lauren said. "That's why we're here—trying to piece things together."

"But I don't understand why my experience at the zoo has anything to do with the animals getting loose. Do you think someone working there did it?"

"We don't know yet," Lauren said.

"Just give us a basic recap," Ernie said. "Along the lines of what you told me earlier."

Rory accommodated them, telling a glowing story of a tight group of employees who were basically like a big family. To hear Rory tell it, he loved every minute he spent there. Loved the job. Loved the animals. Loved his coworkers. And they all loved him.

If Lauren hadn't known better, she would've bought every word of it. Of course, she was assuming Tracy's description of Rory was accurate and honest.

Lauren tried not to make snap judgments, but her own opinion of Rory was that he was probably the type who sailed through life fairly easily, thanks to his good looks and charming personality. But what happened when that combination failed him? How did he respond when things didn't go his way?

When Rory was done talking, Lauren said, "Sounds like a great group of people."

"It really is. We have a lot of fun."

"So everybody gets along okay?" Lauren asked.

"Well, sure. Did someone say we didn't?"

"It's just a routine question," Lauren said.

Rory shifted in his chair, which signaled his anxiety, but he smiled. "I'm guessing somebody told you what Albert did yesterday," he said.

"What happened?" Lauren asked.

"You haven't talked to him?"

"Not yet, no."

"But I'm guessing you will, right?"

Was this a ruse? He really didn't know Albert hadn't been located?

"We certainly will, but why don't you tell us what happened yesterday and we'll go from there?"

"Okay, well, Albert got a little out of hand. Lost his temper a little bit." Rory was shaking his head as if it were one big regrettable mess.

"What set him off?" Ernie asked.

Lauren wondered if Rory's account would match Tracy's.

"It wasn't that big of a deal," Rory said. "What did you hear?"

"I'd rather have you tell us about it," Lauren said. She was becoming impatient with his hemming and hawing, but she concealed it.

"Did Tracy say something? She's kind of judgmental."

"She is?"

"She's in the next room, right?"

"We're talking to a lot of different people," Ernie said.

"The thing about Tracy—she kind of has a superior attitude. I was trying to be nice earlier, but if you want someone to come along and criticize everything you do, she's real good at that. Just ask anybody who works at the zoo."

"Who should we ask?" Lauren said.

"Like I said, anyone else who works there. Well, she does have some friends there who probably won't say anything bad about her, but if you talk to more than a few people, you'll see. She thinks she knows everything. She's bossy."

"That's good to know. In the meantime, tell me more about what happened with Albert yesterday."

"Nothing happened, really," Rory said. "We had a discussion, that's all."

Lauren felt her phone vibrate with a text, so she quickly checked it. Callie Young, the new deputy, said, *Photo of victim doesn't match anyone who works at the zoo.* Disappointing. An ID would've helped them move the case forward.

"What did you and Albert talk about?" Ernie asked.

"You know, this conversation feels a little weird. Like I'm about to get roped into something I didn't do. I didn't release the animals, okay? Albert got uptight and sent me home early, and that's the last time I was there."

"See, that's exactly the kind of thing we need to know," Lauren said. "That's why we're asking questions. We certainly wouldn't accuse you of doing something you didn't do. In fact, our goal here is to cross you off the list."

"That's good to know, because I didn't do anything."

"Okay, so, did you go anywhere last night or early this morning?" Lauren asked.

"Is that when the animals were released?"

"We're not sure. Did you go anywhere after your shift yesterday?"

"I stopped at Chicken E on the way home."

"Chicken E?"

"Chicken Express. Everyone calls it that. I got some food to go."

"And then you went home?"

"Yep."

"Where do you live?"

"Chandler Place."

"That's the apartment complex?"

"Right. I like it okay. It's pretty new and they have a pool."

"Did you go anywhere after you got home with your supper?"

Rory opened his mouth—about to answer—but he changed his mind.

Then he said, "You know what? I definitely want to help you clear this up, but I think I'd better talk to my mom before I answer any more questions."

"Your mom?"

"She's an attorney. You might've heard of her."

"Cassandra Grafmiller is your mother?" Lauren asked.

"That's her."

Well, crud.

8

Marlin was following the blood trail, moving through an area thick with cedars, when he spotted a dilapidated box blind tucked under a large oak tree. The blind was built from plywood, now warping, and coated with green paint that had faded over time. It had been here a long time—well before Darren Meyer had bought the place. Small horizontal windows on every side of the blind were open, allowing Marlin to see straight through the front of the blind and out the back. As far as he could tell, the blind was unoccupied, but the open windows made him think the blind had been used recently.

"State game warden!" he called again, with his .357 still in his hand.

No response.

Watching for movement inside the blind, Marlin slowly made a wide circle to the rear. The small door in back was open and it was clear by now that nobody was inside.

Marlin took a step closer and peered inside. He spotted a lighter and half a joint resting on a small shelf underneath the front window of the blind.

Any benefit of the doubt Marlin had been holding for this guy was quickly disappearing. Had the man been too stoned earlier to understand the situation? Or had he recognized that Marlin was a game warden but pointed the rifle because his judgment was impaired?

Marlin holstered his .357 and snapped several photos of the lighter and the joint, but he left the items where they were.

While he still had his phone out, he opened Google Maps and saw that he was no more than two hundred yards from the house, which was to the southwest. Not a surprise, because a worn path behind the blind led in that direction.

Marlin pulled his revolver again and followed the path slowly, stopping every few minutes to listen. He kept his eyes open, too, but the land was thickly wooded and he couldn't see farther than thirty or forty yards in most places. When he was roughly one hundred yards from the house, he still hadn't been able to spot it through the trees.

He pressed on, keenly aware that, with each step, he was moving farther away from Bobby Garza and his deputies.

When he was perhaps seventy yards from the house, he saw movement through the trees. Something brown or gray. A deer? Some other animal? The man with the rifle? It had been nothing more than a quick glimpse, and now it was gone.

Marlin took a few more steps, and then he heard the boom of a rifle shot from somewhere fairly close.

Marlin quickly ducked behind an oak tree and waited.

Was that a warning shot meant to scare him? Time to request backup.

Marlin reached for his microphone, and at the same time, he heard a vehicle door slamming, then the sound of an engine starting, followed by a flash of white visible through the trees. A Chevy truck was coming this way fast on the caliche driveway.

Marlin stepped into the roadway with his revolver in his hands.

Now the truck was thirty yards away and closing fast.

Marlin raised the revolver and yelled, "State game warden!"

The driver accelerated, slinging gravel as he gunned the engine.

Marlin's finger tightened on the trigger, but there was too much glare off the windshield to see the driver. Marlin darted to his right, off the driveway, and the truck roared past him.

Marlin holstered his revolver again and began to run after the truck.

The Chevy rounded a bend and disappeared from view. Just a few seconds later, Marlin heard a loud crash.

He knew exactly what the noise was. The driver had just plowed through the locked gate.

"Problem is, I didn't get a good look at the guy when he pointed the rifle at me," Marlin said.

"That'll shake you up, having a carbine aimed in your direction," Bobby Garza said.

"Tell me about it. My hands are still shaking, but don't tell anybody."

"Our little secret," Garza said. "Don't want to ruin your reputation as the steel-nerved badass."

Thirty minutes had passed since the white Chevy had burst through the gate, and deputies had already located the truck three miles south on a quiet county road. It had significant front-end damage and a busted radiator. But no driver. The license plate on the truck came back to Darren Meyer, so that was no help—not until they could talk to Meyer.

Right after the truck had fled, Marlin and Ernie Turpin approached Meyer's house, guns drawn, but they hadn't seen anybody else around. They weren't able to search the house, because, despite the circumstances, they had no legal authority to enter. Could be someone inside. Or maybe not. They pounded on the door, but nobody responded. Marlin had called Meyer again and left another voicemail, stressing that it was urgent that they talk as soon as possible.

Now Marlin said, "He was wearing a baseball cap and sunglasses, and it looked like he had a week's worth of stubble or maybe a full beard. If he shaves that off and loses the cap and glasses, I don't think I could pick him out. In fact, I know I couldn't."

"But you're sure it wasn't Darren Meyer?" Bobby Garza asked.

They were standing on the shoulder of the highway, not far from the destroyed gate.

"Yeah, it wasn't him. This guy was younger. Too tall. Different build."

"How tall?"

"I'd say six three," Marlin said. "Not skinny, but slender."

"That helps," Garza said. "We can work with that."

Marlin was skeptical. The sheriff was trying to be optimistic.

"I'm hoping Meyer knows who it was," Marlin said.

If the man had been a trespassing poacher, it might prove impossible to identify him.

"Tell me about the shot through the trees," Garza said.

"Didn't see who fired it. I have no idea if it was a warning shot or what. I couldn't see the shooter and I doubt he could see me, but I don't know for sure."

"How much time between the shot and sound of the truck starting?"

"Two or three seconds. And he came at me—the guy in the truck—I can't say if it was the same guy who pointed the rifle. I didn't get a good look. Glare on the windshield."

They both knew they couldn't just assume it was the same guy. It very well might be, but Marlin would need to back it up with evidence.

"What's happening at the zoo?" Marlin asked.

"Lem just removed the body a few minutes ago," Garza said, referring to Lem Tucker, the medical examiner. "He put the time of death at about four or five this morning, but he might tweak that estimate later, after the autopsy."

"When will that be?"

"Tomorrow. I'm hoping he can figure out what caused the wound to the neck."

"Gunshot?" Marlin asked.

"Maybe, but if it was, it didn't exit."

Marlin was interested in the details of Garza's case, but right now, with adrenaline still pumping, he was focused on identifying the man who'd aimed the rifle at him, and determining whether the same man had tried to run him down.

9

"Nice place you've got," Garrett said in the late afternoon. "How long have you owned it?"

"A damn long time," Red said. *And why is that your business?*

Earlier, Red had started a fire from cedar stumps in the fire pit behind his trailer, and now the three of them were sitting in tattered lawn chairs, drinking Keystone Light tallboys and enjoying the cool afternoon as the sun began to drop lower in the sky.

"You can't hardly buy land out here anymore," Billy Don said. "People from Austin and San Antonio buying up parcels left and right and driving up the prices."

"And the property taxes," Red added. "Don't forget the damn property taxes."

"It's the gover'ment stealing, is what that is," Billy Don said.

"That's what they do," Red said. "Steal your money and then waste it."

"Seems like everybody around here has an ag exemption 'cept Red," Billy Don said.

"What's an ag exemption?" Garrett asked.

"It's where you get a big ol' tax break if you're a rancher or farmer," Billy Don said.

"Except a lot of people just pretend to be ranchers to get the exemption," Red said. "They get a few goats and say, 'Hey, I'm a rancher!'"

"You can get an exemption nowadays for keeping beehives on your place," Billy Don said. "Is that crazy or what?"

"Meanwhile, suckers like me pay through the ass," Red said.

"How many acres do you have?" Garrett asked.

Billy Don laughed. "Okay, we'll give you a break, since you ain't from around here, but in Texas, you don't ask that question. It's like asking a man how many head of cattle he owns."

"Off limits?" Garrett asked, obviously amused.

"Pretty much. Might as well ask a man what size bra his wife wears."

Garrett had insisted on buying the beer when they'd passed through Blanco, and he'd even asked what brand Red and Billy Don preferred. Of course, he was using money Red and Billy Don had given him after working for the day.

"Speaking of which, either of you guys married?" Garrett asked.

"Nope," Billy Don said, "but there was a time we was married to the same woman at the same time."

"Wait a sec. Is that legal down here?" Garrett asked.

"Hell no, but we didn't *know* we was both married to her," Billy Don said. "We figured that out later. Long story, but if you want me to—"

"He don't need to hear all that," Red said.

"Whatever," Billy Don said. Then, to Garrett, in a lower voice, he added, "I'll tell ya later."

"They should do a documentary about the two of you," Garrett said, entertained at this new tidbit of information.

Was he as easygoing as he seemed? Red figured it could be an act. But so far, despite Red's shrewd yet subtle questioning throughout the day, Garrett hadn't given any indication that he knew anything about the loose animals or the dead guy at the zoo. Red decided it was time to be a little more direct.

"So you're not a fan of zoos, or what?" Red asked.

"Huh?" Garrett asked.

"I was thinking about that animal you saw crossing the highway, and you said you hoped something got loose from the zoo," Red said. "I was just wondering why you said that."

"Oh," Garrett said. "I guess I just thought it would be kind of funny, you know?"

Red didn't really see the humor in it, but he played along. "Yeah, I guess so. Like some big ol' African cow running around. People driving on the highway would be like, what the hell is that damn thing?"

"Exactly. That would be hilarious. As long as nobody got hurt," Garrett said.

Red was coming to grips with the fact that Garrett was probably nothing but a hitchhiker. There was nothing mysterious about him. He didn't turn the animal loose. He didn't kill anyone.

"They got cows in Africa?" Billy Don asked.

"Of course they got cows, but different than the ones we got around here," Red said. "That's why somebody would wonder what it was when they saw it."

"I think there's a breed of African cattle called Watusi," Garrett said.

"I thought that was a kind of music," Billy Don said.

"You mean a dance?" Garrett said.

"Okay, I guess," Billy Don said.

"It's both," Garrett said.

"It's music and a dance?" Billy Don asked.

"No, it's a kind of cattle *and* a dance," Garrett said.

"But not music?" Billy Don asked.

"Y'all are driving me nuts," Red said.

"You were already halfway there," Billy Don said.

Red was about ready to go inside and get something to eat, but first he took out his phone and slowly typed a text to Billy Don.

You know he can't stay here tonight right?

Let Billy Don figure out what to do with him. Give him a ride to town, or something. Or let him hike back to the highway. But right before Red sent the text, Billy Don turned to Garrett and said, "You said you was gonna tell us why you left Michigan."

"Oh, yeah. I guess I did."

"We could use a good story to liven things up around here," Billy Don said.

"If I tell you, can we keep it between us?" Garrett said. "Does that sound fair?"

Billy Don said, "I can keep a secret."

Red said, "Pfffttt."

"I can, too!" Billy Don said.

"I can't think of a single time you kept a secret," Red said.

"Well, if I did, how would you know, because I wouldn't of told you."

"Just forget it," Red said, shaking his head. He looked at Garrett. "Go right ahead."

Garrett took a long drink of beer, stared at the fire for a moment, and said, "I was born and raised in Quincy, a tiny little town in the southern part of Michigan. Spent my whole life there. But I left because everybody thought I murdered my father."

Albert reached the city limits of Roswell, New Mexico, before five o'clock, and he was ravenous, since he hadn't eaten since last night. He knew he had to get food, and then supplies, and later a place to sleep, and that he would have to interact with people to accomplish those things.

Driving north on Main Street, he saw plenty of places to eat—places where he could pop in, eat quick, and move on. He chose a Denny's, and he wasn't sure why. Maybe because bacon and eggs sounded good right now. Comfort food. Maybe some pancakes, too.

He went inside, keeping his lightly shaded sunglasses on. It was early for dinner, so half the tables were open and the hostess seated him right away. She said his server would be with him in just a minute and gave him a big smile. A reassuring smile. The kind of smile that makes a fugitive forget his troubles for just a few seconds and feel like a normal human being again.

Then she walked away and Albert felt a deep funk settle in again. How depressing to be in this situation. His world was in turmoil and it would never return to normal, or what had been normal for him in the past nineteen years.

He glanced at the menu for about ten seconds, made a decision, then put it on the tabletop.

When he left Denny's, he would need to buy a phone somewhere. He'd left his Samsung at home, obviously, because the quickest way to get caught would've been to bring it with him. But he couldn't continue without a phone. Not because he wanted to contact anyone—that was out of the question, at least for now—but because he wanted an easy way to keep up with the news.

What did the cops know by now?

What did they theorize?

Were they confused?

What were they telling the public?

Had they asked everyone to keep an eye out for a neon-green Ford Fiesta?

The waitress was a slender woman in her fifties. She took his order—the Lumberjack Slam—without any small talk and went about her business. A few minutes later, she brought his iced tea and said, "Your order'll be right out."

"Thanks."

She lingered. "Do you by chance have photophobia?"

"Pardon?"

"I was just wondering about the sunglasses. My son has something called photophobia, and that means you're sensitive to light. He gets headaches from it all the time."

Albert said, "No, but they're prescription and I forgot my other glasses in the car."

"I think I have a touch of that condition myself," said an eavesdropping older man in a booth across the aisle.

"Oh, Horace, you do not," said the woman with him.

They both had a thick Midwestern accent.

"I get headaches, Annie!" the man insisted.

"So you're saying you have that condition? Photo-whatchacallit?"

"Photophobia," the waitress said.

"Yeah, that," Annie said. "You're saying you have that?"

"No, you're right," Horace said. "My headaches aren't from light, they're from sound." He winked at the waitress.

"You're talking about my voice, aren't you?" Annie asked.

"I never said that."

"But that's what you're implying."

It was playful banter, and Albert thought it sounded particularly comical because of their accents.

As the couple continued with their back-and-forth, the waitress said quietly to Albert, "Sorry about that. I'll go get your food."

"Thanks."

After she left, Albert tried to sit quietly, but after a moment, he could feel eyes on the side of his head. If Albert had a phone, he would look at it, or even just pretend to look at it, to avoid any further interaction. These people were nice enough, but Albert needed to maintain a low profile. He grabbed a dessert menu and studied it.

"You from this area?" Horace asked.

Albert didn't respond. Pretended he didn't hear.

"You from this area?" Horace asked even louder.

"Just passing through," Albert said, turning his head a quarter of the way toward the couple. His body English plainly said he didn't want to talk, but he wasn't downright rude about it. That would be memorable, and he didn't want to be memorable.

"Oh, yeah? Where from?"

Just great, Albert thought.

"Louisiana," he said, and he wasn't sure why. It just came out.

"Which part?" the woman said. "We've been through Louisiana plenty of times."

"New Orleans," Albert said. He had never even passed through New Orleans.

"We love New Orleans!" the woman said, as if loving New Orleans was some kind of novelty that would help them create a lasting emotional bond. "What's your favorite restaurant?"

This was getting worse and worse.

"There's a little place near my house that serves the best po' boys, but I can't remember the name, because they just opened up," Albert said, and he quickly added, "Where are you from?"

Maybe the best way to avoid answering questions was to ask questions of his own.

"Madison, Wisconsin," Annie said proudly.

"I'm Horace Norris," the man said. "And yes, I've heard all the jokes about my name. This is my wife Annie."

"Hello!" Annie said, adding a small wave.

"You're probably wondering what we're doing down here," Horace said. "The truth is, we've been nomads for several years now."

Albert could tell Horace desperately wanted him to ask why he had used the term "nomads."

"How are you, uh, nomads?" Albert asked.

Horace pointed past Albert to the window. "See that Winnebago on the far side of the lot?"

Albert looked.

"That's ours!" Annie said.

"She's a beaut, huh?" Horace said.

"Sure is," Albert said.

"Our little home away from home," Annie said.

"*Big* home away from home," Horace said.

"Just the right size," Annie said.

"Yeah, but you aren't the one driving it," Horace said.

"I'd drive if you'd let me!" Annie said, and she rolled her eyes at Albert.

"You should come take a look at her when we're done eating," Horace said. "You wouldn't believe all the features. Features out the wazoo."

"Horace!" Annie said. "That word!"

"There's nothing wrong with it, Annie," Horace said.

Right then, Albert made a new rule about getting food. Drive-throughs only.

10

Everybody thought I murdered my father.

Red had no idea how to respond to a statement like that.

Billy Don spoke first. "Well, did you?"

"Of course not," Garrett said. "But I guess I'd say I didn't do it even if I did, right?"

Garrett was grinning, like he enjoyed the fact that they didn't know for sure.

"But he was murdered, right?" Billy Don said.

"Well, of course he was," Red said. "Would they think somebody murdered him if he *wasn't* murdered?"

"Hey, it could've been some sort of accident that looked like murder," Billy Don insisted.

They both looked at Garrett for confirmation.

He said, "At first they thought it was suicide, but—"

"Suicide!" Billy Don said. "See, Red? That means it coulda looked like murder when it really wasn't."

"But the medical examiner said it was inconclusive," Garrett added. "So we don't really have an answer. It could've been an accident."

Red wanted to ask for more details, but only a moron would be that insensitive.

"Did he shoot himself or what?" Billy Don asked.

Like that.

"He fell off the roof of our house," Garrett said. "Might've slipped, or maybe he jumped. Nobody knows for sure."

"So you musta been up there with him, right?" Billy Don asked. "I mean, if they thought you—"

"Yeah, I was up there," Garrett said. "That's what made it so weird. It's a metal roof and we were replacing some of the screws. It's a two-story house and it backs up to a ravine, so it's a pretty big drop from that side of the house. At least forty feet."

"Your dad was some kind of financial guy, but he was up there on the roof, replacing screws?" Billy Don asked.

"He liked to do that sort of thing himself," Garrett said. "He was kind of old school."

Billy Don nodded approvingly.

"Did you see him fall?" Red asked.

"No, I was facing the other direction, driving a screw."

Likely story, Red thought. He couldn't wait to share all of this with Mandy, who was coming over later.

"But why would he suddenly jump off a roof while y'all are working on it?" Billy Don asked.

"That's the thing—it wasn't sudden. Well, *I* thought it was, but I didn't know what was going on, which was that my mom was about to divorce him. In fact, when we were up there, she sent him a text saying the papers were all drawn up and she'd be getting those to him. A few minutes later, he jumped. Or slipped. Personally, I think he slipped. It's a steep roof and you have to be careful up there."

"Dang," Billy Don said. "That's rough. Did he holler?"

"Jesus, Billy Don," Red said. "That's morbid."

"But I figure if he slipped, he'd holler. But if he jumped, he probably wouldn't."

Red couldn't believe it, but that was actually a good point.

"Yeah, he did," Garrett said. "He sounded surprised."

They all sat quietly for a moment as the fire popped and hissed.

"But wait," Billy Don said. "Why did they think you did it? Did you have a reason to kill him?"

Red realized he still had his phone in his hand, the text to Billy Don unsent. He deleted it and stuck his phone back into his pocket. He wanted to see how this played out.

"Not really, no," Garrett said. "But what the cops said—their stupid theory—was that my dad and I started talking about the divorce, and my dad told me he'd been cheating on my mom, which is why my mom wanted the divorce, so I got mad and shoved him off the roof. It wasn't true, though. I mean the affair part was true, but it wasn't true about me shoving him."

Red said nothing.

Billy Don emitted a grunt that basically meant, *Damn, that's pretty wild.*

"It would've been really easy, to be honest," Garrett said. "I mean, think about it. If you're on a roof, or a cliff, or a ledge of some kind, and it's just the two of you, what's to stop you from shoving the other guy off? How could they prove you did it without any witnesses or cameras or a confession? Sure, they could suspect you did it, but proving it beyond a reasonable doubt? How the hell are they gonna do that?"

Now the pendulum had swung back in the other direction, and Red was more convinced than ever that Garrett wasn't as innocent as he claimed. Red had known men who enjoyed bragging about the crimes they'd committed. This was a slightly different angle. Garrett seemed to enjoy talking about a possible crime he claimed he didn't commit.

"Who was your daddy cheating with?" Billy Don asked.

"The mayor's wife," Garrett said.

"Sounds like a damn soap opera," Billy Don said, chuckling.

"Pretty much. I can't believe I never knew until the day he died."

"What about your mom? When did she find out?"

"A couple of months earlier. She never told me. I wasn't living with them, so I had no clue they were having problems. Mom said she didn't want to make me worry, and she thought I'd try to talk her out of it—and she was right."

"So did you ever get arrested?" Red asked.

"No, it never got that far. The case is still open. But they don't have any other suspects, obviously, and they had no way of proving it was or wasn't suicide, so a lot of people made up their minds that I did it. That gets old real quick—people calling me a murderer. I said it was tough for the cops to prove what really happened in a situation like that, but the reverse is true, too. How was I supposed to convince people I *didn't* do it? Meanwhile, the cops didn't give a rat's ass what people thought about me."

"We've been there," Billy Don said. "Accused of stuff we didn't do. It's a bitch." Then he laughed. "But most of the time, we done it, just like they thought."

"It gives you a whole new perspective on what happens to people who are falsely accused," Garrett said. "A lot of gossip was flying around, and everybody was treating me differently—like I was a killer—so I decided to take off. Who needs that shit, right? That's why I hate the cops. They screwed me around bad. Ruined my reputation. Next time I deal with a cop…" He shook his head instead of finishing his thought.

"Does your mom think you did it?" Red asked.

"Well," Garrett said, and then he didn't say anything for several seconds. "She said she believed me, but I could tell there was a tiny bit of doubt. I mean, come on—who could blame her? We've all done stupid shit in the heat of the moment."

"That musta hurt," Billy Don said. "Your own momma wondering if you killed your daddy."

"Yeah, it did," Garrett said. "It hurt a lot."

Red pondered all of this new information, and tried to square it with the dead body at the zoo. Wasn't it a hell of a coincidence that Garrett had been near the zoo and he also happened to be a suspect in his own father's murder?

After he finished eating, Albert told Horace and Annie he had to go to the bathroom, and when he was done, he quickly paid his tab at the register and snuck out to the Ford Fiesta.

He drove north on 285, looking for a place to buy a prepaid phone with cash, but once again, he glanced in the rearview mirror and saw a cop behind him. New Mexico State Police unit in one of their marked Interceptor SUVs.

Jeez. Bad luck? Or had they been on the lookout for him?

Albert took a right on Berrendo Road. So did the cop.

Maybe it was time to give up. The cops might offer to protect him. But how would they do that? Was it even possible? Could *anyone* protect him?

Albert reached a stop sign and came to a complete halt. The cop was still back there. Albert took a left on North Garden Avenue, careful to use his blinker. He passed Broken Arrow and Swinging Spear and Twin Diamond and the cop stayed right behind him.

He passed Sunrise Road and Mission Arch Drive and Three Cross Drive, and by now it was obvious the cop was following him. Right? But why wasn't he pulling Albert over? Waiting for backup?

Albert was approaching a T intersection with Tierra Berrenda Drive, and now he had a decision to make. He took a deep breath, then flipped his blinker for a left turn. Came to a stop. Made the turn.

The cop took a right.

Oh, thank God.

11

"That right there is one hunk of a man," Nicole Marlin said.

"He looks kind of awkward to me," Marlin said.

"I don't see that, but even if it were true, he's still a total beefcake. The viewers won't care if he's a smooth talker or not. They might even turn the volume down."

It was 6:03 in the evening and they were seated on the couch in their living room, watching the Kitty Katz interview from that morning.

Marlin had spent the rest of the day searching for the man on Darren Meyer's ranch and trying to interview other landowners in the area. He'd also loaded the carcass of the axis deer into the bed of his truck and taken it to a local butcher, who'd agreed to keep it in his meat locker for the time being.

All in all, he hadn't been able to make much progress.

He still hadn't been able to contact Darren Meyer. Throughout the day, he'd left several additional voicemails, but Meyer hadn't called back. Marlin had spent a few minutes on social media, hoping to contact Meyer through a Facebook or Twitter account, but Meyer had no online presence that Marlin could find.

Now Bobby Garza appeared on the TV screen, having been interviewed later in the afternoon.

"We haven't been able to identify the deceased person yet, but we do know it is not a zoo employee. We haven't been able to contact the owner of the zoo, but we've spoken with several employees. Unfortunately, we just don't have many answers yet."

Marlin was hoping Lem Tucker's autopsy tomorrow would determine how the man had died—murder or some kind of accident? Marlin had been wondering about the possibility of a gore injury from a horn or antler, but at this point that would be pure speculation.

As for the loose animals, Lauren had put Marlin in touch with a woman named Tracy Lavelle, the assistant zookeeper, who had confirmed that the axis deer shot on Darren Meyer's land by the unidentified poacher had been from the zoo. Beyond that, four animals were still missing. Not ideal, but Marlin was thrilled to hear the number was that low.

He would head back out this evening to continue contacting landowners in that area, and to make sure no zoo animals were lingering on the highway. He could envision some of the animals returning to the zoo, hungry and tired, only to find a closed gate. Even worse, now that it was dark, drivers would have a tougher time spotting the animals on the highway before impact.

Tracy Lavelle had also agreed to visit the zoo several times throughout the evening and in the coming days, so she could watch for returning animals, and she was asking other zoo employees to help her out, watching in shifts. She'd said there were no plans to reopen the zoo until Albert had been located.

In the interview, Kitty Katz said, "Sheriff, if the animals were released on purpose, can we assume that the body found on the zoo grounds was the victim of some sort of foul play?"

"We'll go where the evidence leads us," Garza said, "and I'm afraid we just don't know the answer to that yet. If anybody has any information to share, as always, we welcome calls to our office."

"Can you share with us the nature of the victim's injuries?"

"I'm not prepared to go into that right now," Garza said.

"But no obvious cause of death?"

"It's undetermined at this point," Garza said, and the interview ended after a few more questions.

"He's better in front of a camera than I am," Marlin said.

"But not as cute," Nicole said.

"Not that you're biased," Marlin said.

"Of course not," Nicole said. "Have they searched Albert's house?"

She knew the routine, having been a deputy for many years. Now she was the county victim services coordinator—a job that suited her perfectly.

"His house, his truck, and his office, all this afternoon," Marlin said. "Found nothing. Well, one thing. There was a note on his desk that said, 'Zoos are prissons,' with 'prisons' spelled wrong. That's all it said. None of the employees knew anything about it. The envelope was postmarked from Dallas."

"No return address, I assume."

"Nope."

"So maybe from some type of animal-rights activist?"

"Maybe so. Or totally unrelated. The assistant manager Tracy said they got a note like that occasionally."

"Doesn't seem likely that a person would send a note like that first if they were going to visit the zoo and, say, let all the animals out," Nicole said. "Why telegraph what you're about to do?"

"I agree."

"Maybe Albert will still show up," Nicole said. "Maybe he's been out running errands all day, or he had some type of emergency."

Nicole was just being an optimist, and she knew it wasn't likely at this point.

"Without his truck or his cell phone?" Marlin said.

"They found his phone?"

"Yep. Not password-protected, but there wasn't anything good on it. And they found his wallet."

"That's not good."

"Nope. But at least they haven't found his body."

Nicole turned the TV off. "You hungry?" she asked.

"Absolutely," Marlin said.

"Then get in there and whip us up some supper," she said.

"I'm telling you, something ain't right," Red said, his voice low, because the walls were thin in the trailer.

"You're just distracted, is all," Mandy said. "It's usually very reliable."

They were lying in Red's bed together.

"I'm not talking about *that*," Red said. "We'll get to that in a minute, and then you'd better hang on to something heavy."

"Promises, promises," Mandy said.

"I'm talking about that kid Garrett," Red said.

"You really think he shoved his own dad off that roof? Why would he tell you about that if he had something to hide? It don't make sense."

It was currently 9:14. Mandy had joined Red and Billy Don and Garrett around the fire pit about an hour ago, so she'd had a little time to form her own opinion about the kid, even though he'd become more tight-lipped when she'd shown up. Or maybe he had a hard time talking to pretty women.

"Could be he's just plain psycho," Red said. "Some of those crazies get off on playing mind games with people. Maybe he *wants* us to think he did it. Maybe that's how he gets his jollies."

"Let's focus on getting *our* jollies," Mandy said. "How 'bout that?"

"It woulda been the perfect crime, or damn close to it," Red said. "The only flaw I can see is if his daddy woulda lived to tell what really happened. But he didn't."

Mandy snuggled up next to Red and placed a hand on his chest.

"You're a great detective and all, but forget about all that for a while," she whispered.

"He had a big-time motive," Red said.

Mandy began to breathe hot air into his ear. She knew he liked that. A lot.

"He was mad that his daddy had cheated on his momma," Red said.

"You already told me," Mandy said.

"Because it's true. And if it turns out he did kill his daddy, don't that make you wonder about the dead guy at the zoo?"

"Um-hmm," Mandy said, and she began to run her tongue around the rim of his ear.

There was something else Red had been thinking about—something he wanted to check—but now he couldn't remember what it was. His brain was a little foggy for some reason.

He said, "Did you, uh…was…"

"Ssshhh," Mandy said, and she tugged gently on his earlobe with her teeth.

He could feel her breasts pressing against his upper arm. If there was anything—or two things—that could take his mind off other matters, those hooters could do the trick.

Now she was sliding her hand down to his belly button—and then even further downward.

"See, you just needed to focus," Mandy said.

Red said something, but it wasn't actual words.

Mandy swung a leg over him and climbed on top.

"Okay, we're gonna need to keep this kind of quiet," she said. "Can you do that?"

Red nodded vigorously.

"You sure?"

Red nodded again.

He was wrong. He was not able to keep it quiet.

As Albert drove, he remembered a particular conversation with Sylvia—the first time he'd suggested they run away together.

"That's crazy!" she replied. "You're crazy."

"Crazy about you."

"That would never work, so don't even think about it."

He wasn't so sure she was right. This was a long time ago, before technology had evolved so quickly. Back then, you could disappear more easily. Start over. Keep a low profile. Social media wasn't a thing yet. The internet was still fairly new.

"If it would work, would you do it?" he asked.

"Would I run away with you?"

They were lounging in bed together on a Sunday afternoon.

"Yes. That's what I'm asking. You can be honest, you know. I can handle it, whatever the answer is."

She lay quiet for a long moment, and he thought she didn't want to hurt his feelings, and then he realized she was crying. He took her by the hand.

"I'm sorry," he said.

"For what?"

"For bringing it up."

She squeezed his hand.

"I would do it," she said. "I want you to know that. I would, if we could, but we can't."

How could a simple declaration like that simultaneously crush him and make his heart soar?

"He wouldn't hurt you if we got caught," Albert said.

She rolled onto her side to face him. "I *know* that. He would hurt *you*. He would never stop until he found you. Never. Twenty years from now he would still be looking."

"Then he's the crazy one," Albert said.

"That's true," she said. "Very true."

Eerie how prescient her prediction had been. It had been nineteen years and three months since that conversation. Nearly twenty years. Her husband had been every bit as vengeful as she'd imagined.

Then again, Albert had done more than try to steal his wife. A lot more.

12

When Marlin woke the next morning, he had a text from Tracy Lavelle.

Three escapees returned last night! Down to just one!

He replied: *Excellent news. Who's the lone holdout?*

She said: *A greater kudu named Kevin.*

Kevin the kudu. Marlin had to laugh.

When he got out of the shower at 7:15, he had a voicemail waiting from Darren Meyer, plus a text from Bobby Garza sent eleven minutes earlier, with Lauren Gilchrist included.

Still no ID on the deceased. No hits on AFIS. Autopsy today.

Marlin replied: *Thx. Plz keep me posted. Just one animal missing from the zoo now.*

Then he listened to the voicemail.

It's Darren Meyer returning your call. I'm out of the country—in Australia, to be exact, so we've got a bit of a time difference. I believe I'm fifteen hours ahead of you. Also, I've been out in the bush, where cell coverage is spotty. Anyway, feel free to give me a call back if we still need to talk.

So it was late in the day there—10:15 p.m.

Marlin dialed him back immediately and Meyer answered. Marlin quickly summarized the situation—the loose animals, the body at the zoo, the man who shot the axis deer on Meyer's ranch—but he held back several important details. He didn't tell Meyer that the man had pointed a rifle at him, nor did he mention the shot through the trees or the person fleeing in the truck.

When he was done, Meyer said, "I hadn't heard about any of this. You think the man on my property had anything to do with the events at the zoo?"

"Right now, we don't have any reason to think they're connected," Marlin said. "My guess is that the man shot the axis, then panicked and ran when he saw me—but I need to talk to him and get his side of it."

In Marlin's experience, when a hunter panicked, there was generally a reason. Perhaps he didn't have a hunting license, or he had an active arrest warrant for some other offense, or he was carrying drugs. But there was no reason to get into those possibilities with Meyer. Marlin wanted to downplay the potential charges the man might be facing, so that Meyer might be more inclined to share information, if he knew who the man was.

The connection wasn't good, but Marlin could hear Meyer let out a sigh.

"Here's the situation," Meyer said. "I've been gone for two weeks and I'll be gone for two more. Taking a vacation. I told my nephew he could spend some time on the ranch while I was gone—kind of keep an eye on everything for me. I guess there's a chance it might've been him."

"What's your nephew's name?"

"Bryce Cauley."

"How old is he?"

"Twenty-four, I think."

"Is he a hunter?"

"I don't think so. He's never mentioned it. I know he likes to shoot guns, though. I told him I didn't want him shooting on my place. He knows that."

"What does he look like?"

"He's probably five foot nine and a little on the heavy side. And he has blond hair, kind of shaggy."

That didn't match the man Marlin had encountered, but he opted to keep that to himself for now. Bryce might know who the bearded man was. Maybe it was a friend of his.

"Can you text me Bryce's phone number when we're done talking?" Marlin asked.

"Will do."

"What does he drive?" Marlin asked.

"A blue Ford Ranger."

"You know the year model?"

"Just a year or two old."

"Where does he live?"

"That apartment complex in Blanco," Meyer said. "Chandler something."

"Chandler Place," Marlin said.

"Right. He's been there about a year."

"Where does he work?"

"Dairy Queen in Blanco. I have to say, if he shot that deer, I hope he didn't break any laws. I thought he was back on the right track and this would be a setback."

"So he's had some trouble in the past?" Marlin asked.

"Unfortunately, yes. Some drug-related issues."

"Using or selling?"

"Just using, I think. I don't know all the details."

"What kind of drugs?"

"It used to be pot, but then he got caught with some meth early last year. He went through a court-ordered program and I thought he was doing okay. Otherwise, I wouldn't allow him on my place. I don't need that kind of trouble."

Marlin would check to see if Bryce had been convicted of a felony. If he had, possession of a firearm was a major infraction. He didn't mention that to Meyer, either.

"Do you know what kind of firearms he owns?" he asked.

"I'm sorry, I don't. I'm not much of a gun person."

"Do you know if he owns handguns or rifles or both?"

"I know he owns at least one rifle. I saw it once, but I don't know what kind it was."

"Can you describe it for me?"

"Well, it's black. Other than that, don't most rifles pretty much look the same?"

Marlin tried not to laugh. "Maybe a little. Do you know if it has a scope on it?"

"I believe so, yes."

"Do you know what a bolt-action rifle is?"

"I think so."

"How about a lever action?"

"Like the kind they used in the Old West?"

"You could call it that. Do you know which kind Bryce owns?"

"I think it's the lever-action kind. He might own more than one, though."

"Does he have a key to your Chevy truck?"

"He does not—but that question makes me nervous. Was somebody driving my truck?"

Meyer didn't seem to be protecting his nephew or ducking the questions, so Marlin opted to share a little more information.

"The man pointed his rifle at me, and then he disappeared before I could talk to him. A few minutes later, somebody—maybe the same man, but I can't be sure—took off in your truck and plowed it through the front gate. Deputies found it later with some front-end damage. We towed it in for processing, but you'll get it back, and then you can work with your insurance company."

"Jesus. This is not what I needed to hear today."

"If it makes you feel any better, the man who pointed the rifle doesn't match the description you gave of your nephew."

"Oh, thank goodness."

"Do you know any of Bryce's friends?"

"I've never met any of them. Truth is, I'm not particularly close to Bryce, but I've tried to change that recently and help him straighten his life out. Last year I offered to pay the tuition if he went to community college or a trade school, but he wasn't interested."

"Can you think of anyone else who might've been out there other than Bryce or his friends?"

"Absolutely not, and I told him not to take anyone out there."

"Does he have a key to your house?"

"Yes, I left one for him. Maybe that was a huge mistake."

"Is there a key to your truck inside your house?"

Meyer let out another exasperated sigh. "Yep. Sure is. A spare. I forgot about that."

"Can I assume that nobody, including your nephew, had permission to drive your truck?"

"You certainly can."

"So we can treat it as a stolen vehicle?"

"Absolutely."

"Even if it was Bryce?"

"Yes. He needs to be held accountable if he did something that stupid."

"Do you know any of your neighbors?"

"Not very well."

"Have you ever had a problem with any of them trespassing, or anybody else trespassing, for that matter?"

"Not that I know of. I've never caught anybody."

"Do you have any game cameras on your land?"

"What's a game camera?"

"Well, they also call it a trail camera or a scouting camera—the kind that takes pictures when a deer or other animal walks in front of it."

"Oh, right. I don't have any of those."

"Any security cameras?"

"I've thought about getting some, but I haven't done it yet."

"I'd like to go back over there and have a look inside your home. You okay with that?"

There was a long silence.

"Mr. Meyer?"

"I'm still here. I'm thinking. I have no problem with it, really, but it's a little unsettling to have your house searched while you're eight thousand miles away."

Marlin waited.

"Let's say you go inside and find drugs," Meyer said. "If Bryce or his friends left some in there, what would happen to me?"

"If they aren't yours, you wouldn't have anything to worry about—at least in theory," Marlin said. "Besides, I wouldn't be looking for drugs, I'd be trying to contact Bryce or anyone else who might be inside. I wouldn't be looking in drawers or cabinets or anything like that."

"Okay, but what if you see drugs or something else illegal and you can't tell who it belongs to?" Meyer said. "What happens then?"

"We couldn't ignore that, obviously," Marlin said.

"So it's possible I could be creating some legal headaches for myself?"

Marlin had to be honest. "Yes, it's possible. I don't see it as likely, though. Your candor with me would go a long way."

"Let me be clear—I don't do drugs, and I wouldn't allow them in my house, but I have no way of knowing what Bryce might've been doing there. I was foolish to ever allow him on the place while I was gone. I see that now."

"So you won't allow me to enter the home?" Marlin said.

"Right now, no. I'm sorry, I know that doesn't look good, but that's the way it'll have to be, at least until I get home."

Marlin had interviewed hundreds of people over the years, and he was confident Meyer had answered his questions truthfully—but Marlin couldn't blame him for refusing the search.

Marlin said, "I appreciate your help. I'm going to make one other request."

"I'll help if I can."

"If you talk to your nephew, please don't tell him what we talked about. Just ask him to call me or the sheriff's office, please. And let me know if you hear from him."

"I'll do that. I promise."

13

Red was drowsing in bed when he remembered something he'd been wanting to check about Garrett's weird story.

He stretched and yawned. He'd get to it in a minute. It didn't seem so important right now.

Mandy had already gotten up and left for work at about eight. He vaguely remembered her kissing him on the cheek. He also remembered—with much greater clarity—the way she'd distracted him last night. What a gal. To be that beautiful and still do the things she'd do…what were the odds? Most women who would do those things in bed were either homely, drunk, or foreign.

Mandy had also said he was a great detective. And she was right. He'd gotten damn good at figuring things out.

He'd learned to trust his gut, and his gut told him Garrett couldn't be trusted. Something about the situation was screwed up. Or maybe Garrett wasn't presenting it right. Or leaving something important out.

Red rolled onto his right side and grabbed his iPhone off the old whiskey barrel that acted as a nightstand.

He didn't really want to become one of those people who was always relying on his phone for every damn thing, but he had to admit it was handy for looking stuff up. It was like carrying a library around in your pocket. Actually, it was even better, because his phone didn't have a librarian nagging him to keep quiet, or to stop chewing tobacco, or to put his boots back on.

He'd gotten pretty sharp at using Google. Now he typed in "Garrett" and stopped for a second, because he realized he didn't know Garrett's last name. Garrett had never given it. That was kind of suspicious, wasn't it?

What town was he from? Some small town in southern Michigan. Damn it, what was it called?

Oh, right! Like that old show with Jack Klugmann. *Quincy*!

So Red searched for "Garrett quincy father roof." He'd learned that you had to put the right combination of words together to find what you wanted.

Sure enough, he got all kinds of hits to newspaper articles, including references to Garrett, whose last name was Becker. Garrett Becker. His dad's name was Larry Becker. Red clicked the first article listed, and as he read, he realized the facts seemed to match everything Garrett had told them.

Garrett and his dad had been on the roof working. Then Garrett's mom had texted her husband, saying she'd be forwarding the divorce papers. Moments later, he fell, or jumped, or was pushed. Later Garrett told the cops he hadn't known his parents were planning to split, or that his dad had been having an affair, and the cops wondered if those issues had caused an argument on the rooftop.

That was exactly the way Garrett had told it. Red wasn't sure how to feel about that. It would be easier to draw conclusions if Garrett was a big-ass lying son of a bitch.

Red realized it was awfully quiet around here. No sounds of Billy Don snoring. No sounds of Billy Don making ungodly noises in the bathroom. No sounds of Billy Don turning the TV too damn loud because he was halfway deaf from going to tractor pulls without ear protection.

So where was Billy Don?

And where was Garrett?

Screw it. Who cared?

Red kept reading. Despite what he knew already about Garrett and his dead dad, there was one thing in particular Red wanted to find out, but he hadn't seen it mentioned yet. He finished the first article and moved on to another one, published three days later.

In this one, the cops said they'd questioned Garrett at length several times now, and he'd cooperated, but they still couldn't determine what had happened on that roof. Lots of people were mad that Garrett hadn't been arrested, but the cops said you couldn't just charge a man without probable cause.

Red stopped for a minute to look up the meaning of "probable cause." He'd heard it before, on TV and in front of a judge, but he wasn't exactly sure what it meant. Wikipedia said it was "a reasonable amount of suspicion, supported by circumstances sufficiently strong to justify a prudent and cautious person's belief that certain facts are probably true."

Red wasn't sure about the word "prudent," either, but there was only so much time in a day for looking stuff up.

So he went back to the second article, and that's when he found the tidbit he'd been looking for.

At the end of that article, one of the detectives said, "We're a little concerned by the fact that Larry Becker had a life insurance policy for eight hundred thousand dollars, which is to be split equally between his wife and his only child, Garrett Becker."

Boom.

There it was, spelled out in black and white.

Garrett being angry with his dad was one thing, but if $400,000 wasn't big-time probable cause, what the hell was?

Albert jerked awake to the sound of a loud thud and the vibration of a hard impact, but he knew none of it was real. All in his head. Replayed memories.

Where was he? He had no idea. Still groggy.

Strange bed. Not as comfortable as his own. And these weren't his pillows. The paint on the ceiling wasn't the right color. Much darker in this room. Too much noise outside. It even *smelled* different.

Then he remembered. A motel. Some little mom-and-pop place. He couldn't recall the name of it. He couldn't even name the town he was in. Not a city, a town. Small. It reminded him of horses.

Whinny? Halter? Bridle? None of those.

Gallop.

Wait, not Gallop. Gallup. Gallup, New Mexico, a couple hours west of Albuquerque.

When Albert had rolled into town at 10:30 last night, he'd seen several hotels and motels to choose from, including well-known chains, but he'd settled for a place called...

What was it? Desert something? Something of the sun? Or sands? Did it matter?

Just a little blue-and-white two-story cinderblock place on the side of the highway, directly across from the train tracks. The name didn't matter, did it?

The important thing was, last night, Albert had gone inside and told the clerk—an elderly gentleman who may or may not have been an Indian of some kind—that he wanted a room, but he'd lost his ID. Could he give some cash as a deposit instead? Albert had plenty of cash. Over the years, he had slowly stashed a large sum in his getaway bag.

The old clerk hesitated, so Albert said he wouldn't expect the deposit back.

Wink, wink.

Now Albert propped some pillows behind his head, grabbed the remote control off the nightstand, and turned the TV on.

First thing he saw was a photo of Elmer, which made Albert sit up straight.

Jesus! Elmer! There he was!

Elmer, the emu. Loveable Elmer. So much personality. Mischievous.

And there was Elmer on *Good Morning, America*, with Robin Roberts chuckling about the fact that a bunch of exotic animals had escaped from a small zoo in central Texas. The headline on the screen read *On The Loose!*

The video footage showed several of Albert's animals on the shoulder of the highway, with traffic backed up as far as the camera could see. Cops were all over the place, too. Albert could feel his pulse pick up, just seeing his animals in danger like that.

Then the camera showed the county game warden, John Marlin, leading the animals back into the zoo with a bucket of feed. Smart. So smart. Good guy, making sure the animals were safe. Albert owed him one.

Now the camera switched back to Robin Roberts, who said,

"Unfortunately, the chaos at the zoo seems to have come with a tragic mystery, as a body was found on the grounds. The sheriff has not yet been able to identify the victim or pinpoint a cause of death, but experts point out that fatalities among zoo employees are rare, with just four in the past six years. The most recent involved a zookeeper in Sweden who was mauled by a tiger when a gate was left open. That man died later at a hospital."

Albert let out an involuntary yelp when he suddenly saw his own face on the screen.

Robin Roberts said, "To deepen the mystery, authorities have not been able to locate the owner of the zoo, Albert Cortez. He remains missing this morning."

One of Robin Roberts' co-anchors—some guy Albert didn't know—said, "That's pretty wild, Robin."

"Pun intended?" Robin Roberts asked.

He chuckled. "You'll have to forgive me for that. So the body that was found—that wasn't the zoo owner?"

"It was not. The police were clear on that."

"It will be interesting to see how the situation plays out. Taking a look at the weather now, record temperatures across the country continue to turn your average autumn into a hotter, sweatier—"

Albert switched to other channels, but he found no other reports. He scrolled through the channels nonstop for twenty minutes, but nobody else was covering it. Yet. Maybe that *GMA* report would be the extent of it. Maybe the story would be nothing more than a quick blip on the national radar.

If only he had access to the internet. After that state cop had shaken him up in Roswell, Albert had been too nervous to do anything but drive. The idea of going inside a store to buy a cell phone was more than he could handle. He would have to get over that and just do it.

He left the TV tuned to GMA, got out of bed, and went to the only window at the front of the room. He pushed the curtain aside by two inches. There was the neon-green Ford Fiesta, parked right out front. Several other vehicles were scattered around the parking lot, but the motel was obviously far from full. Same with the town itself. Not much traffic on the highway.

If there were a perfect place to hide out, this might be it.

But for how long? He couldn't just stay here indefinitely. He had plenty of cash, but he had to start coming up with a plan. He didn't have to figure it all out at once, though.

One step at a time.

14

At 8:45, Marlin was on his way to the Chandler Place apartment complex when he got a text from Nicole.

Good Morning America just ran video of you at the zoo. You're going national, you big stud.

He replied, *Maybe it's time to get an agent.*

She sent a laughing face.

Two minutes later, Marlin got a call from Rance Powell, a rancher who owned several hundred acres to the west of the exotic zoo.

"I just saw something I ain't never seen before, but I cain't tell you what it was," Powell said.

"An animal from the zoo?" Marlin said.

"I hope so, or my vision is going."

"Is it still there?"

"Nope. It run off. It might still be over there in the brush somewhere."

"What did it look like?"

"Well, it was some kind of big goat or sheep or something. I'm talking big, like the size of a small cow. Probably four or five hundred pounds."

"What color was it?"

"Kinda tan or light brown, with some white stripes running down from its backbone and across its rib cage. And it had long spiral-shaped horns. I wasn't about to mess with it."

"That's a greater kudu," Marlin said.

"If you say so."

"It's an antelope from Africa. His name is Kevin."

"He's got a name?"

"And just a friendly reminder, but you shouldn't shoot it."

"Dang it," Powell said, laughing. "I was already picturing it on my wall, but then I remembered you saying it was a state jail felony and I figured I wouldn't look good in an orange jumpsuit."

"It's not a good look for anybody," Marlin said. "If you see it again, will you call me?"

"Sure will. I've never been over to that zoo. Are the animals tame or what?"

"More or less, but don't get too close. It might be kind of rattled at this point. Don't approach it or lasso it or anything like that."

"Can I give it a stern lecture?"

"If it will listen."

"I got a little one-acre pen and I might be able to lure him into that."

"That would work."

"Will it eat corn or cattle cubes?"

"Probably either one. Call me anytime, day or night, okay?"

"You got it."

"And let me give you the number of a woman named Tracy Lavelle, the assistant zookeeper. Can you call her after this and let her know you saw it? That's the last loose animal."

"You bet. Happy to do it."

"She might want to come over to your place and look around."

"No problem."

They finished their call, and fifteen minutes later, Marlin pulled into the Chandler Place apartment complex, where he found the parking lot mostly empty. Apparently most of the residents had already left for work or school.

The complex consisted of two long parallel rows of buildings, with Bryce Cauley's unit in the center building of the westernmost row.

Marlin had checked Bryce Cauley's criminal history earlier and found that Cauley had pled guilty to a class-A misdemeanor in connection with his arrest for possession of a controlled substance eleven months earlier. No felony. He could possess a firearm. And there was still the chance that Bryce had had nothing to do with any of the incidents at Darren Meyer's ranch.

Bryce's driver's license photo had confirmed that he was not the man who'd pointed the rifle at Marlin yesterday. Could he have been the person driving the white truck? Probably not, considering that none of the fingerprints lifted during processing matched Bryce's, whose prints were definitely in the system.

Marlin parked and got out of his truck. As he was walking toward the complex, he stopped for a moment. There on the rear window of a silver BMW coupe was a small sticker for Safari Adventure. What were the odds of that?

He turned and went back to his truck. Got on the radio and asked Darrell, the dispatcher, to run the plate.

A moment later, Darrell said, "Comes back to a 2019 BMW M2 registered to Rory Grafmiller. Negative twenty-nine."

So the vehicle wasn't stolen and the owner had no warrants. Marlin didn't recognize the name. Was Grafmiller a zoo employee? Or simply an enthusiastic supporter?

He sent a text to Bobby Garza and Lauren Gilchrist. *Know the name Rory Grafmiller?*

Lauren replied within thirty seconds. *Yes. Will call you shortly.*

Marlin waited. His phone rang one minute later.

Lauren said, "He's a tour guide at the zoo and had a run-in with Albert Cortez on Tuesday morning. Albert sent him home after that. Where are you seeing that name?"

Lauren was already up to speed on the events that had occurred at Darren Meyer's ranch, so Marlin quickly explained that Bryce Cauley and Rory Grafmiller both lived at the Chandler Place apartments.

"Could be a coincidence," Marlin said.

"Sure it could," Lauren said.

"Am I crazy, or are you a tad bit skeptical?"

She laughed. Lauren understood they had no reason—yet—to conclude that the trespassing poacher on Meyer's ranch was involved with anything that had happened at the zoo. Same with the person driving the white truck, whether it was the same person or someone else. But she'd always been the type to follow her instinct, and more often than not, she was right.

"Plenty of places to live around Blanco County," Lauren said. "What're the odds that Meyer's nephew is neighbors with a zoo employee?"

"Yeah, raises some questions, but I still don't even know if Bryce Cauley was on the ranch. If I can ID the man with the rifle, I might get somewhere. Or if I can talk to Bryce and get his side of it."

"I'll bet you lunch there's a connection somehow," Lauren said.

"I'll take that bet, mostly because we haven't had lunch in a while."

"Yeah, what's the deal? You ducking me?"

"Every chance I get."

"Smart aleck," Lauren said. "I'm gonna win this bet and rub it in your face."

Truth was, Marlin hadn't socialized much with Lauren one-on-one when she'd first started working at the sheriff's office, if for no reason other than to avoid the appearance of impropriety. Many people in Blanco County knew about their history, and he didn't want to provide fodder for gossip. Lauren, on the other hand, was never concerned about such things. She would've laughed if he'd told her his concerns.

"Fair enough," Marlin said. "What's the story on Grafmiller?"

"He was kind of dodgy in his interview yesterday, and then he lawyered up," Lauren said. "Convenient that his mother is Cassandra Grafmiller."

"Ah. I was wondering about that last name."

"She said her son has no interest in talking to us any further because he thought we were trying to pin something on him. Tracy Lavelle said Rory has a temper and isn't a great fit at the zoo, whereas he said she is basically a know-it-all with a superior attitude. We've talked to maybe eight or nine employees and they all back Tracy—every one of them. He's the one with the problem, not her."

"What was the run-in with Albert?" Marlin asked.

"Rory was late to work, which is apparently a habit, so Albert called him on it. Later, Tracy saw Rory getting a little rough with an antelope, so she told Albert, and when Albert asked Rory about it, it got heated."

"Any sign of Albert?" Marlin asked.

"Nothing. Hate to say it, but I figure he's either dead or on the run. If he's on the run, well, that doesn't look good. Still no hits on his debit and credit cards, so I'm guessing there won't be any."

"And no ID on the victim?"

"Nope. If we don't nail it down soon, we'll get a sketch drawn up and send that out to other agencies in Texas. Hoping to hear from Lem real soon about cause of death."

Right then, the door opened to Bryce Cauley's apartment. Cauley stepped out and locked the door behind him.

"Okay, great," Marlin said. "Right now I've got my eyeballs on Bryce Cauley, so I'm gonna let you go."

"Good luck," Lauren said.

"Thanks."

"And don't get hit by a truck or anything like that, okay?" Lauren said. "You're gonna owe me lunch."

"Oh, but I'm the smart aleck?" Marlin said.

Red woke again at 9:17.

He got up, opened his bedroom door, and stood there for a moment in nothing but some elastic-banded gym shorts.

"Billy Don?"

Nothing.

"Garrett?"

Nobody home.

Red walked to the kitchen at the other end of the trailer.

Empty. He didn't even smell coffee. What a bummer.

But he did see a note on the dinette table. Good to see that Billy Don was still following Red's "no texts before nine o'clock" rule. Of course, that rule didn't apply to Mandy, especially if she was sending one of those special photos he liked so much.

Red stepped over and picked up the note.

Went to town for brekfast tacos. Back in 45 minutes. Will bring you a cupple.

That showed Billy Don's typical sloppy thinking. Red didn't know what time they'd left, so how could he know when 45 minutes had passed?

Red dropped the note back onto the table and headed back down the long hallway.

As he was passing the spare bedroom with Garrett's things in it,

Red stopped.

He stood in the doorway and just looked.

There was Garrett's backpack, resting on the futon that folded out into a bed.

Ten seconds passed.

Red was wondering exactly what was in that backpack, just like he'd wondered when they'd picked Garrett up on the side of the road. But Red no longer thought there might be drugs or booze or scabies medication in there. Maybe there was a big roll of cash. Or maybe not. Garrett was essentially homeless, so Red had a hard time picturing a guy like that carrying an ATM card, but maybe he did.

Which brought up an important question: Had Garrett already received the $400,000 in life insurance, or would the insurance company wait until the police closed the case? Red had no idea how that worked, but Red figured an insurance company would use any excuse to hold on to that money for as long as possible, stalling until a judge or somebody ordered them to release it. Greedy bastards. Almost as bad as banks.

But if Garrett *had* already received the $400,000, why was he living like a vagrant? Who would choose to do that? And why? Red knew that even if he somehow ended up dead broke, he wouldn't be homeless. Well, technically, maybe he would, meaning he might not own a home, but he wouldn't be sleeping under a bridge or in the woods, taking a dump behind a tree. He'd sleep on friends' couches at first, and then he'd find some kind of job working for a wealthy rancher who had some little shack or cabin where Red could bunk. And then he'd work damn hard to get his life—

Damn it, he was getting sidetracked.

None of that mattered right now.

The backpack. That's what mattered.

It was so calm and quiet in the trailer, all alone like this. He could pop in there, take a peek, and never get caught. If Billy Don and Garrett came back, Red would hear Billy Don's old Ranchero bouncing up the driveway, and he'd have plenty of time to clear out.

Red stepped slowly into the spare bedroom and stood by the futon. He studied the backpack for a few seconds, noting the way it was resting on the blanket, because he'd need to put it back exactly the way he'd found it.

He reached down and unzipped it. Looked inside. There were a couple of T-shirts on top. Then some socks. Some underwear. None of it folded, just shoved in there. Red pulled it all out of the backpack, glad the items were clean, because Garrett had asked to do a load of laundry last night. Still, it felt a little weird handling some other dude's skivvies.

He dug deeper and found a little sleeve of saltine crackers, a can of tuna, and a granola bar.

Then he found a small zippered bag that would be perfect for holding a bunch of cash, but it contained various toiletries—a disposable razor, toothbrush, deodorant, and things like that.

Then, digging to the bottom, he saw the butt of a handgun.

15

Red froze for a moment, just staring into the backpack.

He couldn't blame a homeless guy for carrying a gun around, for protection and whatnot, but it made Red wonder if the dead guy at the zoo had been shot. The cops hadn't shared that information yet. The truth was, Red wasn't real comfortable knowing that a suspected murderer was now an armed guest in his house.

Red didn't want to touch the gun and leave his fingerprints on it, so he shifted the backpack around to get a better look. It was a black Glock semi-automatic in a nylon holster. A real gun, not a toy or a BB gun. Not a big gun. Maybe a .380, but it was hard to—

He flinched as he heard someone climbing the back steps of the trailer. Then the back door opened!

Red quickly began to stuff everything back into the backpack, but he was panicking, and he wasn't sure if he was doing it in the proper order.

The back door closed and now he heard someone walking down the hallway!

The socks and underwear and shirts were a jumble, but Red shoved it all in as fast as he could, and he zipped it up and—

"What're you doing?"

Red turned to see Garrett standing in the doorway. *Be calm. Deny everything.*

"Hey," Red said. "I thought you went to town with Billy Don."

Garrett took one step into the bedroom.

"No, I was taking a walk out back. Just looking around."

"A walk?" Red said. *Who the hell just walks around?*

"Yeah," Garrett said. "What, uh, were you doing just now?"

Red had always been pretty good at making up excuses fast—mostly because he had a long history of engaging in behavior that required that sort of thing. Had Garrett seen him handling the backpack? Red figured it was fifty-fifty.

"I was checking the bed sheets," he said. "I got to thinking this morning that we might need to change the sheets so you can sleep in a clean bed."

Garrett stared for a long moment. Then he said, "That's thoughtful of you. The sheets seem okay to me."

"Just trying to be a good host," Red said.

"Yeah, okay, but why were you—"

"Hang on," Red said. "Hear that?"

"What?"

"That's Billy Don getting back with breakfast tacos," Red said. "You hungry? I sure am."

Red moved past him and out the bedroom door before Garrett could ask any more questions.

"Bryce?"

"Yeah?"

Marlin was catching him just as he was opening the door to a blue Ford Ranger. Nice truck. Had a silver toolbox mounted in the back.

"I'm John Marlin, the county game warden."

Marlin extended his hand and Bryce shook it.

"How's it going?" Bryce asked.

He was exactly as Darren Meyer had described him—five-nine or so, and just a bit heavy, with shaggy blond hair. He was wearing blue jeans, a purple T-shirt, and sunglasses.

"Just fine," Marlin said. "Got a minute to talk?"

"Actually, I need to be at work in ten minutes. I've got a ton of prep work to do before we open."

Marlin thought it was odd that Bryce didn't ask what he wanted to talk about. Most non-hunters would be confused, or at least curious, if they were approached by a game warden.

"I'll keep it short, then," Marlin said. "You been out to your uncle's ranch lately?"

"My uncle?"

A red flag already. Marlin's experience was that people repeat your question, or part of it, when they want to stall.

"Yeah, Darren Meyer, your uncle."

"Well, yeah, I mean I know my uncle, but no, I haven't been out there."

"He said he gave you permission to go out to the ranch while he's in Australia."

"Yeah, he did."

Marlin could smell marijuana coming off him. Faint, but it was there.

"But you haven't been there?" Marlin asked.

"Not yet, no. I've been pretty busy. Did you talk to him?"

"Yeah, this morning. Have any of your friends been out to the ranch?"

"Can I ask what this is all about? I heard about the weird stuff happening at the zoo across the highway, so..."

"So...?" Marlin prompted him to keep talking.

"I heard somebody on the news say people shouldn't shoot any of those loose animals. Is that why you're here? To tell me not to do that?"

"Not just that."

"I wouldn't anyway," Bryce said. "Even without the warning. I'm not into shooting animals. I'm not a hunter or anything like that. I don't even like to fish."

He had his hand on the truck door, eager to leave. Marlin wished Bryce wasn't wearing sunglasses. It would be interesting to see if he could maintain eye contact.

"How about any of your friends?"

"I think a couple of them hunt, but I'm not sure. I really need to—"

"Which friends hunt?"

"Can I call you later and talk about this? I need to go. I'm already late for work."

"Won't keep you much longer," Marlin said. "Which friends of yours hunt?"

"I don't see why it matters, because none of them were at my uncle's ranch."

"But if you weren't out there, how would you know that? One of them could've gone out there without telling you."

"My friends aren't like that. They wouldn't just go."

Marlin grinned. "I can't tell you how many times I've heard that. You never know. Sometimes there's a misunderstanding—maybe a friend thought you said he could visit the ranch anytime he wanted, but you didn't mean that at all."

"Okay, well, I'll ask if anybody went out there, and if they did, I'll let you know."

It was time to be more aggressive.

"I'd rather talk to them myself," Marlin said, "but it seems you're dead set on keeping their names from me—which makes me wonder why."

"But I'm not. I just don't know what you—"

"Bryce, I want you to listen to me for a second, and then I'll let you go. No matter what happened at the ranch or who was involved, we'll find out eventually. By 'we' I mean me, the sheriff's office, and even the Texas Rangers, if we need to call them in. If you were at the ranch anytime in the past few days, we can get the location data on your phone, plus the texts between you and your friends. We'll go that route if we have to. But if you step up like a man and take care of business right now, I'll work with you on this. You understand what I'm saying?"

Bryce was staring at the pavement. Finally he raised his head and said, "I don't know what happened out there, but none of it was my fault. I wasn't even there."

"If that's true, I'll do my best to keep you out of it. But I need to know who was there."

Bryce looked around, as if to make sure nobody could overhear. Then he said, "I work with this guy named Trevor at Dairy Queen and sometimes we hang out. I told him about the ranch and he said we should go out there. Then on Monday, he said we should go out there on Tuesday or Wednesday, because he was off on those days. But I had to work, so I told him he could go by himself, just as long as he didn't do anything stupid."

"He's that kind of guy—who might do something stupid?" Marlin asked.

"I don't know him well enough to be sure."

"What's Trevor's last name?"

"Larkin."

"Do you know if he took you up on it?"

"I don't know. I haven't talked to him since then."

"Did he have the gate code?"

"Yeah."

"Was he planning to hunt or just shoot guns or what?"

"He said he wanted to kill a deer, which is part of the reason I let him go by himself. I'm not into that. It's kind of cruel, in my opinion."

"Have you talked to your uncle in the past few days?"

"No, I haven't talked to him since he left."

"Has he called you?"

"No. He didn't know about any of this. He didn't give me permission to take anyone else out there. I screwed up and I'll admit it."

"Do you know what happened out there yesterday?" Marlin asked.

"I heard some rumors, but I don't know what's true and what isn't," Bryce said.

"Tell me what you heard."

"That there was a game warden on the ranch and somebody stole my uncle's truck and then wrecked it on Highway 281 and ran away."

"Anything else?"

"No, that's all. Was that what happened?"

Apparently word hadn't spread about the man shooting an axis deer and then pointing the rifle at Marlin. Or Bryce wasn't being completely honest about what he knew.

"That's part of it," Marlin said. "He plowed through your uncle's gate on the way out, and the truck is banged up pretty good."

"Jeez," Bryce said.

"You weren't there?"

"No, I swear. I was at work."

"And you haven't talked to Trevor about this? Not a word?"

"No way. I was too worried it might've been him—but I was hoping it wasn't. We haven't talked or texted. The truth is, for the past couple of days, I've been trying to avoid him."

"Why's that?"

Bryce shook his head. "There's something not right about him. He's just strange. Creepy strange. I see him staring at girls sometime."

"Sounds pretty normal to me," Marlin said. "Being that age and staring at girls."

"But it's more than that—like he's fixated and he's *watching* them, not just checking them out. There's something in his eyes that just isn't normal. Oh, and then—this is really weird, but he has this leather bracelet that says 'WWCD,' and when I asked what that meant, he said, 'What Would Charlie Do?' Apparently Charlie was some famous killer. So I was like, dude, that's a sick joke, but he just looked at me."

"Charlie?"

"Right."

"Think he was talking about Charles Manson?"

Technically, Charles Manson hadn't killed anyone himself, but Marlin had to wonder if Trevor Larkin—or Bryce—would even know that.

"I have no idea," Bryce said. "He never told me who it was. Maybe it wasn't really even what those letters stood for. It was just friggin' weird, to be honest. I think he's kind of a nutcase. Either that or he likes to pretend he is, because he doesn't really fit in anywhere. He doesn't seem to have any friends."

"So why do you hang out with him?"

"I'm pretty easygoing, but then I saw how weird he is. You always hear about loners snapping and going on a killing spree. That's the kind of guy he is. Like all this stuff about him stealing my uncle's truck and plowing it through the gate? That doesn't surprise me at all."

"If it was him," Marlin said.

"Right, if it was."

Marlin had to remind himself that Bryce's evaluation of Trevor could be way off base. Even if Bryce could be trusted, he wasn't trained to do any kind of risk assessment on a person like Trevor Larkin, or anybody else, for that matter.

"When you heard somebody wrecked your uncle's truck, why didn't you call the sheriff's office?"

"I just wanted to stay out of it, especially since I don't know who did it."

"But the information you just gave me would've been helpful

earlier."

"Yeah, okay, I'm sorry about that."

"What does Trevor look like?" Marlin asked.

"He's tall and thin. Has a beard, sort of. Like long stubble. That's the way he keeps it. Oh, hang on."

Bryce took his phone out and a moment later turned the screen toward Marlin, showing him a photo of a man from the waist up. It wasn't a great photo—taken at night and kind of blurry—but Marlin was fairly certain it was the man who'd pointed the rifle. "Fairly certain" wasn't much of a legal standard, though. He couldn't swear to it in court.

"Got any others?" Marlin asked.

"Sorry, no."

Marlin felt confident he could find additional photos online, along with Larkin's driver's license photo—and any mug shots that might exist.

Marlin asked at least a dozen more questions, gathering as much information about Trevor Larkin as he could. Then he said, "Go ahead and text me his contact information, along with that photo," and he gave Bryce his number.

"I will," Bryce said.

"No, I mean right now," Marlin said.

Bryce took his phone out again and a moment later the items arrived on Marlin's phone.

"I really need to go now," Bryce said. "I'm way late."

"One more question," Marlin said. "You know a guy named Rory Grafmiller?"

"I know a guy named Rory," Bryce said. "I've seen him at the pool and we've talked a couple of times. I don't know what his last name is."

"Do you know where he works?"

"Yeah, that little zoo on 281," Bryce said. "Where all the animals got out."

"Does Trevor know Rory?"

"I have no idea," Bryce said. "I don't remember him mentioning Rory."

"Thanks for being straight with me," Marlin said. "I might be in touch with more questions."

Bryce did not appear pleased by that prospect.

"One other thing," Marlin said. "I smell pot. Have you been smoking?"

"No, sir."

"But I'm smelling it, right?"

"Uh…"

"Shoot straight with me, Bryce."

"You might smell it, yeah."

"When was the last time you smoked?"

"Last night."

"You promise? I don't want you driving stoned."

"No, I promise. Really."

16

Albert couldn't remember ever feeling elated to see a Walmart anywhere, but there was one on the west side of Gallup, and it filled Albert's heart with joy. Not a small Walmart, either, but a supercenter. They would have plenty of cell phones to choose from, plus other supplies he'd need.

Albert parked between two trucks, walked inside, and grabbed a cart. There was a greeter, of course—an elderly woman who said, "Welcome to Walmart!" She gave him a big smile, but…was there something else on her face? A flicker of recognition? Had she seen the segment on *Good Morning, America*? Albert was wearing sunglasses, but that wasn't much of a disguise.

Albert had no choice but to continue on his way, moving with purpose and confidence, and completely unlike a fugitive. But then, a few seconds later, he casually ducked into an aisle with his cart and looked back at the elderly woman. She wasn't watching him at all. She had already forgotten him. She was, in fact, greeting other shoppers. That's what paranoia will do to you.

He made his way through various departments to reach the electronics section and found an aisle filled with prepaid no-contract cell phones hanging in plastic-encased packaging. Burner phones. Pay with cash. Buy plenty of data in advance, via a card also hanging on a rack. No ID required. No name associated with the phone. Just one more phone in a sea of cell phones across the country and around the world. Total anonymity.

He reviewed all of the choices carefully, then picked a Samsung Galaxy, even though it was one of the most expensive phones. This phone would be critical to his future, so it would be ridiculous to skimp. He also picked out an external battery and several wall chargers and charging cables.

What else would he need? Clothes. All he had was what he was wearing.

He went to the men's section and grabbed about thirty casual shirts, intentionally choosing styles and patterns he wouldn't normally wear. Then he picked a dozen pairs of cargo shorts in various colors. He stacked up a bunch of blue jeans in his size, and several pairs of khakis, and then he grabbed a bunch of multi-packs of underwear and socks.

Next he went to the shoe department and picked out three pairs of comfortable sneakers in different brands and colors, plus two pairs of canvas loafers.

Next were toiletries. Shampoo, soap, deodorant, razors, shave cream, toothpaste, toothbrush, mouthwash, dental floss, but no hairbrush. Instead he bought a Wahl hair clipper for nineteen bucks.

Then he went to another department and found one large rolling suitcase capable of holding everything he was about to buy.

Five minutes later, he was standing in line with his basket and the suitcase and he began to panic again. Now it seemed obvious that the items he was buying couldn't have been a larger red flag. How could he have been so stupid? The contents in his cart, when viewed as a collection, practically screamed, "I'm on the run! Notice me! Ask me questions! Call the cops, for God's sake! Be a hero!"

Should he get out of line and put some of the items away? Maybe come back later for those?

He started to do that, but the customer in front of him completed her purchase and now it was Albert's turn. The cashier—some young kid with spiked hair—was looking at him, waiting.

Albert moved forward and began to put his items on the conveyor belt.

"How are you doing today?" the kid asked as he began to scan each item.

"Real good," Albert said. "Thanks."

"Did you find everything you need?"

"Sure did."

The kid smiled. "This is a lot of shirts."

"I'm helping a homeless guy get back on his feet," Albert said spontaneously.

"Pardon?"

"I'm buying all of this for a homeless man. Just helping him out."

"I was wondering," the kid said.

"God bless you," said the woman behind Albert.

Albert turned his head halfway and said, "Thank you."

"Are you with a church group or something like that?" the kid asked. "I can get you a discount if you are."

"No, just me."

"Rotary Club? Kiwanis? Lions Club?"

"Nope."

"First responder? Military? Over 55?"

"Sorry, no. I'll just pay the regular price."

The kid said, "I bet my manager would give you a discount anyway."

This was turning into a nightmare. Albert was becoming the center of attention. Someone might recognize him from the report on *Good Morning, America.*

"That's okay," Albert said. "Let's not worry about it."

"You sure?" the kid asked.

Since when were kids his age this helpful and proactive? Albert had hired plenty of young tour guides and most of them were merely adequate on a good day. Some, like Rory, were essentially a liability.

"Yeah. Thanks, though," Albert said.

The woman behind him said, "Here, let me pay for some of it," as she was opening her wallet.

Oh, Lord. When would it stop?

"You don't have to—"

"You're a good man to be helping somebody out like that," said an elderly gentleman behind the woman offering money.

"Yeah, it's really cool of you," said the kid cashier.

"So much better than having them people standing on the corner, asking for money," the elderly gentleman said. "How do we know they ain't using it for drugs or booze?"

"Here you go," said the woman, shoving a twenty-dollar bill at Albert. "It's isn't much, but—"

"No, that's very generous," Albert said, taking the money. "God bless you, too."

"Yes, bless you—again!" said the woman cheerfully.

"This way he can get a job and pull his own weight," the elderly gentleman said.

"Oh, there's Mike," the cashier said. "Mike!" Now he was waving Mike over. "Let's get you that discount," the kid said to Albert.

"But I—"

"It's no trouble at all," the kid said.

Albert's heart was racing by now—pounding, actually—and he resisted the impulse to drop everything and run. Did the expression on his face show the panic?

Mike, the manager, came over, listened to the kid, then gave Albert a big smile. "Sir, we're gonna knock ten percent off your total today. How does that sound?"

"That's very generous. Thank you."

"The least we can do to show our commitment to the community," Mike said as he moved to the kid's register and hit the right keys to apply the discount. When he was done, he gave Albert another big smile. "You have a great day."

"Thank you."

"God bless," said the woman behind him.

"Thank you," Albert said.

The kid eventually finished ringing everything up, and then he began to fold each and every item of clothing.

"You can just toss everything into the basket and I'll fold it later," Albert said.

"You sure?"

"Absolutely," Albert said. "I'm supposed to meet him in, like, five minutes."

"Okay, gotcha."

Albert paid with cash and finally got the hell out of there, pushing the cart with the suitcase stacked on top.

He threw it all into the trunk of the neon-green Ford Fiesta and had to resist the urge to gun it all the way back to the motel.

But he maintained the speed limit, and a few minutes later, he took

a right into the parking lot and—
What the hell?
Somebody was seated in a chair right in front of his room.
Albert coasted slowly across the lot, and as he got closer, he realized it was the old man. The clerk. He appeared to be waiting for Albert to return. Why else would he be sitting there?
Albert eased into the same parking spot and killed the engine. The old man appeared to be napping. There was an empty chair next to the one the old man was occupying.
Albert got out of the Fiesta and closed the door, which roused the old man.
"Hey, there," Albert said. "Sorry to wake you."
"The morning sun always makes me drowsy," the old man said.
Albert chuckled, but he didn't say anything more. He assumed the old man would get out of the chair and go back to the office—but he didn't.
But he was staring. The old man was staring. Just sitting there—and staring.
"Is something wrong?" Albert asked.
Then the old man said it. He said the words that almost buckled Albert's knees.
"Albert, right?"
The pleasant smile on Albert's face slowly melted away.
Last night, when checking in, Albert had given his name as Alexandro Coronado. Same initials. Easy to remember.
"I'm sorry?" Albert said.
"Your name is Albert," the old man said.
"No, it's Alexandro."
The old man grinned. "We shouldn't play this dumb game. Your face is turning white, which isn't easy for a Mexican."
"My name is Alexandro Coronado," Albert said.
It was so hot out. Only seventy degrees, but hot.
"It's Albert Cortez," the old man said, "and you should be grateful I'm sitting here instead of calling the cops. But the story was…they left out so many details. I wanted to talk to you first."
Albert was getting lightheaded. He felt like he might pass out. His vision was spotty.
The old man nodded at the empty chair. "You should sit down

before you fall down."

Albert realized there was no sense in denying it anymore. The old man wasn't guessing. He knew. But he hadn't turned Albert in. Why?

Albert walked over to the chair and eased himself into it. Took a deep breath and tried to gather himself. Tried to think of a good lie that would explain everything, but good God, there was no chance of that.

So he'd tell the truth. All of it. But where to start? There was one important point he wanted to make—not just to defend his own honor, but to put the old man at ease.

"I'm not a criminal," Albert said. "I didn't do anything wrong. Well, not illegal. I might've crossed some lines ethically, a long time ago, but I didn't do anything illegal."

The old man nodded slowly. "Tell me your story."

In nineteen years, Albert had never shared it with anyone. But now it was time.

17

"Damn, these are good," Garrett said, lifting a breakfast taco. "Can't get anything like this up in Michigan."

They were seated around the small square dinette table in the kitchen. If Garrett was suspicious about catching Red in the spare bedroom, he wasn't showing it now, so Red relaxed a bit. The excuse about bed sheets had worked, apparently.

"That's a damn shame," Billy Don said, exposing a mouthful of chorizo, egg, and cheese, with salsa mixed in.

Red swallowed what he was chewing and said, "You gotta do that?"

"Do what?" Billy Don replied.

"That. You just did it again, on purpose."

"Did what again?" Billy Don asked, shrugging, acting all innocent.

"Talking with your mouth full," Red said.

"I like to eat and I like to talk," Billy Don said.

"Tell me about it."

"And sometimes they happen at the same time."

"It's gross."

"Well, if you don't like it, don't look," Billy Don said.

"That's a great solution," Red said. "Suppose I was taking a big dump with the door open, and you said it was gross, and I said, okay, well, just don't look. How would you feel about that?"

"I'd be fine with it," Billy Don said, speaking yet again with a full mouth, complete with food lodged between his teeth.

Red shook his head. "I know I ain't no country-club gentleman, but you've got the manners of a donkey."

"I've seen you dip snuff at a funeral," Billy Don said.

"Well, the guy was dead," Red said. "Wasn't like he could get offended. Plus, it was an *outdoor* funeral, so the rules were different."

"Then there was the time you told that nurse with the big hooters you had some swelling you wanted her to look at."

Red grinned at the memory. "But you laughed, didn't you?"

"Yeah, but she sure as hell didn't. I mean, who gets kicked out of a hospital? You've gotta own that one."

"They say laughter is the best medicine, right?"

"Point is, don't be trying to teach me manners. We're both pigs."

"I can agree with that," Red said.

The three of them ate in silence for a moment.

"One thing I've been wondering about," Red said, talking to Garrett now. "Seems like you're just sort of traveling around the country, going wherever you feel like going. Does that basically sum it up?"

"Yeah, I guess," Garrett said. "I figure once I get married or have kids or whatever, I won't be as free to travel. I'd been thinking about doing this for a long time, but all that mess back home sort of inspired me to get out on the road. So at least that's something positive that came of it. I think, in a weird way, my dad would be glad about that part. He always told me to do things while I was young, because before you know it, your time is up."

Yeah, because somebody shoves you off a roof, Red thought.

"So did you, uh, save up for the trip or what?" he said. "I mean I know you're not staying at four-star hotels, but if you're mostly just traveling and not working, I figure that's gotta eat up a pretty good amount of money."

Red wanted to see if Garrett would reveal that he was rolling in cash from life insurance.

"Being nosy," Billy Don said.

"I'm just curious, is all," Red said.

"Not your bidness."

"It's a fair question," Red said.

"None of your concern," Billy Don said.

"Hey, if you don't like it, don't listen!" Red said, feeling pretty smart for throwing Billy Don's nonsense logic back at him, but with a twist.

"That's okay," Garrett said. "I don't mind. And the truth is, I'm really enjoying myself, but I can't travel much longer before I'll need to get a job again."

Red didn't say anything, because he wanted to make sure Garrett was done answering. Billy Don didn't say anything because he was starting on yet another taco—his fourth, according to Red's count.

Garrett didn't add anything else, so Red said, "Money getting tight, huh?"

"Yeah," Garrett said, grinning. "I can stretch the hell out of a dollar, but it only goes so far."

So there it was. A kid his age with $400,000 in the bank doesn't think about stretching dollars. So that meant Garrett didn't have the money yet...or he didn't want to admit he had it.

Red decided he needed to push harder, even if it meant crossing a line or ruffling some feathers. It's what a real detective would do. Ask the hard questions, as they say.

"I hate to pry," he said, "but didn't your daddy leave nothing to you in his will? Or maybe life insurance? Nothing like that?"

"Jesus, Red," Billy Don said, apparently so appalled that he actually stopped eating for a moment. "You're way outta line."

Before Red could defend himself, Garrett spoke up.

"Hey, I think I'd be wondering the same thing," he said. "Unfortunately, no. He didn't have much to leave behind. But that's okay. He was a great dad and that was good enough. I didn't need anything else from him."

The kitchen went quiet for a long moment.

Red was wondering why Garrett was lying about the life insurance. Even if Garrett hadn't gotten the money yet, that wasn't the same as his daddy leaving nothing behind.

"You guys shouldn't feel sorry for me," Garrett said. "It's all good. I have great memories of my dad, and I still have my mom, and now I'm out exploring the world. When my cash gets low, I'll just work for a while. And when I've had enough of life on the road, I'll just go back home. By then, maybe everything will have blown over. If it hasn't, well, I'll deal with it."

When Albert was finished with his story—including revealing his real name and explaining why he was hesitant to seek assistance from the cops—the old man didn't say anything for the longest time. Then he finally said, "I will help you."

The relief was enormous. Not because the old man offered to help—what could he possibly do?—but because he wasn't going to turn Albert in.

"Thank you," Albert said. "I mean it. Really. And, hey, if you doubt anything I told you, just google my real name."

"I don't know how to google," the old man said. "But I believe you anyway. If you weren't being truthful, I would know."

How would you know? Albert wondered. But he believed the old man.

"Thank you for believing me," Albert said.

The old man nodded. "What would you like to be called?"

"Albert. Please. Always Albert. Never my real name. I've been Albert for nineteen years. That's who I am now. Albert Cortez."

"What are you planning to do? Run forever?"

Albert thought about that. "I don't know. I don't have a lot of options. In fact, that's the only option I can think of—running. And starting over."

"Here, or somewhere else?"

"You mean a different country?"

"Yes, that's what I mean."

"I don't know that, either. I've been thinking a lot, but I don't know what to do. I just know that I don't want to die."

Across the highway, a train rolled north on the tracks, creating enough noise that Albert and the old man sat silently for a few minutes. After the train had rolled out of sight and the noise was dissipating, Albert spoke again.

"What's your name? I never got it."

"It's Bob."

"Bob?"

"Yes, Bob."

"Oh."

"Unless you want to call me Soaring Eagle."

Albert looked at him. "Soaring Eagle?"

"Just kidding," the old man said. "I'm not Soaring Eagle. Just Bob."

"That's funny. You got me."

"I'm a laugh a minute," Bob said, with no hint of sarcasm.

"I'm sure you are."

"But I shouldn't be making jokes right now. Instead, you need to make some decisions."

"I know," Albert said.

"And then I will help you."

Albert nodded somberly to show his appreciation and agreement, but he said, "I don't know if anybody can help me. But it's nice of you to offer."

"I grew up in this town," Bob said. "Been here all my life. I know people. If the people I know can't help you, you're right—nobody can."

Now Albert was nervous. Bob was talking about involving more people, and the more people who knew who he was, the greater the chance that someone might turn him in. And how would anyone in a little town like Gallup be able to help?

"What kind of people?" Albert asked.

"You'll see," Bob said. "Do you trust me?"

"I do," Albert said.

"Because you have no choice," Bob said, grinning. He was missing several teeth, and the remaining ones were the color of caramel.

"That's true," Albert said. "But I'd trust you anyway."

A car pulled into the motel parking lot and stopped at the front office, prompting Bob to rise slowly out of his chair.

"We'll talk again later," he said.

Albert nodded. "Thank you."

Bob walked slowly across the parking lot and Albert remained in the chair, enjoying the sunshine for a moment. He might've even dozed off—which showed how much the conversation had eased his worries—but suddenly Bob was jostling his arm.

"You need to get into your room," Bob said. "They're talking about you on the local news."

"What the—"

"Somebody spotted you," Bob said. "An older couple in an RV.

Said they ran into you at a Denny's in Roswell. That ring any bells? They showed a security video of you in the restaurant and your green car in the parking lot."

Just like that, the feeling of renewed hope was gone.

18

After lunch, Marlin sat at his desk within the sheriff's office and did some research.

Trevor Larkin was 27 years old and had been born in Sweetwater, Texas, about forty miles west of Abilene. There, he had compiled a minor criminal record for possession of marijuana and hunting from a public roadway—both more than five years earlier.

He'd never been married.

He'd moved to Blanco twenty months ago. He owned no property in the county.

He'd gotten a speeding ticket nine months earlier, but his driver's license was current.

He had no warrants.

He had a valid hunting license for the current season.

Three years ago, a woman in Sweetwater had gotten a protective order against him. The order had remained in effect for one year, and it appeared Larkin had had no contact with the woman in that time.

Marlin checked social media and came up empty. Trevor Larkin had various accounts, but none of them were visible to the general public.

Larkin might've thought aiming a weapon at a law enforcement officer was no big deal, but in reality, it was a felony. The trick would be getting Larkin to admit he knew Marlin was a game warden. If he claimed he thought Marlin was a trespasser, and that he didn't understand what Marlin had yelled at him, that would change the scenario. Marlin also had to remind himself that it might not have been Larkin out there on Meyer's ranch.

When Marlin finished with his research, he called the Dairy Queen in Blanco and asked for Trevor.

"He's not here," said a young woman who identified herself as Caitlin.

"Oh, I thought he was scheduled," Marlin said, winging it.

"He was, but we haven't seen him."

"What a slacker."

"I know, right?"

"Has he called in?"

"Uh, I...who is this?"

"This is John. I'm supposed to meet up with him later."

"You could try his cell," Caitlin said, "but I called it myself earlier and he didn't answer. Anyway, if you reach him, tell him he's supposed to be at work, okay?"

She laughed and hung up.

Interesting.

The fact that Larkin was a no-show at work supported the theory that he'd been the poacher on Meyer's ranch. He was afraid to show his face, because the cops would find him there. Or, another possibility—he'd been injured when he'd plowed the truck through the gate and he wasn't capable of working. All speculation, of course.

Marlin set his phone down, but right then, he received a text from Lauren Gilchrist, so he picked it back up.

Lem isn't done yet, but he just said our DOA was shot. One round in his neck that struck a carotid artery, then the spine. No exit. He says .380.

Which meant her case had just officially become a homicide.

He replied: *Thanks. FYI, Bryce Cauley said Trevor Larkin is a nutcase, loner, the type who goes on a spree. Have no idea if that's accurate. Will let you know my thoughts when I finally track him down. He didn't show at work today.*

Thx, Lauren replied. *I'll be thinking where I want to go for that lunch you'll owe me.*

"They said you are a 'person of interest' in the death of that man at your zoo," Bob said, "and that you might be armed."

Oh, Jesus. This was getting crazy.

"I don't know what to do," Albert said. "This is hopeless."

He was feeling panicked. Overwhelmed. Scared. They were in Albert's hotel room. Bob didn't seem too worried about tending the front office. What if a customer needed him? He appeared totally relaxed, seated in the padded chair in the corner, near the little table that cheap motels always seemed to have.

Albert, meanwhile, was peeking out the window. The car, sitting right in front of the room, now felt like a giant flashing neon sign. Luckily it was a fairly common kind of car. On the other hand, on his drive from Blanco to Gallup, Albert hadn't seen a single other Ford Fiesta the same color as this one. Why would the rental companies buy cars that garish?

"Nothing is hopeless until you give up hope," Bob said.

Albert thought that sounded like some cheesy nonsense you'd read on a motivational poster.

"I hope you're right," Albert said.

They both stopped talking for a moment as a state trooper passed on the highway and disappeared from view. Albert couldn't tell whether the officer inside had looked in this direction or not. Had he seen the rental car? Was he turning around right now? Albert held his breath for a moment and waited for the marked unit to reappear. Thirty seconds passed.

"First thing we need to do is get your car out of sight," Bob said.

"I was just thinking about that. But what can I do with it?"

"We'll move it around back," Bob said. "It's gated off back there. Nobody will see it."

"Maybe I should ditch the car," Albert said. "Get on a bus and go somewhere else."

"Risky," Bob said. "The other passengers might recognize you. They'll be sitting for hours on a bus with nothing to do but look at the other people on the bus. But we can figure that out later. We need to hide the car now, then we need to come up with a plan. Or I can butt out."

"No, please don't," Albert said.

Bob nodded.

"What kind of plan?" Albert asked.

"One step at a time," Bob said.

"I have to ask," Albert said. "Why are you so willing to help me?"

Bob seemed to contemplate the question for a long moment. "I've been there myself," he finally said.

"Been where?"

"In your shoes. In a similar situation. Sometime soon I'll tell you my story. It's not as good as yours, but it ain't bad. me the keys and I'll move the car. Then I'll make a phone call to a friend of mine."

"How much do I owe you for the tacos?" Garrett asked Billy Don later. They'd been sitting around the dinette for a good while, just bullshitting. Mostly Billy Don was doing all the talking, while Red was contemplating everything he'd learned.

"Don't worry about it," Billy Don said.

"You sure?"

"It's on me," Billy Don said.

"I appreciate it," Garrett said.

"You, on the other hand, owe me five bucks," Billy Don said to Red.

"I'll take it off your rent," Red said.

"But I don't pay rent."

"Exactly."

Garrett said, "Thanks for letting me stay here last night. And thanks for the work yesterday."

"No problem," Billy Don said. "Red wasn't gonna stop the truck, but I insisted."

"I don't blame you," Garrett said to Red. "But I'm glad you did. Anyway, guess I'll be hitting the road later this morning."

Red was surprised that he was somewhat sorry to hear this. How could he continue his investigation if Garrett was gone?

"No reason to rush off," Billy Don said. "Unless you got somewhere you need to be."

"Not really. Just don't want to overstay my welcome."

"We'd let you know if you did," Billy Don said with a guffaw. "Ain't that right, Red?"

Red grunted.

"We'd probably just toss you out the door," Billy Don said. "Then you'd know for sure."

"That's usually a pretty good clue," Garrett said, laughing.

"You ain't there yet," Billy Don said. "Stick around, if you want. Or not. Up to you."

"I just might," Garrett said. "Thanks. Hey, is it okay if I take a shower?"

"Ain't my day to take one, so go right ahead," Billy Don said.

"Okay, cool."

"Towels are in the cabinet," Billy Don said. "Might even find a clean one."

Garrett rinsed his coffee cup, then left the kitchen and went down the hallway.

"Good kid," Billy Don said.

Red didn't say anything.

"Don't you think?" Billy Don asked.

"Sure."

"That stuff about his dad dying is pretty wild," Billy Don said.

Red decided it was time to share some of his suspicions with Billy Don—in just a few minutes.

"Poor guy," Billy Don said.

"Umm-hmm," Red said.

"He's been through a lot," Billy Don said.

And Red finally heard the water running in the bathroom, which would prevent Garrett from hearing their conversation.

"Maybe so, but he can afford to pay five bucks for some breakfast tacos," Red said.

"So what? I was just being nice."

"In fact, he could probably afford to pay five *thousand* bucks for some tacos. Or fifty thousand."

"What're you babbling about?"

"Let me tell you something about your new friend Garrett," Red said.

19

Marlin drove slowly along Althaus-Davis Road, in the northwest corner of Blanco County.

This was a quiet road in perhaps the least populated area of the county. That was saying something, since the entire county was sparsely populated—somewhere around ten or eleven thousand people in seven hundred square miles. Compare that to neighboring Travis County, with about 1,300,000 people in one thousand square miles.

Trevor Larkin's current address matched a mobile home on ten acres—a rental, apparently. Marlin had never met the owner, whose mailing address was in Georgetown.

He crossed a cattle guard and tapped the brakes as he saw a mailbox with Larkin's address. The property was fenced and gated, but the gate was open. The land was too thick with cedar and oak trees for Marlin to see the trailer from the road.

Marlin sat in his truck for a moment, thinking.

There was a good chance Larkin wasn't home. If he was home, he probably wouldn't open the door. Marlin couldn't force him. Also couldn't make him talk.

But there was something else bothering Marlin.

He knew he should probably let someone else question Larkin. Maybe ask another game warden to tackle it. Or a deputy. Or even a Texas Ranger. After all, Larkin was possibly, if not likely, the person who'd pointed a rifle at him. That meant Marlin's emotions—his desire for justice—could impact his objectivity. Or a defense attorney could make that claim later.

On the other hand...

The man with the rifle might not have been Larkin. That was why Marlin was here—to find out. No harm in that. If Larkin appeared to be the right guy, Marlin could then turn it over to somebody else.

Marlin pulled his truck through the gate and eased along the caliche road leading to the mobile home.

Albert stood in front of the mirror in the small bathroom and ran his palm over his smooth head for the tenth time, but it was still an unusual feeling. Totally bald. Gleaming bald. Light bounced off his mocha-colored skin. The freshly shaven portion was somewhat lighter. He'd have to get some sun or wear a hat.

The shape of his head surprised him, but he wasn't sure why. He'd never seen it like this before. Why had he been expecting a pronounced roundness, almost to the point of looking like Charlie Brown? In reality, it was a nice shape. Not too circular. Not pointed on the top or anything like that. Some nice angles that made him look like he'd lost weight. Weird.

Before Albert had shaved his head, he'd used a comb and the Wahl hair trimmer to groom his eyebrows—and what an amazing difference that had made. He'd always had bushy brows, but now he had trimmed them shorter. Then he'd used a bit of hair color to get rid of the gray. Amazing. He should've done that years ago.

He hardly recognized himself. Add sunglasses and his own mother, God rest her soul, would've walked right past him on the street without so much as a nod.

When Bob returned to the room later, he studied Albert for a moment, then said, "Well, I guess you can forget making a plan. You don't need to do anything now. You can go anywhere on the planet. Nobody will know who you are."

"Not bad, huh? I might grow a goatee, too. I've never had one, or even a mustache."

"Too bad you can't change your fingerprints," Bob said. "Or your DNA."

"If it comes down to that, I'm screwed anyway."

Bob sat down in the chair in the corner again. He seemed to always sit, when there was an opportunity to sit.

"I made a call," he said. "I talked to a good friend about the situation. He doesn't think it's hopeless."

"Well, that's good news," Albert said. "It's not hopeless. Before you know it, we might decide I shouldn't be steeped in gloom and despair—but let's wait and see."

Bob grinned. "It's harder than it used to be to build a fake identity, considering the way technology has changed, but it can be done. You can start over, if that's what you want to do."

"How do they do it?" Albert asked. "How do they create the new ID? What name do they use? How do they match it to a Social Security number? They have to do that, right? I just don't understand how they can do it."

"Take it easy," Bob said. "And you might want to stop rubbing your head. That's a pretty good signal that you recently shaved your scalp and you aren't used to it yet."

Albert lowered his hand. He hadn't even realized he was doing it. He sat down on the edge of the bed and faced Bob.

"I guess I don't need to understand how it works," Albert said, "but I'm confused. You're saying you have a friend who can create a new identity for me?"

"No."

"Then what?"

"He can't create it—not all of it—but he can help you obtain it."

Alarms were ringing in Albert's head.

"This is all making me very nervous," Albert said.

"I can understand that," Bob said. "It might make you feel more comfortable if I try to explain it."

"Please do."

Bob nodded slowly. "My friend says the government used to assign Social Security numbers in a very methodical and sensible manner, based on geography and date of birth. Then, they began to assign those numbers randomly, and—"

"Why?"

"Why what?"

"Sorry to interrupt, but why did they begin assigning the numbers randomly?"

"I don't know. I didn't ask. He didn't tell me."

"Okay."

"But once they began to do that—assign the numbers randomly—it made it easier for people like my friend to take an unused number and start to build a new identity around it. They almost always use numbers assigned to kids—ones that haven't been used yet—and I can see you have another question."

"Why would a parent get a kid a Social Security number if he isn't about to start a job or earn money somehow?"

"You can't claim a child as a dependent on your taxes without a Social Security number."

"Oh," Albert said. "I didn't know."

"There are other reasons, like opening a bank account in the kid's name or getting government services. A lot of people get a number right after their kid is born."

"Okay, so this guy gets a Social Security number for me. Then what?"

"Actually he gets you a signed Social Security card and two other supporting documents, like a utility bill or a library card or even a fishing license. You can use those to apply for a replacement birth certificate, and once you have that, you can get a driver's license, or a passport, or both."

Albert let that sink in for a moment.

"If he gets me a Social Security number for some kid, won't it say I'm that kid's age—like five or ten years old, or whatever?"

"I don't know. I think he has a way around that. He can make it your birth date or some other date."

"But how?"

"I don't know."

"And how does he match my name with the Social Security number? Isn't there a record somewhere that shows the real name that goes with that number? Or do I use the real name?"

"I think you use the name that goes with the number."

Albert stood and went to the window again. Peeked outside. Nice to see an empty spot where his rental car had previously been parked.

Bob had been very helpful so far.

"How much does all this cost?" he asked.

"A thousand dollars."

Albert wondered if Bob was keeping a cut for himself. Did it matter? Albert could afford it. And it seemed like a reasonable price for a new identity.

"That's fair," Albert said.

"But you're hesitant."

"Honestly, yeah, but only because I don't know your friend."

"I vouch for him."

"Okay."

"He's a good man."

Despite the reassurance, Albert was feeling overwhelmed. It was all too much. But what else could he do?

"Questions?" Bob said.

"Several, but I don't know where to start."

"First get the ID, then worry about the rest."

"That makes sense."

"Although it would probably be wise to start thinking about where you'll go."

"Agreed."

"You speak Spanish?" Bob asked.

"Un poco."

"So...no?"

"Not really, no."

"Got relatives in Mexico? Or friends?"

"No."

"That's unfortunate."

"Maybe Canada would be better," Albert said.

"Maybe so."

"Is it nothing but white people up there?" Albert asked.

"I'm not sure. I've never been there."

"I might not fit in so well up there, either."

"At least you speak the language," Bob said.

Albert realized now that he would miss Blanco County. He'd always thought he could live there quietly for the rest of his days.

"You want my friend to proceed?" Bob asked.

"Yeah, that seems like the best way."

"You got that thousand bucks? He needs it up front."

"Oh, sure. Hang on."

Albert pulled his suitcase out from under the bed. There was no point in trying to keep Bob from knowing where Albert kept his cash. Albert had already made the decision to trust Bob completely, and if didn't work out—if Bob screwed him or was simply not competent enough to help—so be it.

Albert opened the little leather case that held his money. He had nearly forty thousand dollars in here, all in hundreds. He had slowly tucked it away over the years, just in case. Now he wished he'd stashed more. How long would forty grand last him if he couldn't work? Couple of years, if he was careful and frugal?

He removed ten bills and handed them to Bob. Then he removed two more bills and held them out.

"What's this?" Bob asked.

"For your trouble," Albert said.

Bob shook his head. "No. I don't need it."

"But you've been—"

"No," Bob said again. He folded up the thousand bucks and stuck it in the front pocket of his jeans. "You hungry?"

"Starving," Albert said.

20

When Red was done sharing everything he had learned about Garrett, Billy Don said, "Well, that explains it."

"Explains what?"

"Why you've been acting like a jerk lately. More than normal. I figured maybe you just didn't like him."

"If I didn't like him, he wouldn't still be here."

"So you *do* like him?"

"That don't matter either way," Red said. "The only real question is, did he shove his own dad off the roof?"

The water was still running in the bathroom.

"You think he's got four hundred thousand bucks in insurance money?" Billy Don asked.

"Well, not on him, but yeah, in a bank somewhere, probably."

"Why probably?"

"Because they might be holding that money back until the cops close the case."

"So you don't know if he's got that money yet or not," Billy Don said. "Or if he'll ever get it."

"No, but I'm damn sure a lot of people would kill someone for a shot at that much money."

"Even their own daddy?"

"Things like that happen all the time. Just look in the news."

"Know what else happens all the time?"

"Huh?"

"You come up with crazy ideas. Maybe his daddy slipped and that's all there is to it."

"Hey, I'm just following the facts," Red said. "And there's more. When y'all were gone for tacos—I mean, when I thought y'all were gone for tacos, but Garrett was walking around out back—I decided to take a little peek into his backpack and—"

"Jesus."

"Know what I found?"

"You shouldn'ta looked, Red. That's his own private property. Can't believe you did that."

"Wanna know what I found?"

"Not really."

"Sure you do. Take a guess."

Billy Don, trying to be funny, said, "A pair of women's panties?"

Red started to say no, but then he thought about it and said, "Do they make men's panties?"

"What?"

"You said it was women's panties, which made me wonder if—never mind. It wasn't any kind of panties, it was a gun. Looked like maybe a three-eighty."

Billy Don shook his head but didn't say anything.

"Why's he got a gun?" Red asked.

"That ain't so weird. You'd carry a gun if you was hitchhiking around the country."

"Damn right I would, but it's just the combination of everything in totalness—his dad died, and then Garrett ran away, and then he acted like money was tight, despite all that insurance money, and then I find out he's got a gun."

"I wouldn't say he ran away."

"He left town."

"That ain't running away."

Red let out a big sigh. "I just knew you'd argue with me about this."

"I ain't arguing."

"Now you're arguing about arguing."

"Am not."

"It never stops."

"Does too."

"And what're the odds he'd be right near that zoo when another dead body was found?" Red asked. He knew he should just drop it, but he couldn't help himself. The fact that Billy Don thought he was wrong made Red more intent than ever on proving he was right.

"So now you're thinking he had something to do with that?" Billy Don asked.

"I don't know if he did or not. That's the point."

"What possible reason could he have for killing that guy?"

"Ain't no way of knowing until we know who the dead guy is. Maybe it was somebody Garrett knew. Maybe they was traveling together. Maybe it was a stranger and Garrett killed him just for the thrill of it. Lot of sickos out there that would do exactly that. Most of the time, people say, 'Oh, he was such a nice guy. I never figured he'd do something like that.' Garrett could be like that. Maybe he got a thrill when he killed his dad and it turned him into some kind of psycho."

"I think you're letting your 'magination run away from you."

"Maybe so, but it's usually right."

Billy Don opened his mouth to reply, but right then the shower cut off.

Red waved his hands, meaning it was time to shut up.

"You're nuts," Billy Don said quietly.

"Leave my nuts out of this," Red said.

Marlin rounded a bend in the driveway and saw a brown dust-covered Chevy Tahoe parked in front of a singlewide mobile home that appeared fairly new. It had a covered wooden porch—a deck, essentially—that stretched at least twelve feet to each side of the front door. A nice place to hang out and enjoy a cool autumn evening.

You always hear about loners snapping and going on a killing spree. That's the kind of guy he is.

That's what Bryce Cauley had said about Trevor Larkin. Was it accurate?

Marlin knew from experience that the vast majority of people who appeared to pose a threat rarely did. Some of those people purposefully cultivated that sort of reputation. They wanted to appear tough or dangerous or unpredictable. Why? You'd have to ask a psychiatrist.

He tapped the brakes and stopped about forty yards from the trailer. Then he grabbed his radio microphone and let the county dispatcher know he'd be out for a few minutes at this address.

He saw no movement. Nobody outside. The trailer was tucked into a small open area surrounded by walls of towering old-growth cedar trees. Lots of privacy. A guy like Trevor Larkin could do just about anything he wanted out here, as long as he didn't disturb the neighbors, the nearest of whom was roughly a quarter-mile away.

Marlin eased forward and parked his truck behind the Tahoe. He stepped out and closed the truck door firmly. He had no intention of sneaking up on Larkin. After all, he wasn't serving a warrant or trying to catch him in the act of committing a crime. He was here merely to ask questions. Make Larkin give a statement and commit to a story. Had he been on Darren Meyer's ranch yesterday morning? If not, where had he been? Who had he been with?

Marlin walked alongside the Tahoe's driver's-side window and looked inside. Cluttered and messy, but nothing unusual. Some beer cans on the passenger-side floorboard. Marlin took another step and placed his hand on the hood. Cold. This vehicle hadn't moved today.

He moved toward the covered porch.

It was quiet out here—no dogs barking, no traffic noises—but as Marlin mounted the front steps, he heard muffled music through the thin walls of the trailer. Not loud. Nothing he recognized. Nothing catchy or commercial or even with any sort of discernible melody. He wasn't sure how he would classify it, except that it wasn't good. The lead singer should've looked into a different line of work.

Marlin stepped forward and knocked on the flimsy aluminum door.

The music continued, but he heard nothing else. If anyone moved around inside the trailer, he would almost certainly feel it and hear it.

The song ended, and for three seconds, there was nothing but the sound of a jet passing high overhead. Then another song began to play. Something familiar about the intro. Then a woman sang about liking dollars and diamonds and million dollar deals.

Marlin raised his hand and rapped again.

"State game warden!" he called out. "Trevor, you in there?"

No response. The music played on.

"Trevor Larkin!"

Ten seconds passed. Nothing. Marlin rapped even harder.

He waited a full minute, then moved to his left and looked through a window with slightly parted curtains. A nearly empty bedroom. Nothing in it except a group of stacked cardboard boxes and a padded armchair.

He moved to his right, to the window on the opposite side of the door. Same thing here—slightly parted curtains. He peered inside and saw a body facedown on the floor. A man. Couldn't see his face. Wasn't tall or slender enough to be Trevor Larkin. But he was wearing blue jeans and a purple T-shirt, which now had a large bloody spot on the back. And he had shaggy blond hair.

Marlin pulled his phone from his pocket and called it in.

21

Bob returned to Albert's room with a large pepperoni pizza and a twelve-pack of Bud Light.

"Damn, this is good," Albert said, wolfing down a slice. He hadn't had much to eat lately.

Bob nodded.

"You aren't going to eat?" Albert asked.

"I ate earlier. That's for you."

"Thank you. I was starving."

Bob opened a beer and took a long swig.

"Who mans the front desk when you're gone?" Albert asked.

"I leave a sign saying I'll be back in ten minutes. It says they can grab a room key and we'll handle the check-in later. They seem to like that—the casual arrangement. Most of them are from a big city somewhere and they never do things that way."

"You have any employees?" Albert asked, grabbing a second slice of pizza.

The TV was tuned to CNN with the volume turned down. Albert left it on all the time, in case they mentioned him or the body at the zoo.

"No, it's just me," Bob said. "My wife used to help me, but she's been gone a long time."

Albert wasn't sure what that meant. Had she left him, or had she died?

"Mind me asking how old you are?" Albert said.

"I'm ninety-three," Bob said.

"No way," Albert said. "You look about seventy-five."

Bob shrugged, as if his appearance—or maybe his longevity—were of no importance to him.

"Your health seems good," Albert said.

"My father lived to one hundred and six."

"That's amazing."

"My mother lived to one hundred and one."

"Great genes," Albert said.

He grabbed another slice. He might eat the whole damn pizza.

Then, without any sort of preamble, Bob said, "I was nineteen years old, living right down the road. I'd graduated from high school one year earlier, but my girlfriend at the time was still in school, a year behind me, just about to graduate. There was a big party to celebrate. Lots of beer and liquor. Probably two hundred kids there. It was out in a big field, with a bonfire, and some people had set up tents. It was a wild night."

Bob finished his beer and opened a second one.

"Somebody must've complained, because the cops showed up at about three in the morning and began running everybody off. Apparently—I only learned this later—they caught a couple having sex on a blanket, out in the dark, beneath a tree. The guy got up and ran. They talked to the girl and it turned out she was fifteen years old. A freshman. White girl. Very drunk."

Bob shook his head at the memory.

"I knew her. Everybody knew everybody, because this town is so small, and even smaller back then. Anyway, the cops called her parents, and of course they were furious, because the girl had told them she was spending the night with a friend. They wanted the name of the boy. They wanted to know who he was and—the important part—how old he was. Guess who she named?"

Albert didn't have to guess. "But…why would she do that?"

"What I heard is she had a boyfriend a year younger than me, but still eighteen—an adult—and she didn't want him to get into trouble. So she named me."

"Why you?"

"I have no idea. I guess I was the first person to spring to mind. I kind of looked like her boyfriend, so maybe that was it."

"And what happened?"

Albert knew it couldn't have ended well or Bob wouldn't be telling the story.

"Remember this was all a very long time ago, back when the cops probably would've let it go, except that the parents pushed and pushed and wouldn't drop it. They were wealthy people with power. The father had been a councilman a few years earlier."

"But I'm sure you denied it was you."

"Well, sure. You think they were going to believe me over her? A bunch of white cops and a white girl accusing an Injun?"

"Couldn't anyone back you up? Where were you when the cops showed up?"

"Asleep. I'd wandered off to take a piss and I fell down. I decided I was comfortable right where I was, so I stayed there for a minute. Next thing I knew, I was waking up. I could hear all the commotion, because the cops had arrived. So I just walked home. Left my truck there. That didn't look good, considering they were looking for someone who'd run away, but I didn't know that at the time."

"That's terrible. What happened?"

"I got arrested a week later—can't even remember the exact charge, but it wasn't as bad as it could have been. The lawyer they gave me haggled it down even lower, but I had to plead guilty to it, which I did, and then I spent six months in the county jail."

"Jeez," Albert said. "That's fucked up."

He didn't have to ask why Bob would plead guilty to something he didn't do.

"That stupid charge and all the gossip followed me around for nearly sixty years," Bob said. "Early on, I thought about moving away, but screw all those people. I stayed right here. And then…"

Bob grinned.

"What?" Albert asked.

"The girl—she was an old lady now—finally told the truth. First she came to see me and apologized—she cried a lot—and then she did an interview with the newspaper and told the truth. She'd been lying to protect her boyfriend."

Albert didn't know what to say. "All those years…people thinking…"

"Yeah," Bob said. "But what can you do?" An odd expression crossed his face, and he pointed at the TV. "You'd better turn that up."

Albert looked, and suddenly he couldn't breathe.

It was Sylvia. Right there. Sylvia. Still beautiful. Still capable of capturing his heart. Being interviewed outside her home. She must've seen the *GMA* segment and decided to speak out.

The caption on the lower screen said THE MISSING ZOOKEEPER. A smaller caption identified her as Sylvia Golino, her maiden name. Did that mean what he thought it meant?

He quickly grabbed the remote and turned up the volume.

"...about nineteen years ago," Sylvia was saying. "That's why I wanted to come forward and tell my story. Miguel and I had a relationship back then, and the truth is, I was married. I'm not proud of that, but I had no choice about staying in the marriage or not. I'll just leave it at that. The way I handled the situation back then is something I'll always regret."

Was married? That was ambiguous. Was she still married?

Someone off camera said, "Did you know anything about his disappearance nineteen years ago?"

"Not at all," Sylvia said. "He just disappeared, and I felt like I was lost on a deserted island."

A deserted island? He couldn't believe she said that. Was it a message?

She continued, saying, "But I'm glad to know he's been okay for all these years, and I hope he still is. Back then, like a lot of people, I figured he was dead, and I figured my ex-husband did it."

Ex-husband! Ohmygod! There it was!

"Miguel Lopez struck and killed your brother-in-law with his car, and he fled before he was prosecuted," the same voice said. "Do you still want him held accountable?"

"I never did, even back then," Sylvia said. "That wasn't his fault. My brother-in-law was trying to shoot him, and Miguel was just trying to get away. They never should've charged him. Read the articles from back then. You'll see."

"Do you know where he is now?"

"I have no idea. That's the truth."

"Do you know if the man who was killed at the zoo in Texas is somehow connected to this incident from nineteen years ago?"

"I don't know that, either. You should talk to my ex-husband about that."

Ha. She was sending them after Anthony Carducci. Sylvia had always had nerve.

She said she had nothing further to say, then turned away from the camera, ending the interview. They cut back to the anchor, who made a final comment about the story, but Albert wasn't listening. His mind was still spinning from seeing Sylvia. Good God. She hadn't changed a bit.

"She's a captivating woman," Bob said.

Albert nodded.

"Speaks her mind."

"She always did."

"Did you know she was divorced?"

"Not until just now. I used to check her Facebook page now and then, but I couldn't see very much, and it was just too…"

Bob nodded. He knew. Too painful.

"You okay?" he asked.

"I think so."

The way I handled the situation back then is something I'll always regret.

That raised so many questions.

Did she mean she wished she'd run away with Albert when he'd suggested it? Or that she never should've gotten involved with him in the first place? Or maybe she meant she should've mustered up the courage and gotten a divorce before starting her relationship with Albert.

Was she ready to run away with him now, after all these years? Maybe he was deluding himself to even entertain that question—but what if the answer was yes?

What if she'd been regretting her decision for a long time, and they could've been together if only Albert had reached out to her? It was heartbreaking to contemplate that possibility.

Lauren Gilchrist couldn't believe what she had just seen. Fortunately, a deputy had been watching CNN during his lunch break and had alerted Lauren to Sylvia Golino's interview. She'd backed it up and watched it three times, taking notes.

The bottom line was that Albert Cortez—quiet Albert, the zookeeper—had been on the run for years, living in Blanco County under an assumed name. His real name was Miguel Lopez. He'd apparently killed a man with his car in Massachusetts nearly two decades ago. Mind blower.

The first question that popped into Lauren's mind: Could Sylvia Golino identify the dead man found at the exotic zoo?

Lauren needed to speak to her immediately, and she'd already asked Darrell to try to track her down. If Darrell couldn't find Sylvia Golino's phone number or contact her via social media, he would try contacting CNN. Maybe the producer would share her phone number, or at least pass a message to Sylvia Golino, asking her to contact the Blanco County Sheriff's Office.

Lauren began to search for the archived articles Sylvia Golino had referred to, but her phone rang right then. Did Darrell have news already?

Nope. It was John Marlin.

Now Lauren couldn't believe what she was hearing. Sylvia Golino would have to wait.

22

After a long nap, Red went into the living room and found Billy Don and Garrett focused on the TV.

"This shit's getting weird, Red," Billy Don said from his usual sunken spot on the couch. Garrett was seated beside him. Wise man, not taking Red's recliner. "Almost woke you up."

"What shit?" Red said.

Billy Don nodded at the TV, like that would explain it all.

There was a lady on the screen, talking in front of a house, but she'd just finished saying whatever she'd been saying.

"That lady was saying some wild stuff about Albert, but you just missed it," Billy Don said.

"Remember how you can back it up?" Red asked.

That was one of the features of their DVR—the ability to rewind what you were watching. Billy Don always forgot, and when he remembered, he seemed to think it was some kind of mystical, magical voodoo trick. How could he operate an iPhone but fail to understand a DVR?

"Oh, yeah," Billy Don said, and he rewound it about a minute.

Now that woman—probably in her late forties, with thick brown hair and a hell of a nice body—was talking about some guy named Miguel, which confused Red at first, until he realized Miguel was Albert Cortez.

"Albert was banging this lady years ago," Billy Don said.

"Yeah, I figured that out," Red said.

"Even though she was married," Billy Don said.

"I pieced that together when she said she was married," Red said.

"And then he took off," Billy Don said. "He's been hiding out for nineteen years."

"I'm watching the same clip you are," Red said.

Red took a seat in his recliner, and from this vantage point, he could sneak a look at Garrett, who had his eyes glued to the TV set. It was hard for Red to read his expression.

Now the lady on the TV was saying she wasn't going to say anything else, but she was glad Miguel was okay. Then she said she didn't know anything about the body at the zoo, but they should talk to her ex-husband.

"Miguel means Michael," Billy Don said to Garrett. "That's the Mexican word for Michael."

"Billy Don is always good at taking these complex issues and boiling 'em down for us simple folk," Red said.

He expected to get a laugh or at least a grin from Garrett, but the kid didn't react. He was too focused on the TV.

"Play that back again," Red said.

"Which part?" Billy Don asked.

"All of it."

Red wanted to watch Garrett more closely. As the interview played again, Garrett appeared almost hypnotized by it.

"Can't believe they still don't know who the dead guy is," Red said. "Ain't like it would be that hard to figure it out. Just run his fingerprints through one of them databases."

"Not everybody's in there," Billy Don said.

Red knew that, of course, because he was a seasoned investigator, but he wanted to see how Garrett might react.

Red said, "Yeah, I know, but if he ain't in there, somebody's bound to report him missing eventually."

"Think the ex-husband sent him down here?" Billy Don asked.

That idea hadn't occurred to Red yet, so he said, "Well, sure. That seems obvious."

If that were the case, there was a good chance Albert killed the guy in self-defense, which would mean Garrett had nothing to do with it.

"Can't believe they haven't even shown us a picture of him yet,"

Billy Don said.

"They usually don't do that until they can notify the kinfolk," Red said.

"Or maybe they can't show a picture, because he got shot in the face with a shotgun," Billy Don said.

Garrett said, "That's not—" But he stopped in mid-sentence.

"What?" Red said.

"Huh?" Garrett replied.

"What were you gonna say?"

"I was just saying that he probably wasn't shot in the face."

"Why do you think that?"

"I think I heard he was shot in the neck."

"Heard it from where?" Red asked.

Garrett kept his eyes on the TV.

"I can't remember. I think I read it online. Or I saw it on the news."

"I don't remember seeing that," Red said. "Did you see that, Billy Don?"

Red and Billy Don locked eyes for a few seconds, and even Billy Don was smart enough to read the message in Red's eyes. *How does Garrett know where the man was shot?*

"Lotta rumors getting spread," Billy Don said. "Can't trust most of it."

"Yeah, you're probably right," Garrett said. "I probably just heard a rumor."

Now Red was more confused than ever.

Trevor Larkin was fifteen years old the first time he heard the name Charles Starkweather. He—Trevor—had been flipping through the cable channels and happened to stop on a grainy black-and-white photo of Starkweather from the late fifties.

There was something compelling about that photo—that face, those wide-set eyes, that terrible flattop haircut—that stopped Trevor cold before he even knew why Charles Starkweather was famous. Then the narrator told him exactly why.

The photo wasn't just a casual snapshot or class picture, it was a mugshot. Starkweather had been arrested after going on a murder spree in Nebraska and Wyoming in 1958. Killed ten people in eight days.

He'd killed his first person, a gas station attendant, two months earlier and had gotten away with it. That changed everything for Starkweather. He'd found a way to transcend the bullying and poverty he'd endured as a kid. A way to express the rage that burned inside him.

Trevor could relate.

On January 21, 1958, Starkweather went to pick up his girlfriend, 14-year-old Caril Ann Fugate, but her parents didn't want him around their daughter. They argued. So he shot them. Simple as that. He hid the bodies for a few days, but family members became suspicious, and Starkweather and Fugate went on the run. Even to this day, there was debate as to whether Caril Ann was a willing participant or a hostage. Trevor always figured—always *hoped*—that she was happy to be along for the ride. It made a better story that way. The two of them against the world.

Starkweather killed eight more people, most at random, and according to him, Fugate participated. They got caught after a high-speed chase. Caril Ann Fugate got a life sentence and ultimately served seventeen years. Starkweather got the electric chair, but so what? He'd had his blaze of glory. His moment in the sun. A lot of people knew his name.

After watching that documentary, Trevor felt as if he'd discovered a fallback plan for his life. It was something he could keep in his back pocket in case things didn't work out, and he'd always found it oddly comforting. He never knew when, how, or if he'd act on it. One thing for certain, though—he'd always assumed it would be under his control. He would choose the time and the place and the exact conditions. He didn't expect it to just happen.

But that's the way it had unfolded. It started with the game warden yesterday. Trevor was in a bad mood at the time—still mad at Bryce—so he'd lost control and pointed the rifle at the warden. It was amazing how good it felt. Came *this* close to pulling the trigger. Could have cut that game warden down easily.

Then he realized what a mistake that had been, because he hadn't followed through, and he would get arrested, and his fallback plan would be ruined.

Luckily, he'd gotten away in Bryce's uncle's truck, but he knew it wouldn't be long before the cops came for him. Then what? Nothing would be under his control anymore. That was the worst possible scenario.

But they never came. Not last night and not this morning. Maybe he'd gotten away with it.

Then Bryce showed up at his house, telling him even more stuff that made him angry, and this time, he totally lost it.

Boom. Amazing.

Also unplanned, but he had some time to think afterward and form a plan.

Now he was parked at the Church of Christ next to the Dairy Queen, trying to work up the nerve to go inside.

He was antsy as hell. Mind racing. Doing his best to keep it under control. Panic was his enemy. He had to keep it in check.

A passing thundershower was dumping rain on Blanco right now, but it would pass soon, and then he'd make his move.

Go get Caitlin. Sweet Caitlin. She laughed at his jokes sometimes. Made him feel as if he belonged. But she also had a rebellious streak in her that he liked. He knew she liked to party, because she sometimes told him what she'd done over the weekend. Other times she mentioned how strict her parents were. They wouldn't even let her date yet. Caitlin resented that. She was mature enough to make her own decisions, wasn't she? She was sixteen. Almost an adult.

Would she want to go with him? He hoped the answer was yes. It would make a better story that way.

I felt like I was lost on a deserted island.

Sylvia had to have said that on purpose. Albert felt sure of it.

After all, he and Sylvia had loved the movie *Cast Away*, and as their time had come to an end, the story had become a bittersweet metaphor for the relationship; they were forced apart by circumstances out of their control.

So he downloaded the Facebook app to his new phone and opened a new account under the name Chuck Noland.

He listed his profession as a systems engineer and his employer as Federal Express.

He indicated that he was in a relationship with a woman named Kelly Frears.

He said his hometown was Memphis, Tennessee.

He used a stock shot of a Wilson volleyball for his profile photo.

Surely that was enough to tip her off. Surely Sylvia would see his friend request and understand who he was. She would accept it, right? What if she didn't? Albert had to prepare for the possibility he might be wrong about all this. She might not want anything to do with him now. She might even turn him in.

But if she did accept it…then what? Would it be safe to communicate with her via Facebook messages? Law enforcement wouldn't have grounds to monitor her private communications. Right?

Now it occurred to him that after her appearance on national TV, she would be swamped with all sorts of people, including weirdos, sending friend requests. Hundreds or even thousands. She'd go through them rapidly and delete them, right? Would she even look at his fake profile long enough to understand who he really was? Would she recognize the name Chuck Noland after all these years?

He hovered his finger over the Add Friend button.

Biggest decision he'd made in years. Could be his downfall. Hell, he could be signing his own death warrant. One killer had already come for him, and Albert had gotten away, and now, did he want to put himself at risk all over again? For what? One slim shot at rekindling a long-lost love? That was downright crazy. Where would they go? How could they ever be together, considering his past?

He touched the button.

23

Four months before a man called the sheriff's office about a loose zebra, Rory met Bryce at the pool in their apartment complex and they got stoned as hell that night. Hung out. Shot the shit. They weren't like immediately best buddies or anything, but Rory thought Bryce was okay, so they'd get together every now and then, usually to get high.

After that, Rory would sometimes sell Bryce some weed. No big deal. It wasn't like Rory was a dealer, but he had a connection with really good pot in Austin, so Rory would buy a little extra and sell it to Bryce, who, as far as Rory could tell, liked to be stoned basically all day long.

Then one day, three months after they'd met, when they were smoking again, Rory randomly mentioned something he thought was kind of weird. Or maybe it wasn't. That's why he wanted to tell somebody about it.

"I was at work today," he said, "and my boss—Albert, who can be an asshole sometimes—he was on the phone with somebody and he said his name was Miguel. Then he—"

"Your boss or the guy on the phone?"

"What?"

"Did your boss say *his* name was Miguel or was the guy on the phone named Miguel? Who was your boss saying was Miguel?"

"I have no idea who the guy on the phone was. All I'm saying is that *Albert*, my boss, identified *himself* as Miguel, but then he corrected it, like he'd accidentally said it or something."

"So Albert accidentally said his name was Miguel?"

"Right."

"Is that like a nickname or something?"

"Is Miguel a nickname for Albert?"

"Yeah."

"No, it means Michael."

"Albert does?"

"Miguel does."

It was really strong weed.

"Oh, *Miguel*," Bryce said. "Duh. Sorry, I wasn't hearing it right."

"What did you think I was saying?"

"I don't know, man."

"That's weird, though, huh?"

"No, I just didn't hear it right."

"I mean Albert saying his name is Miguel. *That's* weird."

"Absolutely."

"Why would he say that, you think?" Rory asked.

"How did the conversation go? I mean, like, what was the context?"

"I have no idea who he was talking to, but they must've asked for his name, and he said, 'It's Miguel O—wait, sorry. It's Albert Cortez.'"

"What was that second part?"

"Albert Cortez."

"No, I mean after Miguel, like was he saying part of his last name?"

"Yeah, it was like he was about to say a name that starts with an O."

"So is he Mexican or what?"

"I mean, he's American and everything, but his, like, roots are from Mexico, I guess."

"So it's probably a Mexican last name that starts with an O."

"Yeah, that's what I was thinking," Rory said.

"Like maybe O'Malley," Bryce said.

"But that's—"

"Just a joke, man."

"Ha. You got me. I thought you were really high," Rory said, impressed that Bryce could even come up with a joke like that.

They were in Rory's apartment with the blinds closed and the lights turned low. Rory knew they wouldn't even be talking about this strange topic if they weren't baked. In fact, Rory had basically forgotten about the whole thing after it happened, but now it seemed very mysterious and intriguing. The more he thought about it, the odder it became, and he was glad Bryce agreed.

"I can't think of any," Rory said.

"Any what?" Bryce asked.

"Mexican last names that start with an O."

"Oh. Me, neither, but I wasn't trying real hard."

They sat in silence for a long time.

"Ortega!" Bryce said, suddenly excited. "It just popped into my head. I knew an Ortega once."

"Yeah, but if Albert was saying 'Miguel Ortega' and he didn't finish the last name, it wouldn't sound like *O,* it would sound like *Or.*"

Bryce thought about it and then agreed. Both of them were quiet again.

"Ortiz?" Bryce said. "Oh, wait. Same problem. It starts with *Or.*"

Another long pause.

"Ochoa!" Rory said.

"That's a good one," Bryce said.

"I wonder if his name is really Miguel Ochoa," Rory said.

"If he's using a fake name...why? Is he hiding something?"

"I have no idea, but how do you start to give someone the wrong name? That's just friggin' bizarre, right? It'd be like if I introduced myself as Todd Johnson or something."

"Maybe you misunderstood what he was talking about. Maybe he thought the person on the phone was asking about someone else, but then he realized he was talking about him."

"Who?"

"Your boss."

"You lost me, bro. All I know is, he was calling himself Miguel something, and then he corrected it, like Albert Cortez is his new name, but he forgot for a second."

"Why would he need a new name? What if he's, like, on the run or something?"

"That would blow me away, because he's this boring middle-aged dude," Rory said.

"Well, he owns a zoo, which isn't that boring, as opposed to being an accountant or something. Or working at a Dairy Queen."

"Maybe, but he's got a stick up his ass sometimes. Always complaining if I'm late."

"You should google 'Miguel Ochoa' and see if you find anything."

So Rory pulled out his phone and did exactly that. There were, of course, lots of hits leading to many people with that name, but none that jumped out at him. Rory spent at least ten minutes checking everything out, to the point where he almost forgot what he was looking for.

"You got anything to eat?" Bryce asked.

"Huh? Oh. Yeah. Check the pantry."

Rory kept surfing while Bryce went into the kitchen and came back with a bag of barbecue-flavored potato chips.

"Not finding shit," Rory said.

Bryce was too busy eating chips to respond. He kept licking his fingers, which was kind of gross, since those fingers would go right back into the bag for more chips—chips that Rory might've eaten later, but not now, he wouldn't.

Rory said, "Even if his name used to be Miguel Ochoa and he changed it for some reason, that doesn't mean it would be easy to find out more about him. I mean, unless he murdered a bunch of people or stole millions of dollars, there wouldn't be a lot about it online, especially if it happened a long time ago."

"Yeah," Bryce said, apparently agreeing. "Want some chips?" He offered the bag.

"No thanks," Rory said. "Hey, wait a second. What if it doesn't start with an *O*? What if it starts with *Lo*, but it sounded like an *O* because Miguel ends with an *L* and it all ran together?"

Bryce said it, and the name practically finished itself. "Miguel Lo...pez."

"Miguel fucking Lopez!" Rory said. "I bet that's what he was going to say."

"What else would it be? Miguel Lo...I can't think of any other Mexican names that would start with that."

"Me, neither."

"Google it," Bryce said, digging into the bag again.

Rory was already on it, and the first thing he noticed was that there was an Argentine soccer player by that name, and a Puerto Rican sprinter, and then he saw an article titled *Without A Trace: The Unexplained Disappearance of Miguel Lopez*. It had been written eighteen years ago for some little magazine in Massachusetts. He began to read it and—

"Holy shit," Rory said.

"What?"

"Hang on." Rory was still reading. Then he noticed there was a small photo of the missing man. He clicked on it.

"You find something?"

"Oh, my God," Rory said. "I can't friggin' believe this."

"What?" Bryce asked. "*Whaat?*"

24

It was just after three o'clock and Rodney Bauer was enjoying the hell out of a basket of honey-glazed chicken strips and gravy when the tall guy with the scruffy beard and an oversized army jacket came through the front door.

Dairy Queen wasn't busy at this time of day. Wasn't dinnertime yet. Sure, some folks might use the drive-through to get a fountain drink or maybe a Dilly Bar, but the dining room inside was empty, except for Rodney and one other person, a young girl eating a hamburger and looking at her phone.

Rodney didn't know that girl, or the scruffy guy who'd just entered, and for that, he was grateful. If his wife Mabel found out he had stopped off for a snack, she'd nag him for a solid week. "You ate a dadgum chicken basket, and then you came home and had a full dinner three hours later?" is what she'd probably say. "That's just flat ridiculous. No wonder you haven't been able to lose any weight. You know how it works, doncha, Rodney? If you wanna lose weight, you gotta eat less. And maybe try some exercise every now and then, and I don't mean twelve-ounce curls." She'd mimic him raising a beer can to his mouth.

That's the kind of thing she'd say if she caught him.

But he loved her, of course, despite her nagging. That was his job. To love her. Wasn't always easy. But he did. No question about it. Definitely loved her.

The scruffy guy in the army jacket was just standing by the door, looking around, as if he was expecting to see a particular person.

The thing was, Rodney wasn't all that interested in losing weight. It was Mabel that was always pressuring him about it, which was ironic, considering her own substantial girth nowadays. She kept a basket full of chocolates tucked away in her sewing room and thought Rodney didn't know about it. Occasionally he'd sneak a few pieces when she wasn't home. He was tempted to leave a note in there— something like, *You on a diet, too, honey?* But then she'd know he knew where the chocolates were, so she'd hide them somewhere else.

Now that Rodney was getting a better look, he thought he recognized the scruffy guy. He was pretty sure the guy worked here at the DQ. He was a cook, which meant he didn't interact with the customers. But Rodney had seen his face in the pass-through window from the kitchen into the area behind the service counter.

"Order up," the guy would call out, when he was working.

But right now he was still standing by the front door. Not dressed for work, obviously. Maybe he was here to pick up a paycheck or something. Looking for a manager. There was nobody behind the service counter at the moment. Rodney didn't know where those employees went when there was nobody to serve, but there had to be a couple of rooms back there. Maybe a small break room. And the walk-in freezer. Some employee bathrooms.

Rodney picked up his last chicken strip, dipped it into the gravy, but didn't stuff it into his mouth just yet.

Something wasn't right. He didn't know what it was, but his radar was going off. Something about the scruffy guy hanging by the door. The look on his face. He was holding his right hand in his pocket, like he had an object in there. Rodney was watching him, but the scruffy guy hadn't even looked his way.

"About time, Trevor," a voice said, and Rodney realized one of the girls had emerged from the back area and was now behind the service counter.

"Hey, Renee," Trevor said, but he remained by the door. "Where's Caitlin?"

His voice was shaking. Why the hell was his voice shaking?

"You totally missed your shift and didn't even call in," Renee said. "So thanks for that. We had to scramble. Same with Bryce. He never showed up."

Rodney got the sense that Renee wasn't real fond of this guy.

"Sorry. Where's Caitlin?"

"In back."

Rodney remembered Caitlin. Cute girl. Had a good sense of humor. Always smiling, unlike a lot of teenagers.

"Can you ask her to come out here?" Trevor asked.

"I guess. Is something wrong?"

So Rodney wasn't imagining it. Renee had also noticed that Trevor was acting weird.

"No, I'm fine," Trevor said. "How's your grandmother?"

"What?"

"How's your grandmother?"

"I just—why are you asking about her? That's the second time. You don't even know her."

Yeah, Renee definitely didn't like this guy.

"I'm just trying to be nice," Trevor said. "Who's cooking today?"

Trevor sure was asking a lot of questions—and wanting to know where everyone was. Why was that?

"Craig," Renee said. "We had to call him in when you didn't show."

"Where is he?"

"He's back there somewhere," Renee said. "Maybe in the walk-in."

Now Trevor glanced in Rodney's direction, so Rodney looked out the window, totally nonchalant, while taking a bite of the chicken strip. The girl on the phone appeared oblivious to everything going on—and then Rodney noticed she was listening to music with earbuds.

"I need to talk to Caitlin," Trevor said.

Rodney's revolver was out in his truck. He had a license to carry, but he never kept it on him. Too bulky. Pain in the ass. He felt pretty stupid about that right now. But maybe he was wrong about the situation.

"Hang on just a sec," Renee said, heading for the back of the building.

"No!" Trevor barked, and now he was reaching inside his coat.

Rodney pulled his phone out of his pocket and put it in his lap, under the table.

"Caitlin!" Trevor yelled.

Jesus H. Christ, Rodney was right, because now this guy Trevor was pulling a gun from his pocket, and he aimed it at Renee.

Renee let out a little shriek.

"Everybody just stay where you are," Trevor said, his voice shaking worse than ever.

The girl with the earbuds still hadn't noticed what was happening.

"What are you doing?" Renee said, the fear in her voice obvious.

"You!" Trevor said, now swinging the gun toward Rodney. "Don't fuckin' move."

Rodney showed the kid his palms but otherwise didn't move. Moving would be stupid. The perfect way to get shot. His phone was still in his lap. No way to call 911 and report the gunman. That's what they would call the guy in the news reports later:

The gunman was an employee at the Dairy Queen. The gunman had a scruffy beard and a green army jacket. The gunman shot his first victim, Rodney Bauer, from a distance of approximately fifteen feet.

"Caitlin, get out here!" Trevor yelled.

Don't do it, Caitlin, Rodney thought. *Stay in back. Don't come out. If you come out here, nothing good will happen.*

Well, shit. Here she came. Her eyes were wide, but she didn't look too freaked out. She was standing beside Renee.

"What are you doing, Trevor?" she asked.

Damn calm, under the circumstances. Renee was starting to cry.

"Taking off," Trevor said. "You and me. Let's go."

Trevor wasn't looking at Rodney, but he still had the gun pointed in Rodney's direction.

"What?" Caitlin said.

"We're taking off."

"Who is?"

"Me and you. I'm parked next door."

No way in the world would Rodney let Caitlin leave with this guy.

"Are you serious?" Caitlin asked.

"About what?"

"Put that gun away. Whatever you're doing, it's dumb, and you should just leave before it gets worse."

The girl on the phone hadn't raised her head for even one second, despite the strange scene unfolding around her. Her phone had turned her into a zombie, and the earbuds made it even worse.

"Caitlin," Trevor said, the frustration obvious in his voice.

"What?"

"Don't call me dumb."

She seemed like a smart girl. Good at reading the situation. So she changed her approach.

"I didn't, and I'm sorry if it came across that way. But I care about you and this is just a bad idea. I don't want to see you hurt anyone or get into trouble."

"You care about me? Since when?"

"I think you're a nice guy, Trevor. You know that."

"How would I know that? You never said anything."

"Haven't I always been nice to you?"

"That doesn't mean you care about me."

Rodney wanted to do something, but any movement on his part would draw Trevor's attention.

"Will you put the gun down, Trevor? You should leave and we can talk later."

This girl was amazing.

"But I came to get you," Trevor said.

"I understand that, but where are you going? And why would you need to come in here with a gun?"

"I can't explain right now, but you need to—"

"I just called the cops," the girl with the phone abruptly announced, rising from the table.

Everyone—Rodney, Trevor, Caitlin, and Renee—looked at her.

She didn't appear afraid at all. Was she naïve, or simply stupid? Her body language was totally cocky. One hip thrust out, elbow resting on it, and her phone in that hand, the ringing coming through the speaker.

"Hang up!" Trevor yelled.

But it was too late.

"Blanco County 911. What's your emergency?"

Trevor swung the handgun around and fired it. He just shot, with no further warning.

It was even louder than Rodney would've expected in the small, enclosed space, and his ears were ringing as he lumbered to his feet and rushed toward Trevor.

"I knocked several times and identified myself as a state game warden," Marlin said, "and I called out for Trevor, but there was no answer. I heard music playing, which meant anybody inside might not be able to hear me. I'd heard the music earlier, as I climbed the steps."

He was doing his best to remember every detail in the correct order. Wasn't always easy in a stressful situation like this. He was giving his initial statement to Lauren Gilchrist in her marked SUV, which was parked on the county road in front of Trevor Larkin's rented mobile home. Deputies had secured the scene. EMS had already come and gone. Now they were waiting on Henry Jameson, the crime-scene technician.

"I went to the window to the left of the front door and looked in. All I saw was a mostly empty bedroom with a few boxes in it. So then I went to the window to the right of the door, and that's when I saw a body facedown on the floor. He had an obvious injury that resulted in a large bloodstain on the back of his T-shirt. I called dispatch, and then I entered the house through the front door, which was unlocked."

Bryce Cauley was dead—shot in the chest twice with a large-caliber weapon. It appeared Cauley had been right about Trevor Larkin, who was nowhere to be found. Cauley had apparently skipped work to go to Larkin's house, but why? Had Marlin's interview that morning rattled him that much?

How long Bryce had been dead would be a matter for Lem Tucker, but based on Marlin's estimation, not long. Maybe two or three hours when Marlin had found him.

"Right when I opened the door, I called out again, identifying myself, and got no answer. As I made my way through the house, I didn't see anybody else inside and I didn't see anything that struck me as potential evidence. No shell casings or bloody weapons or anything like that. If there was any blood on the floor, I couldn't see it, but the carpet was in pretty bad shape—lots of stains. And I was in a hurry to get to the victim and confirm his condition."

Marlin would have to give his statement again at the sheriff's office, and it would be recorded. Standard procedure.

"I checked the victim—no pulse, no breathing, and he was cool to the touch, or at least not warm. So then I checked the house for any other potential victims. I found nobody else and at that point I—"

Marlin was interrupted by Deputy Ernie Turpin rapping insistently on the driver's-side window. The expression on Ernie's face told Marlin something terrible had happened.

Lauren lowered the window and Ernie said, "There's been a shooting at the Dairy Queen in Blanco. At least two victims."

25

Details were sketchy as every available unit headed toward Blanco.

Marlin was in his state truck, following Lauren's marked county SUV, as they flew south on Highway 281 at ninety miles per hour, lights flashing, goosing the siren occasionally to move any slow-reacting motorists out of the way. Fortunately, traffic was sparse and the roads were dry. Unfortunately, the four-lane divided highway would narrow to a single lane in each direction as they got closer to Blanco.

Ernie Turpin—who'd remained behind to assume command of the crime scene at Trevor Larkin's trailer—had told them that a young woman, still unidentified, had been shot, possibly in the hand or forearm. Rodney Bauer had also been injured, possibly shot in the shoulder or rib cage as he had rushed the shooter, according to witnesses.

The same witnesses said the shooter was Trevor Larkin, currently on the run.

To make matters worse, Trevor had taken a hostage with him—the young woman named Caitlin from the Dairy Queen. The same young woman who had answered Marlin's call earlier that afternoon.

As Marlin drove, he had to wonder what Bryce Cauley had been doing at Trevor's place. Cauley was supposed to be at work. And he'd said he had been avoiding Trevor lately. Was any of that accurate, or had Bryce managed to tell Marlin a good story to divert suspicion from himself?

Marlin had to set that question aside and focus on radio traffic, which was indicating that a search helicopter was en route from DPS headquarters in Austin. Meanwhile, deputies already in Blanco were combing the area, but they hadn't spotted Trevor's Tahoe yet.

Wait a second.

Marlin grabbed his microphone and said, "Did you say a Tahoe?"

"Brown Chevy Tahoe," a voice replied. It was Callie Young, the new deputy. "Witnesses said the subject stated that he was parked next door to the Dairy Queen."

Marlin said, "His Tahoe was still parked in front of his trailer. I think we need to keep an eye out for a blue Ford Ranger. It'll have a silver toolbox mounted in the back."

Bryce Cauley's truck hadn't been parked in front of Trevor's trailer, so Trevor must've taken it. It was just a guess, but it made sense, considering that Bryce had probably driven to Trevor's place. Maybe the Ranger had been parked behind the Tahoe, and Trevor had been in a hurry after killing Bryce.

"I saw one earlier," said Bobby Garza, who had gotten a head start on Marlin and Lauren from Johnson City and was already in Blanco. "Edge of town, heading north on 281, but that was at least six or seven minutes ago. Can't confirm the toolbox."

Marlin and Lauren were passing the T intersection of Highway 290 and Highway 281, about eight miles north of Blanco. If that Ranger had continued north—

Right then, Lauren hit her brakes hard, so Marlin did, too.

"Got my eyes on a blue Ranger northbound on 281," Lauren said, and now Marlin saw the truck coming this way, going at least eighty.

Lauren took a hard left, jumping her SUV over the curb and onto the grassy median, and Marlin followed right behind her.

The Ranger zoomed past.

Three weeks before things went so wrong at the Dairy Queen, Renee had mentioned to Caitlin and some of the other girls that her grandmother had been moved to an assisted-living facility in Dripping Springs the previous weekend, and since the girls were talking near the kitchen, Trevor could hear it all.

"She didn't really want to go, but Daddy says she'll like it after she's been there a while," Renee said. "He says it's a nice place with a lot of activities, but I haven't been there yet."

"What's wrong with her?" Caitlin asked. "I mean, like, physically?"

"She can't get around very good. And she can't see much anymore. She hasn't been able to drive for about a year, so I've been doing a lot of her errands, which is a total pain in the ass, to be honest. Not that I mind doing it."

Trevor thought Renee didn't sound sympathetic at all.

"What are your parents gonna do with the house and all that land?" Caitlin asked.

"They don't know yet. Daddy said he might sell it, but that would be sometime next year. He grew up in that house, so I think it's gonna be hard for him. Plus, there's so much stuff to get rid of first. We have to go through it all. Some of it will have to go to the thrift store or wherever."

"That's so sad."

"He's wanting me to go through all her clothes and decide what to toss. She won't need much stuff at the nursing home. A lot of it is like a hundred years old and completely out of style."

Caitlin said, "If you need any help, let me know."

"That's sweet."

"I mean it, though. It'd be easier if you had a friend there with you. We could order pizza or something. Have a little party. I bet she has some cool old stuff."

Maybe thirty minutes later, when Renee was picking up an order from the pass-through counter, Trevor said, "Sorry about your grandma."

Renee gave him a weird disgusted look, like *Were you listening to our private conversation? How creepy are you?* Finally, she said, "Thanks," but Trevor could tell she didn't mean it at all.

The blue Ford Ranger took the feeder lane onto Highway 290, heading east toward Austin.

Lauren bounced off the median and back onto the pavement, and Marlin stayed with her, just catching a glimpse of the Ranger as it rounded the curve and disappeared from view. If the truck had a silver toolbox, he hadn't seen it.

Lauren gunned it and quickly began to pull ahead. Marlin's truck simply wasn't fast enough to keep up. She swooped onto Highway 290 and gained even more ground.

"Lauren, you see a toolbox?" Marlin said over the radio as he made the curve and straightened out onto 290. She was sixty or seventy yards ahead of him, and the Ranger was at least that far ahead of her, but that wouldn't last long.

"Not yet," Lauren said.

Marlin's truck began to build up a head of speed now, reaching nearly ninety again, and likewise Lauren was quickly gaining on the Ranger.

"You sure about that toolbox?" she asked. "Not seeing one."

"I'm sure," Marlin replied.

"He could've removed it," Lauren said.

That didn't seem likely to Marlin.

"How many occupants?" he asked.

"Looks like one, but the rear window is pretty dark," she said.

Marlin was fairly certain that none of the windows in Bryce Cauley's truck had been tinted, but before he could say anything more, Lauren spoke again, addressing the dispatcher and all units listening in.

"Got a break in traffic in both directions, so I'm initiating a stop on this Ranger—possible suspect in the shooting in Blanco. We're on 290 toward Austin, approximately half a mile east of 281."

Now she turned her siren on and Marlin did the same.

She recited the license plate number, then said, "Ranger is pulling over on the shoulder."

They followed the standard procedures for a felony stop.

Lauren stopped behind the truck, but slightly angled to the left, so her engine compartment would provide cover. Marlin angled his truck to the right, so he could cover the passenger side.

They got out of their vehicles, both armed with their M4 rifles. From this distance, it appeared to Marlin that there was only one person in the truck. If there was another person, he or she was either very short or had slid low in the passenger seat.

Lauren used her microphone and PA system to order the driver of the Ranger to stick his hands out the window with the keys and drop them to the pavement. The driver complied.

Lauren instructed the driver to open the door from the outside and exit the vehicle. The driver complied. A beer can fell to the pavement as he stepped out.

There wasn't any letdown or disappointment, because Marlin had already concluded that it wasn't the same Ranger, and Trevor Larkin wasn't driving it. He was right.

The driver was a shirtless Hispanic man in his fifties with a potbelly and a walrus mustache. He was unsteady on his feet and had his hands raised halfway.

"I didn't do nuthin'!" he called out.

Marlin heard Lauren mutter, "Damn it."

26

Rory wasn't much of a reader, but he was riveted by every word of the article about the missing man named Miguel Lopez. With each new detail, fact, and revelation, Rory got more and more stoked. He'd figured something out that had puzzled the cops for years.

"What?" Bryce said. "You gonna tell me what's going on?"

"He's been missing for nineteen years," Rory said.

"Albert?"

"Yeah. Hang on." He read some more. "He used to live in Framingham, Massachusetts, which isn't far from Boston. I always thought he sorta had a weird accent—but like he was trying to hide it."

"They do talk funny up there," Bryce agreed. He'd gone back to eating chips.

"He owned a kennel where you board dogs, and he was a trainer, too. He built the place on some land his dad bought back in the sixties. His dad left him that land when he died."

"When who died?" Bryce asked.

"His dad," Rory said. "Anyway, things were going great for him, but then—Jesus—he ran over some dude."

"Albert's dad?"

They were both still pretty high. Plus, Rory had learned over the past few months that Bryce wasn't super swift.

"No, Albert. He hit a guy with his car. Hold on." Rory read a few more paragraphs. "He was speeding and he ran over the guy, but Albert later said the guy was carrying a gun and was planning to kill him. He was trying to get away, and he ran over the guy in the process. He was about our age, this guy—the one Albert hit. Oh, wow. He was the brother of a mob boss. A Mafia guy."

"Albert was?"

"No, the guy he ran over."

"No shit? Like the Sopranos and all that?"

"Looks that way. Anthony Carducci."

"That's the guy he hit?"

"Are you not listening to me?"

"I'm trying."

"Anthony Carducci is the mob boss. It was his brother that got killed. That brother was supposedly trying to kill Albert."

"I thought the Mafia wasn't a thing anymore."

Rory kept reading.

"This article says that's a myth. The FBI was hammering them pretty hard and might've been able to wipe them out, but then 9/11 happened and they had to focus more on terrorism. So the mob was able to rebuild. They aren't as powerful as they used to be, but they're still around. Anyway, Albert killed this guy, and then he was arrested, but he disappeared before his trial. It says Albert knew he was gonna be killed, so he supposedly hauled ass, but some people think the mob guy got to him and made sure the body couldn't be found. Nobody knows for sure. Or knew. But we do."

Bryce said, "Why were they trying to kill him? Just for hitting the guy accidentally?"

"I'm looking for that."

Rory wasn't sure any of this would actually make sense later, when he wasn't stoned, but for the moment, he thought it was the coolest thing ever.

He said, "The cops said Miguel Lopez—meaning Albert—couldn't or wouldn't explain exactly why he thought the guy was trying to kill him. Oh, here we go. The author of this article says there is 'unproven speculation' that Miguel might've been having an affair with Carducci's wife."

"That's the mob guy, right?"

"Right, and the rumor is Carducci's brother was gonna kill Albert because of it. Maybe Carducci put him up to it, or maybe not."

"So Albert might've run over him on purpose?" Bryce asked.

"Hell if I know. Or maybe Albert was just trying to get away."

"But once he ran over the brother, he was fucking doomed. The mob guy wasn't going to let that go, especially if Albert was banging his wife."

"Exactly."

"You sure it's really Albert?"

"Here, look at the picture." Rory turned his phone toward Bryce.

"But I don't know what Albert looks like," Bryce said.

"Oh, right. Hang on."

Rory went to the Facebook page for Safari Adventure and looked around for a few minutes. Then a few more minutes.

"This is weird. I just realized something. Albert was always posting photos on the zoo's Facebook and Instagram pages, but he never wanted to be in any of those pictures himself. We'd, like, do a staff photo, but he'd always take the photo instead of being in it. He said he hated the way he looked in pictures, but, duh, it was because he didn't want anyone to recognize him. That's obvious now."

"So you don't have a photo of him?"

"No, but I'm telling you—this is the same guy in this photo. He's a lot younger, of course, because it was nineteen years ago, but it's him."

"I believe you."

Bryce reached into the bag of chips for the last few crumbs, shoved them into his mouth, then got off the couch and went into the kitchen. Rory could hear him in there opening one of the cabinets under the sink, and then the other cabinet. "Where's your trash can?"

"In the pantry," Rory said, wondering how Bryce hadn't noticed that when he'd gotten the chips in the first place.

Rory heard the pantry door open, and the crinkling of the bag as Bryce shoved it into the trash, and then the door closed, and now Bryce came into the living room again—with another bag of potato chips. This one was sour cream and onion.

He grinned. "You mind, man? I've still got the munchies. I'll pay you back."

Rory waved his hand dismissively, meaning *Whatever.*

Bryce sat down again, opened the bag, and began shoveling chips into his mouth again.

Rory leaned back on the couch and shook his head. What they'd learned was frigging amazing.

"The question is, what can we do with all of it?" he said.

"All of what?"

"This information. It's valuable."

"How so?"

"I bet Albert would pay a lot of money to keep it quiet."

"You serious?"

"Hell, yes, I'm serious. I told you he's an asshole."

"Yeah, but enough to blackmail him? That's what you're talking about, right?"

"It would be kind of funny. Don't you think so?"

"I don't know, man."

"I think it would be funny."

"But why wouldn't he just take off again? I mean, if he found out somebody knew who he really was, wouldn't he run? I would if I was him. It wouldn't be worth the risk to hang around. I'd be wondering if the blackmailer was telling the mob guy."

Rory had to admit that was a possibility. Albert might run, and then what? What was the point of making that happen? It would be fun to screw up the new life Albert had built, but that was pretty extreme.

"What about the mob guy?" Rory asked.

"What about him?"

"I bet he has a lot of money," Rory said. "And I bet he'd still want to know where Albert is. Don't you think Carducci would pay some serious cash for that information?"

27

Trevor wasn't an idiot. Earlier, at the Dairy Queen, when Renee had started to go into the back room, he knew she wouldn't have come back out with Caitlin, because Renee had figured out why Trevor was there. So he'd pulled the gun, because he'd had no choice. Renee had made that happen. It was her fault.

But Trevor had planned ahead, just in case. You couldn't just jump into his kind of thing without planning ahead.

Less than four minutes after driving away with Caitlin in Bryce's truck, they pulled through a gate off Ranch Road 1623, no more than a mile west of Blanco. One minute after that, they were parked inside a two-car garage. A gold Chevy Impala occupied the other bay.

"I hope you're not mad," he said.

Caitlin didn't reply. In fact, she hadn't said a word since they'd left the Dairy Queen.

He could hear sirens in the distance. It would be a massive manhunt. He'd known that all along, and that the odds of getting away were slim, but that was part of the thrill. He was going to outsmart them, or die trying.

"Let's go inside," Trevor said.

Caitlin was looking at him differently now. He saw respect in her eyes. Or was it fear? He didn't want that—not from her. He didn't want her to be scared of him.

"You're not gonna talk?" he said.

"What do you want me to say, Trevor?"

"Anything. Just talk."

She only shook her head, like she was angry.

"I thought you wanted to go with me," he said.

"I'm not sure what that means," she said. "Go where?"

"Anywhere you want."

"We don't—" She stopped for a moment. "I hardly even know you, Trevor. I mean, we work together, yeah, but I'm not sure where you ever got the idea—"

"You're supposed to be my Caril Ann," he said.

"Your who?" she asked.

"Never mind. Let's just go inside."

"I don't understand what we're doing," Caitlin said. "Why are we at Renee's grandmother's house?"

"We had to go somewhere," he said.

"I still don't know what you're talking about. Trevor, seriously. Think about it. You made a mistake, but you can still—"

"You need to shut up," he said, and immediately regretted it. He didn't mean to lose his temper, but why was she being so difficult? Did she want to work at a Dairy Queen in Blanco, Texas, all her life? Couldn't she see what he was offering? "I'm sorry," he said.

She was staring straight ahead with no expression.

"I didn't mean that," he said.

She didn't reply.

"Where's your phone?" he asked.

"What?"

"Give me your phone."

She reached into the front pocket of her blue jeans and passed it to him.

"I just need to turn this off so they can't find us," he said. "You can have it back later."

Red had been thinking hard, but he hadn't come up with any brilliant ways to proceed with his investigation. The best investigators always found clever ways to make people reveal information, whether they intended to or not. You just ask questions, acting all innocent, and eventually the person can't help but let something slip. Or they say two things that can't both be true. But what should he ask?

Red's thoughts kept coming back to the gun in Garrett's backpack. Maybe that was a good angle to explore. See if he could learn anything more about that.

So, shortly before sunset, he grabbed a dozen empty beer cans and lined them up on top of an old, rusty barbecue smoker behind the trailer. Then he retrieved the .22 rifle that was always leaning near the back door, steadied the barrel on the porch railing, and popped a few shots off.

Sure enough, Billy Don and Garrett poked their heads out a few minutes later to see what Red was shooting. After they watched Red knock a couple of cans off the smoker, Billy Don said, "He's always been real good at hitting objects that ain't moving. 'Specially if they ain't no more than spittin' distance."

Red said, "Ask Billy Don 'bout the time he missed a deer from thirty feet."

"It was nighttime," Billy Don said. "And your truck was moving. So was the deer. And I was unebriated."

"Unebriated?" Garrett asked.

"Means drunk as hell," Billy Don said. "I admit I can't shoot so good when I've had a few."

"A few dozen," Red said.

"Whatever."

"Next you'll be saying the scope musta got bumped," Red said.

"It *did* get bumped," Billy Don said. "You was driving like an idiot over them rough roads."

Red shot three more cans off the top of the barbecue pit.

"I could knock 'em over with a fart from here," Billy Don said.

"Please don't," Garrett said.

"Wanna shoot a couple?" Red asked him.

"Ah, no thanks," Garrett said. "It's getting too dark."

"You can still see a little."

"That's okay."

"You don't like to shoot?"

"Sometimes, sure."

"You own a gun?"

Red had set up this whole scenario to ask that one question.

"I've owned a couple," Garrett said. He nodded toward the trailer. "I've got one in my backpack."

Red was surprised. He'd expected Garrett to keep that information to himself.

"Oh, yeah?" Red said. "You've been carrying it around while you're traveling?"

"Yeah, for a while. Probably not real smart, but I figure if I don't give the cops any reason to look in my pack, I'm all good."

"What kind is it?" Red asked.

"A three-eighty."

"No, I mean who made it?"

Red knew it was a Glock, but he wanted to keep Garrett talking.

Garrett opened his mouth, but then he grinned and said, "You know what? I completely forgot what brand it is."

"That's weird," Billy Don said.

"No kidding," Red said. "I don't mean to give you a hard time, but that's like forgetting whether you drive a Ford or a Chevy."

"Well, the reason is, I haven't had it for very long, and I didn't buy it myself. I found it."

"You found it?" Red said.

"Yeah, on the shoulder of the highway. Out in the middle of nowhere."

"Seriously?" Red said.

"Sure did. You'd be amazed at the stuff you find along the road when you're walking. I mean, there's the obvious stuff, like cash and various articles of clothing—lots of shoes—tools."

"Power tools?" Billy Don asked.

"That's dumb," Red said. "You think he's finding a table saw out there?"

"Mostly hand tools," Garrett said, "like wrenches and screwdrivers and hammers and stuff. I never pick that stuff up, because what am I gonna do with it? Carry it around? I don't need the extra weight. Let someone else find it and use it. But I found a really expensive wristwatch once. Also an unopened bottle of whiskey...a cell phone, but it was password-protected, so I just left it there. Oh, I found a diamond ring, but I don't know if it's real. I haven't had it checked yet. I need to take it to a jeweler and see."

"Dang," Billy Don said. "It could be worth thousands of dollars."

"Could be. Or maybe it's totally fake. That would be my guess."

"That's exciting," Billy Don said. "Like buying a lottery ticket."

"True, and I've also found lottery tickets, but most of them are already scratched."

"But that gun had to be the weirdest thing you've found," Red said, to get the conversation back on track.

"Pretty much."

"Was it loaded?" Billy Don asked.

"Sure was."

"One in the chamber?"

"Yep."

"Full clip?"

"I think so. I didn't really check."

"Didn't you wonder if somebody used it in a robbery or something and then tossed it out the window?" Billy Don asked.

"Well, yeah, a little," Garrett admitted, "but what're the odds of that? I figured it just got lost, is all. Somebody probably pulled over to take a leak and it fell out. I'll probably turn it in eventually. Just haven't gotten around to it, like with the diamond ring."

"But if it was used in a crime, now it's got your fingerprints all over it," Red said.

"I can just wipe them off," Garrett said.

"But there's DNA, too," Red said.

Garrett laughed. "You really think these things through, huh?"

"Can't be too careful when dealing with cops," Red said.

"Jackbooted thugs," Billy Don chimed in.

"No kidding," Garrett said.

"Where'd you find it?" Red asked.

"On the side of the road, like I said," Garrett replied.

"No, I mean where were you? Here in Texas?"

"Oh. Uh, I think it was just outside San Antonio."

Red waited for a few seconds to see if Garrett would correct himself or change his story. He didn't.

So he said, "When were you down around San Antonio?"

"Huh?"

"When we were talking the other day, you said this was the furthest south you'd been. So you couldn't have been to San Antonio yet."

"Oh, right, I mean—what's that other town south of Dallas? Not San Antonio. I can't remember the name of it."

"On 281?" Billy Don asked as he got up and turned the porch light on.

"Yeah," Garrett said.

"Lampasas?"

Billy Don sat back down.

"No," Garrett said.

"Burnet?"

"No."

"Marble Falls?"

"I don't think so."

"Stephenville?"

"We gonna guess every town this side of Oklahoma?" Red asked.

"But he's right," Garrett said. "It *was* Stephenville."

"You mixed up San Antonio and Stephenville?" Red asked, and it was damn tough to sound like he believed that crock of nonsense.

"I guess so," Garrett said. "Pretty silly, I know. Hey, what kind of rifle is that?"

Garrett was trying to change the subject. Obvious as hell.

"Savage twenty-two," Red said. "Just a cheapie I bought at a garage sale. Hey, why don't you go get your gun?"

"I don't have any bullets, except the ones that are in there already."

"I think I've got some .380 ammo in the house," Red said.

"Now it's really too dark, though," Garrett said.

"I'll get a spotlight," Red said.

Garrett didn't move. Red stared at him. Garrett stared back.

"You're not gonna get it?" Red asked.

"I don't know what's going on," Garrett said slowly, "but I feel like you don't believe a lot of the things I've been telling you. Not just now, but all along. That gets old real quick, okay? That's why I left home—because I was sick and tired of people thinking I was a liar."

For the first time, Red was seeing some anger in Garrett's face.

28

Albert checked his Chuck Noland Facebook account at six o'clock. Sylvia had not accepted his friend request.

He checked again an hour later. Still nothing.

Maybe she didn't recognize the name and dismissed the request because he had no friends. So he went to her profile to see if her list of friends was visible, or whether she had tightened her privacy settings to keep the list hidden. Nope. He could see her friends. So he sent friend requests to a dozen people on the list. Then he surfed Facebook and sent friend requests to a dozen random strangers.

At eight o'clock, two of Sylvia's friends and four of the random strangers had accepted his request. But she had not.

What were the odds she would even be checking Facebook at a time like this, just hours after granting an interview about her long-lost lover, who'd gone on the run to avoid getting murdered by her jealous husband? After all, Sylvia thought there was a chance Albert was dead all this time. But now she knew better, so her mind would be racing. She'd be talking to her closest friends on the phone. She'd be pacing the hallways of her home, wondering where Albert was at this very moment, and what he was doing, and where he had been all these years. Wouldn't she? She wouldn't be checking Facebook, and considering accepting a friend request from a person presenting himself as Chuck Noland.

But then, at nine o'clock, Albert checked Facebook again.

Still nothing.

"I just want to see your gun, is all," Red said.

"You think I'm a liar?" Garrett asked, standing up.

"Never said that."

"Then what's your fixation on the gun in my backpack?"

"Well," Red said, "it's not so much the gun as it is the fact you said you found it near San Antonio, and supposedly, you'd never been down that way."

"I got confused."

"Weird thing to be confused about," Red said. "Just like not knowing what brand the gun is."

"I'm not a detail person. Besides, what would it matter if I'd been down near San Antonio? I don't understand why you're so focused on that."

"So you have been down there?" Red asked.

"No!" Garrett said, plainly getting worked up now. "I told you that already. But it's like you have some weird point to make, except I don't understand what the point is."

"Everybody settle down," Billy Don said.

"A lot of stuff you've told us doesn't seem to match up," Red said.

Garrett moved forward a step. "So you *do* think I'm a liar. Just go ahead and say it."

"I don't know if you're a liar or not," Red said. "But if you make me get up out of this chair, we're gonna have a problem."

"What does that even mean?"

"You getting your chest all puffed out like that," Red said. "This is *my* house. You need to remember that."

"So I'm supposed to let you call me a liar?"

"But I never did."

"You sure as hell implied it," Garrett said.

"Don't be such a snowflake," Red said.

"That's what assholes say so they can pretend they're not really assholes," Garrett said.

"If you're calling me an asshole, you're about to cross a line."

"I don't know if you're an asshole or not," Garrett said, parroting Red's words back at him.

"Who needs a beer?" Billy Don said.

"You know what?" Garrett said. "I'm gonna take off now, so you don't have to worry about whether I'm a liar or not." He looked at Billy Don and gave him a wave. "You're a good man. Don't let him rub off on you."

"You don't have to go," Billy Don said. "He's just bein' on'ry. Ignore it like I do."

"No, I'm going. Time for me to move on."

He turned and went inside.

"That was some damn good advice," Billy Don said. "You know, about not letting you rub off on me."

"Don't you start," Red said. "I was about to have to kick his ass. Calling me an asshole on my own back porch?"

"You was pushing him pretty hard. And calling him a liar."

"That's 'cause his story don't hold together. Too many contradictancies. On the other hand…"

"What?"

Red kept his voice low.

"I gotta be honest, I have no idea whether he killed that guy outside the zoo. He's not acting guilty in that kind of way. But he ain't innocent, neither, though. What I'm thinking is that he prob'ly stole that gun from somewhere, which is why he never mentioned it, and why he don't want to bring it out. That's why he's been acting kinda weird all along. And it explains why he didn't want to admit he'd been down that way."

Red was proud of himself for figuring all this out.

"I disagree," Billy Don said.

"You disagree with what? You don't think he stole the gun?"

"No, I think he did kill that guy."

That was the last thing Red expected to hear.

"You jerking me around?" he asked.

"Nope."

Red heard the front door of the trailer slam shut. Garrett would have to walk for several miles to hitch a ride, which would be even more difficult at night, but Red didn't care. Screw him.

"I was telling you that all along, but you didn't believe me," Red said.

"Sure didn't."

"And now that I've changed my mind, you're changing yours?" Red said.

"Yep."

"You're driving me nuts!"

"You was already nuts."

"Why do you suddenly think he did it?"

"It just seems like he—"

Boom! Boom!

Both men jumped as two quick shots sounded from the other side of the trailer.

"What did that idiot just do?" Red said, standing and cradling the rifle in his arms. It didn't seem like much of a gun at the moment.

"Hell if I know," Billy Don said. "But that shit's way out of line."

Red opened the back door and turned the porch light off. It was good and dark now.

"Don't shoot him," Billy Don said. "Unless you have to."

"Long as he don't shoot at me first," Red said. "But I'm damn sure gonna scare the shit out of him."

Red descended the porch steps and began to move along the rear of the trailer. He knew every inch of this ground and could move quickly and quietly, even without light.

"Better haul ass, Garrett!" Billy Don yelled, laughing. "Hooooeeeeeee! Red's coming!"

Red was at the rear corner of the trailer, and now he fired a single shot into the ground several feet away.

"Yeeeehaaaaaw!" Billy Don hollered.

The .22 wasn't as loud and deep as Garrett's .380, but the sound carried a good ways. It would be plenty to scare a kid like Garrett.

Red moved to the front corner of the trailer, and he fired another shot into the ground. Then he stood still and listened—and he heard clumsy footsteps as Garrett hustled down the caliche driveway toward the county road.

"Get ready, Garrett!" Red yelled.

As tempting as it was to fire several shots in Garrett's general direction, Red knew that would place him on shaky ground, legally speaking, if he happened to hit him, and the liberals would love to throw him into jail for it. Plus, there were too many damn cedar trees in the way, so a bullet would stand very little chance of making it through. Instead, he fired several more rounds into the ground in quick succession, and it made him giggle to imagine Garrett flinching and ducking with each shot. He was pretty sure he heard Garrett stumble and then get back on his feet.

Red waited a few seconds, then rounded the corner and walked in front of the trailer, where the area was illuminated by the front porch light, but he wasn't concerned about being seen at this point. With the downhill slope of the driveway, even if Garrett did fire again, the angle would prevent it from hitting Red.

"Billy Don, go get the shotgun!" Red yelled.

"Already got it!" Billy Don called back.

Red fired two more rounds into the ground, just for emphasis.

By now, Garrett would have reached the county road.

"I'm calling the sheriff!" Red yelled, although Garrett might see through that lie, given what Red and Billy Don had said about law enforcement over the course of the past 36 hours.

Red could hear movement in the trailer, and then Billy Don came out through the front door with two fresh Keystone tallboys in his hand, one of which he placed on the railing for Red.

"Well, that was a little extra excitement on a Thursday night," Billy Don said, laughing again. "Guess maybe our boy Garrett has a temper." Then he added, "Oh, shit. Look what he done."

Red looked at him, and Billy Don pointed at Red's truck.

Even at this distance, there was enough light to see the two bullet holes in the windshield.

"That little son of a bitch," Red said.

"Dang," Billy Don said. "That was uncool."

"Let's go after him."

"I don't really think we need to—"

"Grab the shotgun!" Red barked. "For real, this time!"

"I don't understand what we're doing," Caitlin said. "How long are we going to stay here?"

"I don't know. I need to think."

They were in a bedroom at the rear of the house. Trevor was on the bed, but Caitlin was sitting on the floor by the dresser, with her back against the wall. They were watching TV, but the choices were slim, because the house didn't have satellite or cable. He hadn't seen a single news report yet about him and Caitlin. He wished he could use his phone to check online, but that was out of the question, obviously.

Trevor had hung a thick blanket over the window so light would not leak out. Maybe that was overkill, but didn't the cops use drones nowadays for searches? Seems like they would, because it would be fast and efficient. Wouldn't take a drone more than a few seconds to dip down, fly around a house, and look for signs of activity. If they saw light in the window of a supposedly empty house...

"We should leave while we can," Caitlin said. "The longer we stay here, the more likely they'll find us."

Was she coming around? Or was she trying to get him caught? He wasn't sure.

"Why do you think that?" he asked.

"They'll know we're hiding somewhere," she said. "So they'll be checking all the houses."

"They can't check them all."

"Do you know what's involved in a manhunt, especially when you've abducted someone? They'll be bringing in cops from everywhere."

Abducted. What a terrible word.

"That's not what happened," he said.

"What?"

"I didn't abduct you."

"Seriously?" she said. "You came into work with a gun."

"It wasn't like I pointed it at you or threatened you."

She shook her head, as if he just didn't get it.

"You just want to leave now so they'll find us," he said.

"If you're saying I'd rather be at home than here, you're right. But I also don't want you to get hurt. If they have to come into this house and get you, it won't end well."

He wanted to believe her. He really did. But she was lying. Trying to get him caught, even if he did get hurt. Right? There was a way to find out.

"Every cop in a hundred miles is looking for a blue Ranger by now," he said.

"But that's such a common truck," she said. "And they can't just stop you for no reason."

"We could just take the Impala instead," he said.

"What?" she said.

"They won't be looking for an Impala," he said.

The look on her face told him everything he needed to know.

29

"He could be anywhere hunkered down," Billy Don said. "Them cedars are thicker'n cream gravy."

When Billy Don made comparisons, they often had a connection to food.

"Keep looking," Red said.

"Or he's laying down flat in a gully," Billy Don said. "Ain't no chance we'd see him then."

"Keep looking," Red said. "We'll see his orange jacket."

They were cruising slowly along the county road between Red's trailer and the highway. For the fourth time. Billy Don was using a spotlight to sweep the wooded areas on the side of the road. They'd seen at least two dozen deer, three sizeable herds of feral pigs, and a fox with a mouse in its mouth.

But no Garrett.

Both bullets had gone through the windshield and hit the rear glass, shattering it. Red was still steaming. He couldn't remember the last time he'd been this mad. He might actually use the shotgun on Garrett—if they could find him.

"Guy with a temper like that," Billy Don said. "No telling what he mighta done back home in Michigan."

"Yeah, like killing his daddy," Red said. "Like I said all along, but you wouldn't listen."

"I listened," Billy Don said. "Just thought you was wrong. And then I changed my mind."

"And he coulda killed that guy at the zoo," Red said.

"Maybe so."

"That's why he didn't want to admit being further south," Red said. "Especially with a gun."

They rode quietly for another mile.

"You know what we should do?" Billy Don asked.

"Huh?"

"Hate to say it—and I know you ain't gonna listen—but we oughta call the sheriff."

"Screw that. Keep looking."

"Yeah, but what if another hour or two goes by and we still ain't found him? Then we should call. That's all I'm saying. Otherwise, he's gonna get away with it. You'll never get him to pay for the damage to your truck."

"Then you're gonna pay," Red said.

"Why the hell would I pay?"

"Because ain't none of this woulda happened if you hadn't told me to pick him up," Red said. "That makes it your fault."

Billy Don grumbled but didn't object.

Within thirty minutes after the shooting at the Dairy Queen, all available full-time deputies and reserve deputies—as well as law enforcement officers from nearby cities—had formed a perimeter on the outer reaches of the county or were otherwise assisting with the search.

By 7:00—well after dark—the blue Ranger still had not been located, nor had Trevor Larkin or Caitlin McGregor.

At 8:15, the DPS helicopter equipped with forward-looking infrared radar had already searched for two hours, but it had run low on fuel and was forced to return to headquarters. The pilot had offered to come back, but Bobby Garza had declined—at least for now—because the odds were extremely low that Trevor Larkin was still on the move. If he was, that meant he had slipped away before they'd formed the perimeter, and by now he and Caitlin McGregor could be a hundred miles away.

At 9:13, Garza asked Marlin to meet him in the parking lot of a convenience store in Blanco, where they parked driver's window to driver's window. Marlin couldn't recall ever seeing Garza so concerned and frustrated.

Garza said, "Lauren reviewed camera footage from the church next door and they were definitely in the Ranger, just like you said. Good call on that. They went north on 281 from the church parking lot, but that's all we know. She's asking all the business owners in town to check their cameras, but it'll probably be tomorrow morning before some of those folks get around to it."

"They can't have gone far," Marlin said. "Somebody would've seen them, even on the back roads. I think there's a good chance they're holed up somewhere."

He sipped from the cup of coffee he'd gotten in the store a few minutes earlier. It was going to be a long night.

"I agree," Garza said. "So where could he park the Ranger, out of sight, and stay for a while?"

Despite the alarming circumstances in this particular case, Marlin always enjoyed working closely with the sheriff's office when they needed assistance. Marlin had proven time and time again that he was a talented investigator, and Garza was happy to have an extra hand on complex cases.

"Checking their cell phones?" Marlin asked.

"Already did, and we're getting nothing. He must've turned them off. We're interviewing all of the DQ employees right now. Maybe Larkin said something to one of them that'll lead us in the right direction. We'd interview his friends, but he doesn't seem to have any."

Marlin had once read an article that poked holes in the loner-killer myth, but in this case, maybe it was accurate.

"I'm guessing they found an empty house or a hunting cabin or something similar," Marlin said. "And the truck is in a garage or a barn or a large shed. They aren't just parked under some oak trees. The chopper would've seen them or the tracks in and out."

Sometimes simply brainstorming like this could lead to fresh ways of thinking.

"Maybe somebody's out of town on vacation—their house is

empty—and Larkin knew about it," Garza said. "Or it's a house for sale."

Marlin nodded. "But it can't be more than a few miles from the city limits. We had too many units on the roads too quickly for him to have gone any farther."

The radio had fallen quiet in the past hour. Some deputies were parked at strategic intersections and keeping watch, while other deputies continued to scour the city streets and county roads.

"They went north from the church...and then what?" Garza asked.

"I can't imagine they stayed on 281 for long—he'd want to get off the highway as soon as possible."

"He's a local, so he'd know which roads lead out of town."

"Fourth Street and Seventh Street," Marlin said. "That's it. Two choices."

Fourth Street turned into Ranch Road 1623 to the west and Ranch Road 165 to the east. Seventh Street dead-ended to the east, but to the west, it became County Road 105, also known as Rocky Road, which wound for miles in a northwesterly direction all the way to Highway 290, west of Johnson City.

"Can I give you a chore?" Garza asked.

"You know you can."

"Can you figure out a way to map every empty house in the area that has a garage or barn or large shed? Maybe expand it to two or three miles outside the city limits, but no further than that."

"Will do. I bet Jo Virgil can help with that."

"Good idea. I would love to start checking those places at first light."

"I'll call her or drive over there if I have to and we'll make it happen. What else?"

"You staying out for a while?" Garza asked.

"I was planning on it. Just going to roam and see what I can see."

Garza nodded and shifted his SUV into drive. "By the way, Trevor Larkin's dad called me earlier and he said they've known for years—how did he put it?—that Trevor had some sort of serious flaw inside him, but they couldn't figure out what it was. He had problems with impulse control and he went through a stage where he would set fires. He had a lot of therapy when he was younger, but when he turned eighteen, he moved out and they haven't had a lot of contact since then."

None of this was surprising, but it wasn't particularly useful right now, either.

"He have any idea where Trevor might've gone?" Marlin asked.

"Not a clue."

"What's the latest on Rodney?" Marlin asked.

Last he'd heard, Rodney was going into surgery. The other shooting victim—a 17-year-old girl from Mason—had suffered only a grazing wound on her forearm. She'd been every bit as much the hero as Rodney, although she'd been quite upset when she learned that her phone screen had shattered when it hit the floor. The irony made Marlin grin when he'd heard about it.

"He's doing okay," Garza said. "The bullet broke his collarbone but didn't hit any major arteries. Lucky as hell. Now we just need to find Trevor Larkin before he does any more damage."

Lauren Gilchrist was parked along Highway 281 north of Blanco. She was multitasking: watching for the blue Ranger, and calling as many Blanco business owners as possible, asking them to review any security-camera footage they might have from that afternoon. Each time she couldn't reach a particular business owner, she called that business owner's employees, friends, and family members until she made contact. Word was starting to spread.

At 9:30, she took a short break to read an email she'd received earlier from Darrell.

He had not been able to contact Sylvia Golino, and the producers at CNN had refused to provide any contact information. No surprise there. If the situation had been reversed—if CNN had been asking the Blanco County Sheriff's Office for an individual's contact information—the sheriff's office would've declined.

However, Darrell had been able to find an informative article with the title *Without A Trace: The Unexplained Disappearance of Miguel Lopez.*

Too long to read right now, but Darrell had provided a short summary.

Miguel Lopez is Albert Cortez. Nineteen years ago, Albert was sleeping with Sylvia Golino, who was the wife of a reputed mobster named Anthony Carducci. Carducci's brother went to threaten or kill Lopez, and Lopez ran him down with his car and killed him, possibly accidental. Lopez/Cortez was charged with manslaughter. He took off before trial and has been in the wind ever since.

Amazing. So how did the dead guy at the zoo figure in to it? Had Carducci finally figured out where Cortez had been hiding and sent a killer?

Lauren sent a quick reply to Darrell, copying it to Garza and Marlin: *Send the John Doe's photo to Boston PD and see if they recognize him as one of Carducci's crew.*

Then she went back to making phone calls.

30

"You're not stupid, Joey. Don't ever let anyone call you stupid!"

That's what Joey Barella's mother said to him frequently, and it puzzled him, because she was the only person who ever seemed to raise that possibility.

Like the time Mr. Dayton flunked him in algebra, and Joey's mother said, "Don't let him call you stupid, Joey! So you're not a math whiz. That doesn't mean you're stupid!"

But Mr. Dayton never said anything about Joey being stupid. Why did his mother always bring it up?

Sure, Joey knew he wasn't the brightest person living in Framingham, Massachusetts, but he wasn't the dumbest either. He got by just fine. Graduated high school without too much trouble. Never considered going to college. But he didn't need it. His uncle had introduced him to some people, and now he made a damn good living, with plenty of room for advancement. Besides, in his line of work, there were things more important than intelligence. Loyalty, for instance. That was a biggie. Probably number one on the list.

Joey was loyal. Damn right he was. Everybody knew it.

Which probably explained why, six days before a bunch of exotic animals got loose from a zoo in Blanco County, Texas, Anthony Carducci wanted to meet Joey in the parking lot of a strip center on Worcester Road, not far from the Framingham Country Club.

Joey had never met the big boss before and was surprised he even knew Joey existed. But the old man had called Joey up and told him the time and place. And he'd told Joey not to tell a soul about it. Nobody. Not one person. "Not even that girlfriend of yours," he'd said.

How did Carducci know about his girlfriend?

"Lemme ask you something," Carducci said later as they sat in his Cadillac. It was a hell of a nice ride, but it smelled strongly of aftershave and pine air freshener, especially with the windows closed. "You been arrested before?"

"For what?" Joey asked.

Which was a stupid question, but Joey was nervous.

"For anything at all. I'm asking if you ever been arrested before."

"No, sir."

"Never? Not once?"

"No, sir."

"How old are you?"

"Twenty-three."

"Never been fingerprinted?"

"No."

"And they never took your DNA for nothing?"

"Uh-uh."

Carducci nodded approvingly.

"I heard you like to box," he said. "Golden Gloves and all that shit."

"I do, yeah."

"They say you're pretty good."

"I'm all right. Won twenty-seven fights. Twenty by knockout."

"How many you lose?"

"Four. But three of them were right when I started, before I, you know, figured out what the hell I was doing. I had no defense at first. Didn't know how to cover up."

"That how you got that scar on your face?"

"The son of a bitch head-butted me. I knocked him out in the next round. No TKO, either. I knocked him completely out. Sent him to the hospital."

"Nice."

"It was sick nasty. Black guy with a smart mouth."

"Gonna go pro?"

"Thinking about it. I figure it's worth a shot."

Carducci nodded again.

"Got a manager?"

Was that what this was about? Joey's boxing career? He hadn't seen this coming.

"I got a guy I train with. Not sure if he can take me to the next level or not, to be honest."

"Why boxing instead of that mixed fighting stuff?"

Joey shrugged. "I'm not big on kicking. I don't need some skid kicking me. Come at me with your hands, like a man."

Carducci seemed to appreciate that. "And you're getting married next year," he said.

Jeez, they were jumping all over the place. What were they even talking about?

"Yes, sir. November."

"Got some money saved up for a down payment on a house and all?"

"A little."

Joey got the sense that Carducci was trying to get to know him—to gauge what kind of person he was—but why?

"But you could always use a little more—am I right?" Carducci gave him a big smile.

"Hell, yeah," Joey said. "Always. Houses are fuckin' expensive. Even a little one."

Was Joey getting a raise? A promotion? He'd always worked hard and kept his mouth shut. Did what they told him to do. Didn't brag about it to friends. Business was business.

After a long pause, Carducci said, "Here's what this is about. I need you to do something for me. Something really important. You do this, I'll never forget it. You know what I mean? Never."

Joey nodded.

"But you can't tell nobody. And if you decide you don't want to do it, well, that's okay. But you can't tell nobody about this little talk, neither. Not a goddamn word. Not even your girlfriend after she gives you a nice blowjob. You tell anybody and we'll have a big problem. Understand?"

"Absolutely."

"Okay, then." Carducci took a deep breath. "There's a guy who did something to me and my family a long time ago. Then he fucking disappeared for nineteen years. Now I know where he is."

Joey immediately knew what this was about. He'd heard the stories over the years, and he'd looked it up on the internet. Joey didn't know if he was supposed to ask questions now or stay quiet, so he stayed quiet.

"He killed my brother, is what he did," Carducci said. "Ran him down in the street like a goddamn dog. He suffered and then he died."

"That's terrible," Joey said, although he remembered that Carducci's brother had been trying to kill the other guy. Supposedly. The other guy had been trying to get away, but Carducci's brother had stepped in front of his car with a gun. That's what witnesses said, although most of them got foggy memories later, once they learned who the dead guy was. Suddenly they weren't real sure what had happened, and one of them went so far as to say the guy in the car had definitely been trying to kill Carducci's brother. The gun the brother had supposedly been carrying hadn't been found on the scene.

"Then this guy—this scum—he took off like a goddamn coward," Carducci said. "Not right away, but they charged him with manslaughter, and he ran away before they could put him in prison, where he belongs."

"That sucks," Joey said.

"Damn right it sucks!" Carducci barked, plainly getting angry. "There was no justice. He got away with it all. And I have to tell ya…" He looked at Joey. "This is all between you and me. Every word."

"I swear on my mother's life I won't tell nobody nothin'," Joey said.

Joey loved his mother, despite her remarks about his intelligence. In this situation, it appeared Joey had said the exact right thing, swearing on his mother, because now Carducci spoke his mind even more freely.

"What I shoulda done is took care of the son of a bitch myself, instead of waiting for the trial. But no, I tried to be a good citizen. Follow the rules and all that shit. I decided to trust the system, and the cops, and the DA, which is the dumbest thing I ever done. And then he hauled ass, and then I never had a chance to set things right. It tore us all up, but especially my mother. Tore her up. Still does, as a matter of fact. Her baby boy was dead and the killer never paid for it. You know what that does to a woman? To a mother?"

"I can imagine," Joey said. "My mother would—well, I don't know what she'd do, but it would be terrible."

Carducci was staring through the windshield with a sad, glazed expression and they were both quiet for a moment.

"That's why…" Carducci finally said, and then he paused. "That's why I don't want to let this second chance slip away. He's had nineteen years of freedom he never shoulda had, and now it's time for him to pay for what he done. Problem is, the courts can't do nothin' now. Too much time has passed. Plus, I wouldn't trust 'em anyway. They already let him get away once. He could do it again. That means I gotta take care of it myself."

Carducci went silent again. Joey gave him some time to continue, but he didn't, and Joey eventually realized Carducci was waiting for him to speak.

So Joey said, "You just tell me what you want me to do."

The next day, Joey took a flight from Boston to Dallas, and from there he mailed an anonymous letter to Albert Cortez at Safari Adventure. Plain white paper consisting of three scrawled words: *Zoos are prissons*. Just a little something extra to throw the cops off track later. Make them think some animal-rights nut was on the loose. This was all Joey's idea—something he'd come up with on the flight. Carducci didn't know about it. He didn't need to know every detail. He'd said he didn't *want* to know. Just get the job done. Joey made sure not to touch the letter or the envelope with his bare hands, and he damn sure didn't lick the stamp. He used water to moisten the back.

Next, Joey rented a car in Dallas and drove toward Arlington. Yeah, he was leaving a paper trail, or more like an electronic trail, but he wasn't concerned, because he had come up with a cover story. A reason for his trip.

Before he left Boston, he'd bought an overpriced ticket to a Dallas Cowboys football game. Dumb luck, they were playing the Patriots in the next game, which was perfect, him being a Boston boy and all. If things turned to shit on this whole thing and he ever got questioned by the cops, they'd ask why he didn't take his girlfriend on the trip, and he'd say she isn't into football. So he went alone? Sure, why not? He'd never been to Texas. He needed a vacation. None of his friends could go, so he went alone. Anything wrong with that?

So he drove toward Arlington, home of AT&T Stadium, and found a cheap motel that didn't appear to have any security cameras. This was the Saturday before the game. Went to a strip club that night, because that's what he'd normally do on a trip like this—go to a titty bar and see what these Texas women looked like. Paid with a credit card. Would a guy with something to hide go to a titty bar and pay with a credit card? He had a good time, despite the circumstances.

He got up late the next morning, semi-hungover, and went to the game. Cowboys won on a fifty-seven-yard field goal on the final play. Bastards.

On Monday morning, he turned his cell phone off and bought a throwaway phone for cash at an electronics store. Then he drove south in his rental car. He knew from reading online that it was very difficult and complicated for cops to get a warrant for the data from a car's on-board GPS, but he disabled the system anyway by pulling a fuse. Better safe than sorry.

By the time he reached Waco, his gut was in a knot.

Was he ready to do this? Damn right he was. This guy Miguel Lopez was a scumbag, screwing another man's wife. And maybe it was true that he'd run over Carducci's brother on purpose. It was possible. Maybe even likely. So Lopez deserved what was coming his way, even nineteen years later. Paybacks were hell.

The last thing Mr. Carducci had said was, "You get caught, you know how it goes. I didn't know nothin' about it. You acted on your own. Trying to build a name for yourself. You were doing it as a favor to me, but I wasn't involved."

"Absolutely," Joey said, because he meant it, and because he'd have to be insane to ever point the finger at a man like Anthony Carducci.

"But if that happens—and it won't—I'll take care of you," Carducci said, without getting specific.

"I know you will, Mr. Carducci."

"Okay, then. Got any questions?"

"Gotta admit, there's something I been wondering about."

"Yeah?"

"You don't have to tell me, but how'd you figure out where the guy is?"

31

Albert checked Facebook again at 9:37 and nothing had changed.

He set the phone on the nightstand and simply stared at the ceiling, wondering how it had all come to this. After all these years, how had his new life—his safe, normal life—come undone so quickly?

He first knew something was odd during the tour on Tuesday. Albert didn't give many tours nowadays—he was usually too busy with other tasks—but he still enjoyed it, so he squeezed one in when he could. That's what happened Tuesday.

It was a decent turnout, too, for a cloudy weekday afternoon in November. Eighteen people on the trolley, most of them older folks. Retirees. A middle-aged couple that was speaking German. A couple of young moms with toddlers in tow.

And one guy who appeared to be in his mid-twenties. All by himself. No wife. No kids. No friends. A solo customer. That wasn't totally unusual, but for a guy that age, it wasn't typical. Not on a weekday in November. He didn't look very friendly. Had a noticeable scar on his forehead, as if the skin had been split open vertically above his left eye.

Albert didn't think much of it, though, until midway through the tour, when they were feeding the camels, and he noticed that the young guy was wearing a Dallas Cowboys hat. Again, that wasn't unusual at all—there were thousands of Cowboys fans all over Texas—but it reminded Albert of the letter he'd gotten in the mail just the day before.

Zoos are prissons.

That's what the note had said. Those three words, one misspelled, and nothing else. No return address. But it had been postmarked in Dallas. Yes, Dallas. And now this solo male passenger wearing a Dallas Cowboys hat was here for a tour on a cloudy weekday afternoon in November.

Coincidence? Surely it was.

Or was he a troublemaker of some sort?

Albert convinced himself that he was letting his imagination run wild, so he ignored the Cowboys fan for a while. But then Albert noticed that the young man didn't seem to be interested in the animals. He seemed, instead, to be studying the layout of the zoo itself—the perimeter fences, the pens, the various buildings and shelters. In fact, he took several photos without any animals in them at all. Why would he do that? It wasn't as if the zoo was scenic. The animals were the attraction.

So Albert stopped the trolley and played a little game that was always popular with the guests. He asked which town each person was from, and the guest who'd come the farthest would win a $10 credit at the gift shop. One couple was from Fredericksburg. Another was from San Antonio. A young mom with two kids was from Marble Falls.

Albert pointed at the young man with the scar above his eye and smiled. "I guess you're from Dallas, huh?"

"Yep," the guy said, and that was all.

"Nice win against the Patriots on Sunday," Albert said.

"Pretty wild," the guy said.

"Right down to the wire," Albert said. "Heck of a kick."

"I just about had a heart attack!" said an older man in a middle row of the trolley.

"He sure did!" his wife added. "He was screaming like a maniac!"

Everybody else on the trolley laughed—except the Cowboys fan, who didn't look all that comfortable.

"We're from Hamburg!" the German woman said.

"Can anybody beat that?" Albert asked.

"That depends," a retiree said. "Is that farther away than El Paso?"

Everybody laughed again, and Albert had no choice but to move on.

At the time, Albert thought the guy might simply be an animal-rights activist who didn't like zoos. He'd encountered a handful over the years. The few that actually visited the zoo had left with a grudging respect for the way Albert's animals were treated.

But looking back at it now, the truth was obvious. The Cowboys fan had been there to make a positive ID on Albert, and to become familiar with the layout of the zoo so he could carry out his mission in the dark. And his mission had nothing to do with the animals.

After Bobby Garza drove away, Marlin stayed right where he was—in his truck in the convenience store parking lot—and quickly scanned an email from Lauren, which included some mind-boggling details about Albert Cortez's past. Nearly two decades ago, Albert had gone on the run and assumed a new identity after running down a mob boss's brother. Marlin could only shake his head and set it aside for later.

He called Jo Virgil, a friendly local realtor who'd been born and raised in Blanco County. She'd been in the same class as Marlin in school—an intelligent, witty classmate who excelled in every subject.

She answered on the second ring, saying, "Based on what I've been hearing on the news, I know you aren't shopping for a new home right now."

"No, ma'am," Marlin said. "But I am in the market for a favor. A confidential favor."

"What's up? I'll help however I can."

He told her exactly what he needed, and why. And he didn't need word getting out, because the last thing he wanted was a team of civilians deciding to conduct their own house-by-house search.

"When do you need it?" she asked.

"I hate to push it, but how about seven o'clock tomorrow morning?"

He heard a beep and saw that another call was coming in—from Red O'Brien. Marlin let it go to voicemail.

"No problem," Jo Virgil said. "I'll put them all on a map, so you can visit them in an order that makes sense. If you want."

"That would be outstanding," he said. "Oh, I almost forgot. We only want homes that have a garage or barn or shed—someplace a car could be parked. Can you do that?"

"Sure can," Jo said. "That'll narrow it down quite a bit and make your search easier."

"Can you include homes that have already sold but aren't occupied yet?" Marlin asked.

"Sure. Want me to include homes for lease, too?"

"Yes, please. Good idea."

"How big of an area?"

"I'd say a three-mile radius from the center of town."

"Will do."

"Very much appreciated," Marlin said. "And there's one other thing. I hate to ask."

"Ask. Please."

"Can you include the names and phone numbers of the homeowners and the listing agents? We might need permission to search some of the houses. Phone numbers would make things a lot easier."

"You can't just search? With a girl missing like that?"

"Not without a warrant or permission."

"Okay, well, I'll definitely include all that. Won't be a problem at all. Most of those homes are gonna have key boxes on the door, so I'll get the codes, too. That way you won't have to kick any doors down."

"Excellent idea. You are awesome."

"Good luck tonight. I hope you find her soon and you don't even need this map."

"That would be great."

They disconnected and Marlin saw that Red O'Brien had left a lengthy voicemail. He had also received a text message from Tracy Lavelle.

Kevin the kudu just came home! No more missing animals!

Marlin replied: *Thanks for letting me know. Glad to hear it.*

Then he listened to the voicemail.

Hey, it's Red O'Brien. I need to report a guy who shot two bullets through my windshield earlier tonight, and the back glass, too, which is gonna cost me a hell of a lot of money, and I figure that's gotta be illegal, right? Then he just took off. We went looking for him, but no luck. Anyways, I know Garza and all of them guys are busy with that manhunt right now, but you're kind of a cop, so I figured you might could help me out with this thing.

Marlin couldn't help but laugh. *Kind of a cop.* O'Brien always had a knack for making offensive remarks, without intending to. He just didn't know any better. It could be humorous—in small doses. Marlin would call him back to let him know that his problem would have to wait until tomorrow, or maybe later. But Marlin continued listening to the message.

The thing is, there's more to it than just the damage to my truck. This guy Garrett—well, it's kind of a weird situation, and I can tell you more when you get here, but it turns out they thought he killed his own daddy up in Michigan. Shoved him right off a roof, 'cause he was cheating on his mom—the daddy was, not Garrett—even though he denies it, but the cops up there didn't necessarily buy it, from what we can tell, although they didn't have enough to charge him. And now he's been out roaming the country ever since, and we picked him up hitchhiking yesterday morning, which was Billy Don's dumb idea. One of many.

Marlin had been drumming his fingers impatiently on the steering wheel—and noting that the voicemail wasn't even halfway done—but he couldn't help but be a little amused by this strange tale.

So I was kind of suspicious of him from the start, because what're the odds his daddy would fall off a roof a minute or two after telling Garrett he was divorcing his mom? That's a hell of a coincidence, doncha think? But how do you prove a thing like that without a witness, is what I was wondering, because I don't think there's a good way to do it. So then he was staying at my place overnight—I'm talking about Garrett, not his daddy—and it turns out he had a handgun in his backpack.

Okay, now it was getting even more interesting.

Yeah, okay, I peeked and I saw it, but since the backpack was in my house, I figure that's okay, right? Of course, you know I'm a big supporter of our God-given gun rights, and if I was hitchhiking around the country like some kinda hobo, you can bet I'd carry a gun, too. I asked him about the gun later, using a clever cover story, and he said he found it, which is kind of weird, just finding a handgun on the side of the highway. But then he started getting his stories crossed about where he'd been so far. When we picked him up on 32, about a mile or so east of 281, he said he'd been going south on 281 earlier in the morning, but he stopped and turned around when he saw all the cop cars parked near the zoo.

A hitchhiker with a gun near the zoo yesterday morning? Now Marlin was listening intently.

He said that was as far south as he'd ever gone in his life, that spot right there on 281 where he turned around, but then, earlier tonight, when I was asking him about his gun, he said he'd found it down near San Antonio. When I reminded him what he told us earlier—that he'd never been that far south—he got all flustered and said he meant Stephenville, not San Antonio, and if that don't sound like a buncha bullshit, what does? I mean, I'm not necessarily saying he shot that dude at the zoo, but if he's innocent, why did he get all worked up? At a minimum, I'm wondering if maybe he found the murder weapon and didn't want to admit it. So I kept pushing, asking all kinds of smart questions, which only made him mad, and he said I was calling him a liar, and before you know it, he says he's hitting the road, but before he left, he decided to bust a couple of rounds through my windshield. We looked around for the shells, but we ain't found 'em nowhere. Guess he mighta picked 'em up. I figured you'd want to know all this, so call me back. I'd like to see the little sumbitch go to jail for what he done.

Marlin called him back.

32

After Rory asked that question—*Don't you think Carducci would pay some serious cash for that information?*—Bryce had freaked out a little.

"But you're talking about getting Albert killed, right? I mean, that's what would happen, isn't it? Carducci would send somebody to kill him."

"But that's not our problem," Rory said. "We just want the money. It's up to Carducci what he does after that."

"No way, man. That's crazy. You know what he would do."

"Ha," Rory said. "Take it easy, man. I was just kidding. I wouldn't do that to Albert, despite the fact that he's an asshole."

"Okay, good."

"But…"

Rory waited and Bryce said, "But what?"

"That doesn't mean we can't ask Carducci for the money up front… and then never tell him where Albert is."

"So now you're talking about ripping off a mob guy?"

"We just make sure he can never figure out who we are. Not a big deal."

"But what if he does figure it out?"

"He won't. We'll make sure of that."

They went back and forth on that for a few minutes, but eventually Rory's confidence and vague assurances—along with a fresh joint—

brought Bryce around.

They pondered how to pull off their scheme, and later they wrote a simple note.

I know where Miguel Lopez is.

They were able to find Carducci's address in the county tax records. Then they drove to San Antonio and mailed the note in a light-blue envelope with no return address. They were careful as hell. Instead of going to an actual post office, where they would be on security cameras, they found one of those blue dropboxes on the street and slipped it in there.

The postmark would reveal that the letter had come from San Antonio, but there wasn't a way around that, and after some discussion, they agreed it wouldn't be worth it to drive to Dallas or Houston or somewhere farther away.

A week later, they drove to San Antonio and mailed a second note in another light-blue envelope: *Want to know more? I'll be in touch.*

After another week, they figured Carducci, if he had a vengeful streak and could hold a grudge for nineteen years, was just about dying to find out what they knew. He might even have a plan of action ready to go as soon as the anonymous letter writer shared his information.

So they drove to San Antonio and mailed their third note in a light-blue envelope: *If you want to know where he is, send a text to 210-557-1216. Say your name is Glen Johnson.*

The number went to a throwaway phone they'd bought with cash in San Antonio after their second trip down there. It had the San Antonio area code and everything, so it all matched up. Rory had taken the phone to work a few times and snapped several candid photos of Albert throughout the day. It wasn't as easy as you'd think to get a really good photo of a person without that person knowing.

Five days passed. Surely Carducci had received the latest note. Surely he was anxious to make contact and learn Miguel Lopez's location as soon as possible. Right? A guy like that—a fucking Mafia kingpin—wouldn't just let it go, would he?

But the throwaway phone remained quiet. Why? It was frustrating as hell. What value would this information have if Carducci didn't want it?

Maybe Carducci thought it was a trap of some kind. Maybe he thought one of the other mob families was trying to screw him over somehow.

Then, the next day, a text arrived.
This is Glen Johnson.
Rory texted Bryce to tell him what had happened, and Bryce came over to Rory's apartment. Then Rory sent a reply to Carducci. *Good to hear from you, Glen. Is this your boy?*
He sent a photo of Albert.
Ten minutes passed. What was Carducci doing? Did he think it was a scam? Or that Albert wasn't Miguel Lopez? Another ten minutes passed.
Then Carducci answered. *Where is he?*
Rory and Bryce were just about doing cartwheels at this point.
Won't come cheap.
What's your price? Don't get crazy.
Rory and Bryce had already figured out what they would say. They'd decided to start out with a really high number, because the mobster would want to negotiate downward. Where would it end up? What would a guy like Carducci pay? How badly did he want Miguel Lopez? Pretty badly, obviously, considering that his anger was still burning all these years later.
Rory's heart was hammering when he sent the answer. *$100,000.*
This time, a full thirty minutes passed. Rory was convinced they'd blown it, and that Carducci would not respond. But he did. Finally.
Told you not to get crazy. I don't have that much lying around. Not even close.
So Rory waited ten minutes, then said, *50k.*
Ten minutes passed, then: *Still way too high. Can go 20k, with 10k now, the rest when I get the info.*
Well, shit. Rory had figured Carducci would agree to the $50,000, with $25,000 up front.
"So whatta we do now?" Bryce asked.
"We counteroffer again," Rory said.
"You sure, dude? Twenty grand is a lot of money."
"Remember, we'd only get the ten up front and that's all, because we're not gonna tell him where Albert is, so we won't get the other ten."
"Oh, right. But ten thousand is still a lot of money."
"It's not that much," Rory said.
"Maybe not for you, but it sure as hell is for me."

"You'd only get five."

"I know, and that's plenty," Bryce said.

"Worth risking your life?"

"But you said he'd never know who we are! We already agreed on that. So I say we take it."

"Man, this is my thing, okay? So I get to decide what—"

"I helped you figure it all out!"

"Okay, just settle down," Rory said. "But I'm telling you, we've got to counteroffer again. He'll pay more than twenty thou. He's lowballing us. I mean, come on. We start at a hundred thousand and he wants to get us down to twenty? That's an insult."

Bryce didn't say anything.

"I say we ask for thirty, with twenty up front. That means we get ten thousand each."

"Dude," Bryce said, shaking his head.

"What?"

"That's pushing it."

"No, man, it's not. I promise. You've got to trust me. My mom is a lawyer and I've seen how she negotiates. You've gotta be a hard-ass. I've watched her do it, and it totally works. We've got something he wants real bad. Remember that part."

Bryce didn't appear convinced, but finally he said, "Yeah, okay."

"But we're gonna make him wait for a while," Rory said. "Same as he did to us."

Bryce was up and pacing now. So Rory rolled a joint and let Bryce hit it first, to calm him down. Then, of course, Bryce went into Rory's kitchen to get a bag of potato chips. The dude was a straight-up chip junkie.

Finally Rory sent another text to Carducci: *Can't go lower than 30k, with 20k up front. We can tell you exactly where he lives, where he works, what his name is now, what he drives, all of it.*

Carducci replied two minutes later. *We?*

"What does that mean?" Bryce asked, looking over Rory's shoulder.

"No friggin' idea."

"We what?"

"I don't know."

"Should you answer?"

"Oh, crap."

"What?"

"We've been saying *I* all along. In the last text, I said *we*. That's what he's asking about. Now he knows there's more than one of us."

"Shit."

"I know."

Rory realized he should've known better than to handle this texting while he was high. He was bound to slip up eventually.

"You blew it, man," Bryce said.

"Give me a fuckin' break, okay? It's not the end of the world."

"So what do we do now?" Bryce asked.

"I'm thinking. Could you stop eating chips for a minute? It's distracting."

Bryce put the bag down on the coffee table, then he sat in the chair to Rory's right.

Rory thought about it and send a reply. *What?*

Carducci answered immediately: *How many people am I dealing with?*

Two of us.

Then why did you say I earlier?

Rory came up with an answer: *Because it was just me texting. Why does it matter?* Then he quickly sent another. *We need 30k. You in or out? Bet Miguel would pay us more than that to keep the information to ourselves. We're considering that option.*

One minute passed. And another. Finally, a reply.

Okay.

"Yes!" Rory said, and they high-fived. "Told ya."

"That was awesome!" Bryce said.

"I knew he'd friggin' pay," Rory said. "I knew it."

Then his phone dinged with another text.

If you're jerking me around, it will be the biggest mistake of your life.

Rory had to ignore the lump that text put into his throat.

33

"You can go to sleep if you want," Trevor said.

"I'm not sleepy," Caitlin replied.

She was still on the floor, with her back against the wall and knees drawn to her chest. He had offered her the bed, but she didn't want it. He'd made it clear that he wasn't asking her to get in bed with him—that he would get out of the bed and let her have it—but she still didn't want it. When he'd tried to make conversation, she had replied back with just a word or two.

It was becoming increasingly clear to Trevor that he had not found his Caril Ann. He had misjudged. He was disappointed, but he tried not to show it. Not until he decided what to do. Couldn't stay here forever.

"It's cold in here," Caitlin said.

First time she'd opened her mouth on her own and it was to bitch about something.

"It's an old house," Trevor said. "Probably isn't insulated very well."

"Can we turn the heater up?"

"You're that cold?" Trevor asked. "Just get under the blankets."

"I don't want to."

"Then look in that closet for a jacket."

"I will, but I don't understand why you won't turn the heater on."

"I knew from the start that something wasn't right about the guy," Red O'Brien said.

"Me, too," Billy Don Craddock said.

"Oh, hell if you did," O'Brien said. "Don't be changing your story now."

"I ain't changin' my—"

"I 'member you saying I was being nosy when I was asking questions about how much money he had to keep traveling around. And later, when he was in the shower, I said maybe he killed his daddy for the insurance, and you 'member what you said?"

"Nope, but I'm sure you do."

"That I was always coming up with crazy ideas."

"Which is most of the time accurate."

"And I found the gun in his backpack, which seems awfully convenient, considering the dead guy at the zoo was shot. He wasn't stabbed or beaten or hit by a car, he was shot. When I pointed that out, you said I was nuts."

"Still can't rule it out," Billy Don said.

John Marlin finally cut in, saying, "Gentlemen, if you don't mind, can we leave the bickering until later? Right now, I need to ask some questions."

Craddock gave an affirmative grumble.

"Yeah, okay," O'Brien said.

They were standing in front of O'Brien's trailer. Marlin had parked several yards away from O'Brien's old Ford truck. Just minutes earlier, driving along the county road, he'd kept an eye open for anyone walking, but he hadn't seen anybody.

"What's this guy's full name?" Marlin asked.

"Garrett Becker," O'Brien said. "His daddy was named Larry Becker."

"He's the one who mighta got shoved off the roof," Craddock said. "The daddy, I mean. Larry."

"He *knows* that," O'Brien said. "You don't gotta tell him things he already knows."

"I need you to tell me what happened, from the moment you picked him up until he shot your truck earlier tonight," Marlin said.

He wasn't looking forward to hearing these two rednecks give a long rambling account of the past few days, but he saw no way around it. If Garrett Becker was really near the zoo with a handgun, that would make him a person of interest in the case.

O'Brien said, "Okay, well, we was driving east on 32 yesterday morning when—"

"Yesterday morning?" Craddock said. "Was it really just yesterday morning? It seems like a couple days ago."

"Nope. It was just yesterday." O'Brien addressed Marlin again. "We was going to a jobsite down near Canyon Lake when we saw a hitchhiker and Billy Don suggested we should pick him up. I said no at first, but Billy Don started quoting his grandma, at which point I just wanted to shut him up, so I turned around and we went back to get the guy. Really great how that turned out, huh? Anyway, that was about, oh, maybe eight o'clock."

"More like eight-thirty," Craddock said.

"By the time we got to the job site, yeah."

"No, when we picked him up."

"You're wrong, but I'm used to that. So we took the guy to the job site and he actually put in a decent day's work."

"Good helper," Craddock said. "Decent with a chisel."

"But then Billy Don decides to tell him about all the money we won in Vegas, plus all the money we won on that pig-hunting contest, and I don't know about you, but I don't really want a stranger knowing all about the cash we—"

"But you told him we put it in the stock market," Craddock said.

"Well, I had to say something, didn't I?"

"I appreciate you being thorough," Marlin said, "but I don't need every detail. Not right now. Just give me the big picture and then I'll ask questions. That sound okay?"

O'Brien stared at him for a long moment, then said, "Hate to say it, but sometimes you folks are hard to please, you know that?"

Marlin could only laugh. "I'm sure we are, but please continue."

And they did, and it was as painful as Marlin anticipated, but after fifteen minutes, they'd covered all of the pertinent details, including everything O'Brien had learned during his "investigation." Only problem was, Marlin hadn't learned anything that O'Brien hadn't already mentioned during his lengthy voicemail.

Marlin still had no way of knowing if Garrett Becker had ever been in the vicinity of Safari Adventure. According to what Becker had told O'Brien and Craddock, he had seen the swarm of emergency vehicles on Highway 281 yesterday morning and had then turned around and headed north. That was as close to the zoo as he had ever gotten. Was it true? Could it be proven or disproven? Right now, no. Maybe not ever.

What if Garrett Becker was the shooter? Or even a witness? Or what if he was simply in possession of the gun that had been used in the shooting? What if he really had found the gun along the highway, but it had been near the zoo, rather than near Stephenville, as he'd claimed. That could be a tremendous step forward in the case.

Then O'Brien added one more detail. "Oh, we found the shells a few minutes ago," he said.

"*I* found 'em," Craddock said.

"We was looking around after we called you," O'Brien said.

"And I found 'em in some tall grass beside the driveway," Craddock said.

Marlin said, "Please tell me you didn't—"

"We didn't touch 'em," Craddock said. "We know better than that."

"Want us to show you where they are?" O'Brien asked.

"Because I don't want to do anything that might let anybody know we're here," Trevor said.

"How is the heater going to do that?" Caitlin asked.

Caitlin had been trying to decide how hard to push back on Trevor. How would he react if she stood up to him? Or if she stopped letting him make all the decisions? Ultimately, if it came down to it, she would fight like hell. She'd rip his eyes out if she had to. Both her parents had raised her to take care of herself, which included enrolling her in several self-defense classes. If she could get to him when he put the gun down...

"Someone could hear it running," he said.

"Who? The nearest neighbor is a hundred yards away."

"It's not that cold in here," Trevor said.

"Well, I'm cold anyway," Caitlin said.

"Then get into the bed," Trevor said. "Get under the covers."

"Nope."

"Then look in that closet, like I said. Maybe there's a jacket in there."

"So you won't turn the heater on?" she asked, putting some attitude behind it.

"No. You need to stop asking."

She stared at him for a long moment, but he simply stared back. It was irritating, but it was also unnerving. Creepy. There was no empathy in those eyes. No fear, either.

She rose from the floor, went over to the closet, and opened the door. Renee hadn't yet invited Caitlin over to sort through items for charity, and it was obvious nobody in her family had made any progress on that chore. The closet was filled from one side to the other with clothes hanging from the rod and various bagged and boxed items on the shelf above and on the floor.

There must've been thirty or forty blouses, and maybe twenty dresses, all wildly out of date.

Caitlin slid some items to the right and found a bunch of sweaters and light jackets. Most of them were hideous, but it was ridiculous to worry about appearances when—

She stopped. She had almost gotten to the last item on the right, and now she saw something she hadn't been able to see before.

There, leaning in the corner, was a shotgun.

34

"Okay, so how do we get the money?" Bryce asked after they'd finished celebrating the negotiation with Carducci.

"Huh?"

"How will we get him to pay us?"

After Carducci's last text— *If you're jerking me around, it will be the biggest mistake of your life*—Rory had replied that they would be in touch soon with payment instructions. That's how a pro would handle it. Don't rush. Keep control of the situation.

"I don't know, Venmo or PayPal," Rory said. "That seems like the easiest way."

"But is that safe?" Bryce asked.

"Why wouldn't it be?"

"I don't know, dude. Isn't your name attached to those kinds of accounts?"

Bryce was turning out to be a pain in the ass.

"I think we can just use a phone number, and we'll use the same one we're using for the texts. This burner phone. It's not connected to my name or anything."

Saying *burner phone* made Rory feel like a thug. He liked it.

"But you have to connect Venmo or PayPal to a bank account, I'm pretty sure," Bryce said.

"I think that's optional," Rory said.

"Yeah, but if we don't enter it, we won't be able to move the money anywhere. It'll just sit in that account. I think. I'm not sure."

"Okay, then we'll connect it to a bank account. What does it matter? He won't be able to see any of that stuff, like our name and address and all that."

"You're one hundred percent positive about that?"

Rory didn't reply, because the truth was, he wasn't sure. They hadn't planned that far ahead.

"Dude, you're making me nervous," Bryce said.

"Hang on," Rory said, and he did some googling.

He found various forums discussing anonymous payments, but some of the comments weren't necessarily reassuring. A few of the commenters suggested some specific websites or apps that allowed you to get paid without sharing your name or any other private details, but others insisted that those methods might actually leave a paper trail. Were those people right or wrong? And what if the site got hacked and suddenly a bunch of user information got stolen? Rory read some of the comments to Bryce.

"Man, if there's even the slightest chance he can link the account to us, I don't think we should risk it," Bryce said.

"That's what I've been saying."

"We're talking about a mafia guy," Bryce said.

"You don't have to tell me."

"What about an offshore account?" Bryce asked.

Rory had heard that phrase before, of course, but he wasn't completely certain what it meant. So he googled that, too. He read for five minutes, and it all sounded pretty complicated.

"I think we'd be raising a lot of red flags if we did that, and it's probably overkill anyway," he said.

Bryce let the idea drop.

"There's gotta be a way to do this," Rory said. "We just need to figure out what it is."

Rory lit the joint again and took another hit. He knew it muddied his thinking, but it helped him relax.

"Maybe we just need to keep it simple and ask for cash," he said.

"Okay, but how do we get it?" Bryce asked. "He's way the hell up in…which state is he in again?"

"Massachusetts."

"Yeah. Could he, like, FedEx it?"

"We'd have to give an address. Hey, I got it! We could rent a PO box. Make him mail it."

Bryce made a face.

"What?" Rory asked.

"He could send somebody to watch the box. I saw that happen in a movie once. No, wait. It was one of those lockers at the airport. Same kind of thing, though. They watched it until somebody showed up."

"Somebody sat around all day, just waiting?" Rory asked.

"Yup. Then they followed the guy. Or they got his license plate number. I can't remember. And they killed him after that."

"It was just a movie," Rory said.

"I know, but what's to stop Carducci from doing the same thing?"

"Okay, man. Relax. I'm just throwing ideas out there until we figure something out."

Rory was wishing they'd worked on these details in advance, but there had to be a solution. Something simple, but smart.

It took a few more minutes, but he finally nailed it. The idea even made sense later, when he wasn't high.

35

O'Brien and Craddock led the way to two brass shells resting in some tall grass away from the caliche parking area, but not far from O'Brien's truck. Marlin squatted with a flashlight and took a good look. The shells were from a .380—the same caliber that had been used to kill the man at the zoo. Marlin took some photos, then carefully collected the casings into an evidence bag.

"What if we find Garrett tonight?" Craddock asked. "Can we shoot him?"

"You can't just shoot him," Marlin said.

"What if we feel threatened?" O'Brien asked.

Marlin was hesitant to answer that question, because no matter what he said, these two yahoos would twist it around in their minds to justify an armed response.

"I'm guessing he won't be coming back," Marlin said, "and you shouldn't go looking for him. You understand that?"

"What if he does try to come back?" O'Brien asked. "That's trespassing, right? And he's got a gun."

"Then you should call 911," Marlin said.

Which directly contradicted the sign O'Brien had planted halfway up his driveway that showed the silhouette of an assault rifle and the words *Trespassers: We don't dial 911*.

"But we got a right to defend ourselves and our property," Craddock said. "Ever'body knows that."

"Well, you do have that right," Marlin said, "Just remember it's easy to shoot a bullet, but it's impossible to take it back."

"Well, yeah," O'Brien said. "It's a bullet. You probably wouldn't even be able to find it."

"It was a figure of speech," Marlin said. "Just use sound judgment, okay?"

"'Course we would," O'Brien said. "We both got great judgment."

Marlin bit his tongue and said, "I'll need both of you to come to the sheriff's office tomorrow morning and write down everything you just told me. Can you do that?"

"I knew we shouldn't have talked so much," Craddock said, grinning.

"It would be very helpful," Marlin said.

"All right," O'Brien said, sounding like a kid whose mom had just told him to finish his chores. "If we gotta do it."

"Give me a physical description of Garrett Becker," Marlin said.

"About my height," O'Brien said. "Kind of skinny. Prob'ly hasn't shaved in a week."

"What was he wearing?"

"Blue jeans, tennis shoes, and an orange jacket.

"Bright orange, dark orange, Longhorn orange?" Marlin asked.

"Pretty bright," O'Brien said. "Maybe not as orange as that shit they make you wear when you're on one of them public hunts, but pretty close. Oh, hey, I just remembered something else. Can't believe I left this out."

"What is it?" Marlin was ready to return to Blanco and look for Caitlin McGregor.

"Earlier we was all watching that lady talking on TV—that one Albert was banging nineteen years ago—did you see that?"

"I heard about it," Marlin said, remembering the email from Lauren earlier. Apparently Albert Cortez had been having an affair with the woman, who was the wife of a mob boss.

O'Brien said, "Well, we was all wondering why y'all haven't been able to identify the dead guy at the zoo yet, and Billy Don said—"

"I said maybe he got shot in the face with a shotgun," Craddock said. "Which would account for y'all not being able to identify him."

"And Garrett started to say something about that, but he stopped, and I had to badger it out of him," O'Brien said. "What he said was, he heard the guy—"

"—was shot in the neck," Craddock said.

Marlin felt that tingle in his chest that often accompanied a significant step forward in a case.

"You sure he said that?" he asked.

"Damn sure did," O'Brien replied. "Is that right? The guy was shot in the neck?"

"We're not releasing any information about that," Marlin said.

"Which means yes," O'Brien said. "Anyway, I asked Garrett where he'd heard it, since I ain't seen the first thing about that anywhere."

"What that means is he knew something he shouldn'ta known," Craddock added.

"How would he of known it?" O'Brien asked.

It was a good question.

Caitlin had to resist the urge to grab the shotgun, but she pulled a sweater from a hanger instead, and she closed the closet door. Her heart was absolutely pounding.

"What's wrong?" Trevor said.

"Huh?"

"You look like something's wrong."

"Oh, I was just thinking about Renee's grandmother," Caitlin said. "It's so sad that all of her stuff is still here."

Was the shotgun loaded? That was the most important question. Caitlin could handle a shotgun as well as anybody—she'd hunted dove and shot skeet with her parents for several years—but her experience would be meaningless if it wasn't loaded.

She pulled the sweater on and sat on the floor again, back against the wall.

"Warm now?" Trevor asked.

"Not yet," Caitlin said. "And it's only going to get colder in here."

"Then grab another sweater."

If she came out of the closet with the shotgun and it wasn't loaded, that could be a disaster if she needed to actually shoot him. And she *would* shoot him, if it came down to it. She needed to buy some time, so she could check for shells in the shotgun.

She said, "I just remembered something—I think there's a space heater in the kitchen. I think I saw one in there. Nobody would be able to hear that."

"When?"

"When what?"

"When did you see it?"

"I was over here with Renee a few weeks ago."

He stared at her again for a very long moment and she had a hard time holding his gaze.

"Don't lie," he said very quietly. "You don't need to lie to me. It pisses me off that you'd lie."

She didn't say anything.

"You've never been here before. I heard you talking to Renee last week, and y'all were talking about meeting up this coming weekend, and she had to tell you where the house is. That's when she said where the key was hidden."

She looked down at her hands—but she was only pretending to be meek, because that's what he wanted to see.

"What were you gonna do if I left you alone—run for the back door?"

"Yeah," she said, relieved that he hadn't somehow deduced her real motive.

"Don't do that," he said. "You shouldn't do that."

"I won't," she said. "I promise."

"You won't get the chance," he said.

"I'm just scared, you know?"

"Scared of what?"

She didn't intend to laugh, but she couldn't help herself. "Well, you shot a couple of people, Trevor, and now we're hiding out here."

He stared straight ahead at the wall opposite the bed.

"I didn't want it to start this way, you know," Trevor said.

"You didn't want what to start this way? What is *it*? I still don't know what that means."

He was shaking his head slowly and she could tell he wasn't sure how to answer. Finally he said, "Have you ever been driving along and you think, 'What would happen if I just jerked the wheel and went over that cliff?' Or there's a dump truck coming right at you, and you wonder if you can stop yourself from steering into its path. And I know how crazy that sounds, but I wonder about those things, and I can't help it." His voice was getting thicker, like he was about to cry—but he was holding it back. "There are times when I'm at work and I have a knife in my hand..."

Caitlin had no idea how she should respond, or whether she should say anything at all. Instincts guided her and she said, "It has to be hard to deal with those kinds of thoughts."

"That's why I wanted to run away," he said. "And I was hoping you'd want to go with me."

She said, "But why didn't you just ask me?" and immediately realized that was a dumb question.

"Would you have gone?" he said, spitting the question at her—daring her to lie and say she would have.

Dangerous ground. She didn't want him to feel rejected.

She said, "I wouldn't run away with anybody—you or anyone else. I don't want to run away. My family is here. I've lived here all my life. I'm not planning on going anywhere—at least not yet."

His face clouded over, and she had no idea what he was thinking.

"It's not too late to fix all this," she said. "But you need to give up. I think Rodney and that girl are going to be okay." She was guessing, based on what she had seen.

"There's a lot more to it than that," Trevor said.

"What do you mean?"

"It didn't start at the Dairy Queen."

"What didn't start?" she asked.

He laughed. It was a laugh of regret, but it was still a laugh. She couldn't remember ever seeing him laugh before.

Then he told her everything.

Marlin was no more than a half-mile from O'Brien's home when he rounded a gentle curve and saw a flash of orange in some cedar trees along the left side of the county road. Just a quick glimpse. Didn't necessarily mean anything. Maybe it was the text on a NO TRESPASSING sign. Or a logo on a piece of ranch equipment parked behind a barbed-wire fence.

But he stopped, dropped it into reverse, and eased backward slowly, trying to spot the orange again with his headlights.

Nothing.

Had he really seen it?

He drove forward slowly, but this time he swept the area with the spotlight mounted on the outside of his truck. Nothing but cedars and waist-high native grasses. No homes anywhere around here.

Marlin crept along at no more than five miles per hour, looking for any glimpse of orange, maybe a scrap of paper or a tossed soft drink can or surveyor's tape marking a property line.

Then he saw it again for the briefest of moments.

He braked, then reversed again.

And he braked hard. There it was. Orange. Bright orange. Just the tiniest bit, visible through a dense shield of cedar limbs. No more than thirty yards away. Marlin couldn't tell what it was. He grabbed his binoculars and peered through them. Still couldn't tell what he was seeing.

He didn't want to move his truck, so he set the parking brake and left his spotlight trained on the orange object. Flipped the switch for the light bar across the roof. Thumbed his microphone and let Darrell, the dispatcher, know he was going to be out at this location, searching for a possible armed subject. "Code four unless I advise otherwise."

Code 4—*No further assistance is required.*

On almost any other night, Marlin would request backup. It only made sense to minimize risk, considering that Garrett Becker was armed. But right now, every law-enforcement officer within thirty miles was searching for Trevor Larkin and Caitlin McGregor—and Marlin didn't want to pull anyone away from that important work—not for something like this, when he wasn't even sure if there was a person hiding in the cedars.

Marlin took his Bushmaster M4 from the overhead rack, then opened the truck door and stepped out. Closed the door gently.

He crossed the pavement and stepped onto the rough caliche soil of the shoulder. Made his way slightly downhill to the barbed-wire fence separating county property from the ranch beyond. From here, at this angle, he could no longer see any orange.

He found a low point in the fence and was able to hoist himself over quickly, without any snags, thanks to his long legs.

No orange from here, either. The cedars were just too dense.

He moved to his right, and further still, and now he saw it again. Fifteen yards away. Was it the orange fabric of a jacket? Garrett Becker hunkering down behind the thick trunk of an old-growth cedar? Perhaps a shoulder or an elbow poking out? It was certainly possible.

A minute passed and Marlin remained perfectly still, watching the orange object.

Then it moved. Just a little bit, but it moved.

36

When Trevor finished telling Caitlin his story, she didn't know whether she should believe it or not. It sounded so crazy.

She knew that Albert Cortez had gone missing and that the cops had found a dead man at the zoo. And not long before Trevor came to the DQ with his gun, that woman in Massachusetts went on national TV and said Albert had a secret past and had killed a man nineteen years ago.

But the rest of Trevor's story? It came across as some sort of silly movie, like that one called *Fargo* her dad was always watching. It was twisted and gruesome and kind of funny, because all the bad guys were so incompetent, but nothing like that ever happened in real life.

Trevor was dangerous, obviously, and now Caitlin wondered if he was delusional, too. Maybe he was dangerous *because* he was delusional. Had Trevor killed the guy at the zoo? At this point, it definitely seemed possible.

That didn't mean Caitlin was going to let herself be a victim. Time to act.

"I need to get a heavier sweater," she said.

He just stared at her from his place on the bed.

"What?" she asked.

"You don't believe me," he said.

"That's not true," she said. "I'm just cold again, and I need to get another sweater."

Why did her voice sound so weird? Because she was anxious. Like the time she'd had to give a speech in government class. It had terrified her—but now it seemed so trivial. What was there to be scared about back then?

Trevor shook his head and laid backwards, the bed springs creaking beneath him, but he didn't say anything.

"I'm going to get another sweater," she said.

"You need to go to a doctor or something," he said.

"What for?"

"If you're cold all the time like that," he said. "It's not cold in here."

"Sometimes I get a little anemic," she said. "I take iron for it."

Total lie, but it was true for her mom, because of heavy periods.

"What does anemic mean?" Trevor asked.

"That you aren't making enough red blood cells," Caitlin said. "So you get cold. I even get cold in the summer. I need a heavier sweater or even a coat."

"I never noticed it at work."

"Because I'm always moving around."

A long pause.

Then he said, "If you need another sweater, just get one. You don't have to tell me."

Where was his handgun? She couldn't see it from here. It was probably lying on the bed on the other side of him, where he could grab it quickly, if necessary. So it was on his left side, even though he was right-handed. She felt proud to have noticed that, and it meant she might gain an extra half-second.

She rose from the floor and went to the closet door, glancing backward for just a moment. He hadn't moved.

Was she really going to do this?

She had to remind herself that something was seriously wrong with him. He was dangerous. A psycho.

She opened the closet door.

Blood was rushing in her ears as she reached up and slid some hangers to the left, occasionally pausing, as if inspecting the suitability of a particular item.

She could see the stock of the shotgun in the corner, but the barrel was still concealed behind the clothing.

She was going to have to take a chance and pull it out, not knowing if it was loaded or not. If the shotgun was loaded, good. If it wasn't, so be it.

Her hands were shaking. She couldn't help it. The inside of her mouth felt like sandpaper. Her legs felt weak, almost to the point of buckling.

If it was loaded, what was in it? She hoped it was buckshot and not birdshot.

She slid more hangers to the left, one by one. She would hear the bedsprings if Trevor moved.

Her breathing was becoming ragged. She remembered the time she went deer hunting with her dad. Looking through the scope at a big eight-point. Buck fever. *You have to think about your breathing,* he said. *Take deep, slow breaths. That will keep you calm.*

Deep. Slow. Breaths. It wasn't easy.

Sliding hangers. Almost there.

She would hear the bedsprings.

Three more hangers. Now two. And one.

The shotgun was right there, completely exposed now. A pump-action Winchester. Probably twelve-gauge, but she didn't know for sure, and it wouldn't really matter.

She had to do it. Right now.

Deep. Slow. Breaths.

With her left hand, she reached upward and jiggled some clothes hanging from the rod. With her right, she grabbed the shotgun by the barrel.

"What are you doing?" Trevor asked.

The bedsprings creaked.

No stopping now.

She dropped her left hand from the clothes rod and grabbed the shotgun by the fore-end, then swung it up and around, backing out of the closet while placing her right hand under the stock and lifting it to her shoulder.

Her right thumb found the safety button and turned it off.

Trevor saw and reacted immediately, jumping from the bed, lunging for the bedroom door, just as Caitlin pulled the trigger and the shotgun kicked hard against her shoulder.

The orange object hadn't moved much, but it *had* moved, no question about it.

Marlin moved forward with the M4 in the low-ready position—the butt tight on his right shoulder, rifle ready to fire, but with the barrel pointing slightly downward. He had a clear view over the weapon and would be able to raise it and fire in a fraction of a second, if necessary.

Marlin took slow, careful steps, keeping his eyes on the orange object. The area was still brightly illuminated by the spotlight on the truck. Anyone looking in Marlin's direction would be more or less blinded by the powerful light.

After three more steps, Marlin could now see plainly that the orange object was a person crouched behind a thick cedar tree, no more than twenty-five feet away. Marlin could just see the edge of the jacket sleeve. Marlin found a nearby oak tree and positioned himself behind the trunk. He took a deep breath and tried to slow his rapidly beating heart. Then it was time to act.

"State game warden!" Marlin called out. "Show me your hands!"

No movement. No verbal reply.

"Garrett Becker, I'm looking at you right now behind that cedar. There are four of us. Show me your hands!"

"Don't shoot!" Becker finally replied.

"Show me your hands! Right now!"

"I didn't do anything," Becker said. "Just go away!"

"Show me your hands! I'm not asking again."

Marlin could see that Becker was rising from his crouched position and was now standing upright, with his back against the cedar trunk. Stalling. Not following commands. What was he doing back there?

"I dropped the gun at Red's place," Becker said.

"Show me your hands and step out!"

"Red is lying about everything."

"You can tell your side of the story, but first you need to—"

A shot rang out and Marlin quickly ducked behind the trunk of the oak tree.

37

Trevor made it through the doorway and into the hallway just as Caitlin fired the second shot, which ripped a chunk from the doorframe.

Her breathing was out of control. Chest heaving. She had to calm down.

Deep. Slow. Breaths.

She didn't want to take her eyes off the doorway, but she took a quick peek at the bed.

No gun there. Trevor had grabbed the gun when he'd run, or maybe he'd grabbed it right before she'd come out of the closet with the shotgun, because he'd suspected she was up to something.

Or maybe it was somewhere else. What if the gun was under a pillow? She would love to know if he was armed, but moving to the head of the bed and looking for the gun would make her visible from the hallway and the bedroom immediately opposite. Trevor might be out there right now, waiting for her to show herself.

She stood quietly, hoping to hear any sound at all that might indicate where he was. But she heard nothing.

"Trevor?" she called. Now her voice was really wavering all over the place. She didn't even sound like herself.

He didn't reply.

"I didn't want to do that," she said. "I had no choice."

Nothing.

Had she hit him? She had no idea. She glanced at the bed and the floor and the doorway. No blood that she could see. She couldn't believe she'd missed at this distance, but he'd really moved fast.

She studied the damage to the doorframe. Looked like buckshot had done it. Buckshot from this distance would have done serious damage if she'd hit him.

"Trevor, do you need to go to a hospital?"

Thirty seconds passed without a reply.

"I'll take you if you need to go. Or let's call an ambulance."

Then he finally answered from somewhere in the house.

"You didn't have to shoot," he said. "I would've turned the heater on."

A joke. He was making a joke. She couldn't believe it. It made him seem so normal. How could he do that—make a joke, like a regular person—when the other parts of him were so clearly insane?

"Did I hit you?" she asked.

"You ruined everything," he said.

He sounded different. Possibly in pain. Maybe she *had* hit him.

"Let me call for help," she said. Problem was, he had her phone.

"Jesus, I can't believe you did that," he said.

She moved as quietly as possible toward the bedroom window.

"Are you okay?"

Trevor said nothing more. If he approached the bedroom, she would hear squeaking from the floorboards.

She moved the curtain with one hand and saw that the window was of a very old style she had never seen before. It had a handle you cranked in a circle to swing the window open like a door. Would it make much noise? How long since it had last been opened? If she could open it quietly, she could slip into the darkness and run to freedom.

She grabbed the handle, but kept her eyes on the bedroom door, just in case.

"Trevor, are you okay?"

Still no answer.

She turned the handle slowly for one complete revolution—and it came off in her hand.

Five seconds after the shot, Marlin took a quick peek and saw that Becker still had his back pressed against the cedar trunk. He had never extended the gun around the tree trunk, which meant he hadn't fired in this direction.

Marlin placed his M4 in the low-ready position just to the right side of the tree trunk and kept his eyes on Becker.

"That was dumb, Garrett," Marlin said.

In response, Becker fired two more shots, but he was either firing into the ground or into the woods in the opposite direction—a scare tactic. That didn't mean he wouldn't fire at Marlin if it came down to it.

Marlin keyed the microphone clipped to his shirt and requested backup. Darrell repeated the message and asked responding units to identify. The nearest unit—Max, the state trooper—was approximately fifteen minutes out. Marlin was pulling him away from the search for Caitlin, but that couldn't be helped.

"Garrett, you're turning this into something really bad," Marlin said. "There's no need for that."

No reply.

"I didn't even come out here to arrest you," Marlin said. "I just wanted you to tell me what happened at Red's place."

Nothing.

"It's not too late to reel this back in," Marlin said. "Just put the gun down."

Ten seconds passed.

Then Becker said something Marlin wasn't expecting. "I'm sorry, man. I lost my temper."

"I understand," Marlin said. "What happened tonight? What set you off?"

Garrett said something Marlin couldn't understand.

"What was that?"

"I said I'm tired of it all."

"Tired of what?"

"Tired of getting blamed for everything. Tired of people not believing me. Tired of cops."

"What happened at Red's place?" Marlin asked.

"He's an idiot," Garrett said.

Marlin laughed loudly, and it was genuine. "No argument there.

What did he do this time?"

"He just kept pushing me, man."

"About what?"

Another long pause followed, and then Garrett said, "It's a long story. My dad slipped off a roof and died. A lot of people back home think I pushed him, but I didn't."

"Sorry to hear that."

"Hard to clear your name when there aren't any witnesses," Garrett said.

Also makes it hard for the cops to charge you, Marlin thought. *Goes both ways.*

"When did this happen?" Marlin asked.

"Last year," Garrett said.

"What were y'all doing on the roof?" Marlin asked.

"I know what you're doing," Garrett said. "Stalling until backup arrives. I heard you on the radio."

Marlin said, "Wasn't like I was trying to keep it a secret. Eventually you're gonna have to put your gun down and come out."

Marlin was watching closely—waiting to see if Garrett would comply. Marlin knew from experience that reasonable people sometimes made poor decisions driven by stress, panic, anger, drugs, alcohol and a hundred other factors. Garrett had already made several bad choices this evening. Would it continue?

"Garrett?" Marlin called again.

"You'll shoot me," Garrett said.

"Not if you put your gun down and come out peacefully."

"Okay," Garrett said. "But I want to tell you something first."

Still stalling.

"What is it?"

"You probably won't believe me. Nobody ever believes me."

"Try me," Marlin said.

"I'll tell you if you'll forget about the stupid stuff I did tonight."

Wanting to negotiate a deal. Was he about to reveal something about the shooting at the zoo? Or where he really found the gun? He might have valuable information.

"I can't make any promises until I know what you're talking about," Marlin said.

"You know that girl that was taken from the Dairy Queen this afternoon?" Garrett said. "I think I know where she is."

Caitlin returned to the closet and stood inside it quietly with the shotgun. She heard nothing.

She wondered how many more shells might be in the shotgun, but she couldn't count them without unloading. If Renee's grandmother used the shotgun for hunting—which seemed unlikely—there would probably be one shell left, because you are only allowed three shells, and there would be a plug in the tube that stopped you from loading more than that.

If, on the other hand, the shotgun was specifically for home defense, there wouldn't be a plug, and the shotgun would hold more like five shells, so she would have three left. Which meant that—

Floorboards creaked.

Thirty seconds passed.

Then she heard another sound. Something she couldn't identify. Had Trevor bumped against a wall? Had he dropped something? It didn't sound close, though. She stayed where she was, with the shotgun leveled at the bedroom doorway.

Caitlin realized quite suddenly, and surprisingly, that she was crying. Quietly. Letting her emotions take over. She couldn't afford to do that.

Deep. Slow. Breaths.

Now she heard another sound—and this one was unmistakable. A door opening and closing. And from the way the air pressure changed in the house for a moment, it had to be the front door or the back door.

No way. She wasn't falling for it. It was a trick. He was trying to lure her out.

How should she respond? Pretend she bought it? How? What should she do? What advantage could she gain, if any?

She didn't move for a full five minutes. Her arms were growing tired from holding the shotgun.

Finally, she couldn't stand the tension anymore. She couldn't go on like this all night.

"Trevor, I know you didn't go outside."

Nothing but quiet.

"You're not fooling anyone," she said.

"I always knew you were smart," he replied.

"What are we doing, Trevor?" she asked.

"You have to go to sleep sometime," he said. He did not sound wounded.

"Just leave, Trevor, okay? Don't drag me into this any further than you have already. It's not fair. I don't deserve this. I never did anything to you."

Laying a guilt trip on him. Worth a shot.

A minute passed. Then two.

Then she heard the door opening and closing again.

"Trevor?"

No answer.

"I'm not buying it," she said.

No answer.

38

"How'd you figure out where the guy is?" was the question Joey had asked, and it appeared, at first, that Carducci wasn't going to answer. It wasn't really Joey's business, was it? And he damn sure didn't need to know the answer in order to handle the task he'd agreed to complete.

But then Carducci laughed. "Fuckin' amateurs. It's pretty funny, if you want to know the truth. They sent a bunch of notes, one after the other, trying to be clever or some shit. From San Antonio, of all places. First note says they know where Miguel Lopez is. Second note asks if *I* want to know where he is. Of course I fuckin' want to know. No reason to go through all this bullshit. Then the third note finally gives me a cell number to text, which I do, and it's like dealing with a bunch of retards, telling me to say my name is Glen Johnson. It's like they saw a spy movie on TV or something."

Joey was grinning, showing that he was enjoying the story.

"So then they text me a photo, and shit if they aren't right—it's Lopez. No question. He's older, yeah, but it's him. I ask how much they want for the information, and after some back and forth, we come to an agreement—some of the money up front and the rest later. Now, in the back of my head, I'm thinking these assholes might take the first payment and never give up the information, so before I send it, I say it sure as hell looks like Lopez, but send me a couple more photos so I can be sure. Of course, I'm hoping they slip up and give me something in one of these photos that tells me where he is. And you know what happened?"

Joey figured the answer was that Carducci's tactic had paid off, but he simply said, "No, what?"

"It worked like a goddamn charm!" Carducci said. "I get them to send three more photos, and that's when I notice something. Lopez is wearing the same shirt in all of them—a blue polo shirt. Like a, you know, company shirt, but without a logo anywhere. I figure these idiots erased the logo off the shirt in the photos, but just knowing that much—that Lopez worked somewhere that he's gotta wear a blue polo every day—that's helpful."

"That was damn clever," Joey said, and he meant it.

"Maybe so, but these guys are morons, so it's not my greatest accomplishment ever. Anyway, I remember that Lopez liked animals. He owned one of those places, whatdayacallit, where you keep a dog when you go on vacation."

"A kennel?"

"Right, a kennel. So I take a guess that he's working with animals again, somewhere in or around San Antonio, at a place where they all wear blue polos. I start checking kennels, veterinarians, pet stores, all that kind of shit, but I'm striking out. Then I think, hey, what kind of place has more animals than anywhere else?"

He looked at Joey.

"A zoo?" Joey said.

"Damn right a zoo. As it turns out, San Antonio's got a nice, big zoo, so I check it out online, but their employees are all wearing green polo shirts."

"They coulda changed the color," Joey said.

"Huh?"

"The guys who sent the photos coulda played around with the color. Changed green to blue. At the same time they erased the logo."

Carducci chuckled. "Damn. I never thought of that—and it's a good thing, too, because that woulda thrown me off. Instead I looked for other zoos in the area, getting wider and wider, and finally I found this little zoo north of San Antonio, before you get to a little town called Blanco. Safari Adventure is what it's called, and the employees there all wear that exact same blue polo shirt."

"Nice," Joey said, nodding.

"It's just a little place, and the website says the owner is somebody named Albert Cortez. Funny thing about ol' Albert is, I can't find a single picture of him on the zoo's website or Facebook page or the Instagram. I see all of the other employees, but not Albert. But then I finally find a lady who went to that zoo this past summer, and she posted a video, and who do I see giving a tour in one of those little trolleys? Miguel fucking Lopez—now known as Albert Cortez."

"That's epic," Joey said.

Carducci nodded with self satisfaction. "And the best part is, whoever was sending those photos, they was probably gonna screw me, but I screwed them first. Never sent them a goddamn dime."

39

Red and Billy Don were still outside, drinking beer on the porch, when they heard a shot from somewhere along the county road leading toward town. The same direction Marlin had gone earlier. Probably the same direction Garrett had gone.

"That sounded like a handgun," Red said.

Billy Don grunted in the affirmative.

Then the sound of two more quick shots rolled over the hilltops.

"A three-eighty, I think," Red said.

Billy Don snorted.

"What?" Red asked.

"Ain't no way you can get that pacific."

"Sure as hell can," Red said.

"As if."

"As if what?"

"That's just something people say. As if."

"But you agree it was a handgun?" Red asked.

"Well, duh. Any idiot could figure that out."

"So that includes you," Red said.

"It would be great if you was as clever as you thought you was."

"Well, it sure as hell wasn't Marlin's three-fifty-seven," Red said.

"Probably not."

"And it damn sure wasn't his M4."

"Course not."

They waited for more shots, but heard nothing.

"He could be dead right now," Red said.

"Garrett?"

"No, Marlin. If that was Garrett shooting, that means Marlin could be dead."

Billy Don didn't disagree. Instead he said, "Gotta admit I never saw any of this crazy shit coming."

"What'd you expect when you pick up a hitchhiker? And then later he told us how much he hates cops. Talk about a red flag."

"You hate cops."

"I don't *hate* hate them," Red said. "Not like he does. I wouldn't shoot one. I just don't like it when they get all picky about the law."

Billy Don didn't say anything.

Red drained the last of his beer, then said, "I'm thinking we should go see if Marlin is okay—but there's also a chance he might blame us for interfering in cop bidness."

"Yup. We don't get paid to get shot at. He does. Plus, we can't get into trouble if we stay right here."

Billy Don pulled two more tallboys out of the ice chest and passed one to Red.

"Good point," Red said.

"I feel bad for him, though, because it ain't no picnic gettin' shot, I can tell you that much," Billy Don said.

"Yup," Red said.

"'Cause I been shot twice."

"I 'member. I'm sure it hurt."

"Then why are you grinning?"

Red could feel Billy Don glaring at him. "I didn't know I was."

I think I know where she is.

Marlin hadn't expected that.

Was Becker trying to play him? Grasping at straws to get himself out of this predicament? Willing to make something up to use as a bargaining chip? The problem was, Marlin couldn't just dismiss the possibility entirely. Becker might actually have information.

"How would you know that?" Marlin asked.

"You have to promise me first. No charges."

Marlin spoke quietly into his microphone. "Dispatch, be advised that the subject is claiming he might know where Caitlin McGregor is. I'm working on getting that information."

Then, more loudly, Marlin said, "Garrett, you could save her life. Where is she?"

"I lost my temper and fired those shots," Garrett said. "I know how stupid that was."

Marlin was starting to lose his patience.

"Garrett, this is your chance to do the right thing. Tell me where she might be."

"No charges. That includes shooting Red's truck."

Nothing was more important at this moment than extracting the information about Caitlin.

"We'll work something out," Marlin said. "But only if we find the girl."

Garrett didn't say anything.

"The sooner you tell me, the more likely we'll find her," Marlin said. "If you wait, Trevor might take her somewhere else. Then you've got no deal."

"I think you'll charge me anyway."

"I won't. You have my word."

"You'll take the information and then arrest me later."

"I'm telling you, that won't happen. Not if we find her."

"I don't believe you," Garrett said.

"Why not?"

"You're a cop, man."

"So what?"

"I don't think I can trust you."

"Damn it, Garrett, you're gonna have to—"

"See how it feels?" Becker said.

"What?"

"See how much it sucks when people think you're a liar?"

Marlin let out a long breath. "Okay, you've made your point. Now I'm asking you—please—put your gun down and tell me where you think Caitlin might be."

A long moment passed. Then Garrett extended his right hand from behind the cedar tree, bent down, and placed the pistol on the ground.

Caitlin woke with a start, the shotgun cradled in her arms. Unbelievably, she had dozed off. But for how long? What time was it? It seemed like no more than ten or fifteen minutes had passed, but she couldn't be sure.

She remembered sitting down in the closet, because she couldn't stand forever, but she'd vowed not to fall asleep. Then she'd nestled into some of the longer garments—dresses and hanging coats.

Now she was awake, and berating herself for the slip-up.

Where was Trevor? Had he really left when she'd heard the door opening and closing the second time?

She hadn't heard him start the truck, but that didn't mean anything. She probably couldn't hear it from here, or maybe she'd been asleep.

Maybe he was still in the house. Maybe he wasn't. Maybe he had fled on foot. Maybe he'd sprouted wings and flown away. Maybe some buckshot had hit him and he was dead by now.

Making matters worse was that she had to pee—really bad.

"Trevor?" she called, because what was the harm? She gained nothing if he didn't answer, whether he was actually out there or not. Then, on impulse, she added, "I fell asleep for a few minutes and you missed your chance."

The house was quiet.

"On Tuesday afternoon, Trevor Larkin picked me up outside Marble Falls and gave me a ride to Johnson City," Garrett Becker said. "We bought some beer and hung out by the river for a while, just bullshitting, and then he said he knew a place I could crash for a few days. He worked with this girl whose grandmother had gone into a nursing home. Her house was empty and he said he'd take me over there."

Garrett was riding in the passenger seat in Marlin's truck. He had agreed to accompany Marlin back to the sheriff's office and tell his story along the way, then repeat it in front of a camera, if necessary. He would voluntarily remain at the office until Marlin confirmed that Caitlin McGregor had been found. Max, the trooper, had returned to the search.

"Who was the girl?" Marlin asked.

"Her name was Renee," Garrett said.

Renee was one of the Dairy Queen employees who'd been present when Trevor Larkin had abducted Caitlin. So far, Becker's story was sounding legit.

"Where is the house?" Marlin asked.

"Don't know."

"So you didn't take him up on it?" Marlin asked.

"Hell, no. I could tell he didn't have permission to let me into that house, and I didn't want to get shot, or get busted for trespassing. Plus, the more I talked to him, the more I realized he was a pretty strange guy. Like, you know, creepy. I wasn't gonna go with him to some random empty house."

Marlin had a lot of questions, but for now, time was of the essence and he had to keep it short. If Garrett's information was accurate, Marlin wanted to check it out as soon as possible. But he didn't want to pull resources away from the search if Garrett was spinning a tale in an attempt to escape charges.

"How did you hear what happened at the Dairy Queen?" Marlin asked.

"It came up as an Amber Alert on my phone, and the news reports said it was Trevor Larkin."

"Why didn't you call 911 and tell them what you knew?" Marlin asked.

Becker shook his head. "The cops back home really screwed me around, so why should I ever help any of you out?"

Because a girl's life was at risk, Marlin thought. But he held his tongue. There was nothing to gain from arguing with Becker.

"Did you see Trevor or talk to him after Tuesday afternoon?"

"He took me to Blanco and dropped me at a little motel there. That was the last I saw of him."

"No calls or texts or anything like that?"

"No."

"So your only reason for thinking they might be in that empty house is because he mentioned it to you?"

"Yep. It's a hunch, but I bet you'll find them there."

Marlin wasn't quite as confident, but he said, "You did the right thing, Garrett. I appreciate it."

Then he got on the radio and asked Darrell to track down Renee or her parents as quickly as possible.

As they were nearing the sheriff's office, Marlin said, "Where did you get the gun?"

"I found it on the highway," Becker said.

"Where?"

"A couple miles outside Stephenville. I'm sure Red told you I said San Antonio, which is true, I did. But it was Stephenville. I just slipped up. I can't really prove where I found it, though, can I?"

When Marlin pulled into the parking lot, there was plenty of light for him to watch Becker's face closely as he asked his next question. "Why did you tell Red the victim at the zoo had been shot in the neck?"

Becker didn't even flinch. "Somebody said that on Facebook."

"Who?"

"I don't remember the name. I joined a local group as soon as I got into this area. I always do that to learn about restaurants and motels and stuff."

If Garrett was lying, he was good at it.

"What's the name of the group?"

"Blanco County Neighbors."

"That's where you saw the comment?"

"I think so, yeah, but I can't be positive. Might've been on some other page."

Marlin couldn't rule out the possibility that there had been a leak from the medical examiner's office or even from the sheriff's office.

"When did you see it?" Marlin asked.

"That would've been yesterday afternoon. Did the guy really get shot in the neck?"

Marlin was about to give a non-answer, but right then Darrell came over the radio, saying he had Renee's father waiting for Marlin's call.

40

The hole in Trevor's lower rib cage was tiny. Smaller than a pencil eraser. And it hadn't bled much. But what was going on inside him? Was he bleeding internally? He had no way of knowing. He felt okay so far. Perfectly fine, actually. Maybe a little lightheaded. The hole was three or four inches to the left of his solar plexus. Had that one little round of buckshot hit anything? What was back there? The liver?

He couldn't believe she'd shot him. He should've looked inside that closet before letting her get a sweater. Big mistake on his part. Totally screwed everything up.

He wasn't sure why he'd come out to the garage. Maybe it was time to hit the road. Right now he was in the driver's seat of the Impala. They keys were in the ignition. He'd found them hanging on a pegboard in the kitchen.

What would Caril Ann do if he left? She probably wouldn't be able to hear him start the car, because the bedroom was at the rear of the house. She wouldn't see the headlights, either, or he could leave them off until he reached the county road.

How long would she stay in there? A long time. She'd think he was waiting for her somewhere in the house.

He could be hundreds of miles away by daybreak. The cops wouldn't be looking for an Impala.

They cruised slowly past the driveway in Bobby Garza's SUV and proceeded for several hundred yards, until the sheriff pulled to the side of the quiet county road and parked.

They had a plan. Solid, but simple.

Lauren would approach the house from the front. Garza would approach from the rear. Marlin would check the garage.

It was 1:22 in the morning.

Earlier, Renee's father, Joel, had verified that his mother had recently gone into an assisted-living facility and her home was empty. He consented to a search of the property, with no limitations. He told them where a key was hidden and gave them a verbal description of the floor plan. He mentioned that they never bothered locking the door to the detached garage, so they wouldn't need a key there.

Now Marlin, Bobby, and Lauren were preparing to exit the SUV and approach the eight-acre property. No moon tonight. No artificial light emanating from any sources. But they had an advantage they'd be using shortly: night-vision goggles. They would also use earpieces with their radios so the transmissions wouldn't give them away. Each of them was carrying an M4 rifle.

"I'm not a big fan of splitting up in a situation like this," Garza said, "but in this case, I don't want to waste a single minute. If she's in there, I want to get her out ASAP. And I don't want to give him a chance to slip away. So we'll need to stay in touch on the radio. We all on board with that?"

"Absolutely," Lauren said.

"You bet," Marlin said.

"If you see or hear anyone inside the house, just pull back and alert the others. Then we'll probably need to get SWAT out here. We'll check all the windows first—see what we can see—and just listen for a few minutes at each one. Marlin, if you can see into the garage, that'll be a big help. If there's nothing in there but Grandma's Impala—no truck—then we'll know we're probably on a wild goose chase."

"Will do."

"Y'all ready?" Garza asked.

"Let's do it," Lauren said.

They stepped from the SUV and gently eased the doors closed.

Marlin pulled his NVGs into place and turned them on, casting everything around him with a greenish glow. He watched as Bobby and Lauren did the same and made necessary adjustments. Then Bobby gave a hand signal and they proceeded in single file along the county road and up the driveway, toward the house. After another one hundred feet, they branched off in different directions, moving stealthily through the darkness.

Marlin could see the detached garage no more than sixty feet away now, to the left of the house. No sign of movement outside. The garage had one large retractable overhead door in front—the south side—for the two vehicle bays. To the right of the overhead door was a regular door with a small window built into it. There were no other doors or windows in the three other walls.

Marlin was trying hard not to get his hopes up. Odds were good this was a waste of time. Garrett Becker had done his best to provide useful information, but what he'd shared was a guess, and nothing more.

Lauren Gilchrist reached the steps to the wide front porch and paused for a moment. Listened. Heard nothing. Earlier, Joel—Renee's father—had told Marlin there was no alarm system. No motion-activated lights. Nothing to trip them up and alert anyone inside to their presence.

Lauren slowly mounted the wooden steps. Reached the top. Waited a moment. Went left to a window that opened into the living room, although, like every window in the house, it was blocked by curtains or blinds. She stood and listened for two minutes. Silence.

She quietly stepped to the front door and stood to one side. Paused again. No sounds from inside the house.

She continued to the right side of the porch, to a window that opened into the kitchen. Both sides of the blind let her see a small sliver of the room with her NVGs, but there was nothing to see. No movement. She waited a full three minutes.

Quiet.

Bobby Garza was desperately hoping to hear something. Anything. A flushing toilet. Somebody coughing. Music. A TV show. Footsteps on a hardwood floor. The sound of an incoming text.

But he was hearing nothing.

The first window he reached was the bedroom on the back left—the northwest corner of the house. There were only two bedrooms in this small house built more than seventy years earlier. One bathroom. Just over one thousand square feet in total. Tiny by today's standards. The garage had obviously been added later, to the west of the house.

Strange what runs through your mind in these moments.

Garza stood outside that window so badly wanting to hear a voice—but the voice didn't come. So he moved to the second window—the bedroom on the back right. Northeast corner of the house. Waited a full minute.

That's when he heard it.

"Trevor?" the voice said. Muffled, but audible. A young girl.

Caitlin. She was in there.

Curtains completely blocked the window. Garza couldn't even see a sliver on either side. He put an ear close to the glass.

"You gonna talk to me or what?" Caitlin asked.

If Trevor answered, Garza didn't hear it.

"I think I'm about to fall asleep again," Caitlin said. "I bet you're getting sleepy, too."

Garza tried not to jump to any conclusions, but that did not sound like the type of thing an abducted person would say. Had the situation been misunderstood by everybody? Had Caitlin willingly run away with Trevor Larkin? If so, that could change how the SWAT team approached the situation. Caitlin could actually be a threat, instead of a person in need of rescue.

Garza waited for several minutes, but Caitlin said nothing more. He eased himself away from the window. He needed some distance from the house before he could risk talking on the radio.

Marlin was standing outside the garage door—the one with a window built into it—just listening. Hearing nothing.

Unfortunately, he couldn't see anything through the slatted blind, either, although there was a small amount of light escaping through it—enough that he removed his NVGs. Where was the light coming from? Perhaps some kind of power tool or other device was plugged into an outlet. Weed eater. Leaf blower. Something Joel hadn't bothered to unplug. Or maybe it was just a basic nightlight.

Marlin waited several minutes, but he heard nothing inside.

Joel had said the door wouldn't be locked, because there wasn't much crime out this way. He didn't bother. Naïve, but not uncommon.

It was a good, solid door. Metal. Opened inward. Hinges on the left. Knob on the right. Marlin grasped the doorknob with his left hand and—

Garza's voice—urgent but tempered—came through Marlin's earpiece.

"Just heard the female subject through one of the rear windows— the northeast corner. Pulling back now. We need to talk ASAP."

"Copy that," Lauren replied.

Marlin used his free hand to key the microphone clipped near his shoulder and quietly said, "Same here."

Marlin was elated—but what did Garza want to talk about? He obviously had something he wanted to share—something he didn't want to say on the radio.

Marlin's hand was still on the doorknob. He'd go meet with Bobby and Lauren, but first, it made sense for him to take a quick look to confirm that the Ranger was parked inside the garage. The SWAT team might need or want that information. Always good to know where any potential getaway vehicles were located.

He turned the knob and slowly swung the door open.

41

Albert woke at 1:32 in the morning, needing to take a leak, and as he stood there at the toilet, half asleep and swaying, trying not to splash all over the damn floor, his mind continued to process everything that had happened in the past few days.

Zoos are prissons.

That damn note. Albert had been too complacent after nineteen years to understand what it had really meant. The note was bogus—a red herring to fool the cops later. The kid in the Dallas Cowboys hat wasn't some animal-rights activist; he was a hired gun, sent by Anthony Carducci to kill Albert. And he'd come damn close.

But how had Carducci located Albert after all this time? Good question. Albert might never know the answer.

He finished pissing and went back to bed. He could hear an eighteen-wheeler slowly passing on the highway, no more than seventy feet away. Now he was wide awake—and the same question returned to his mind. Had Sylvia accepted his friend request?

He resisted the urge to grab his phone off the nightstand, because he knew it would only lead to disappointment. He was torturing himself by indulging in the idea that Sylvia had accepted the request, and they would make further contact, and who knows what else might happen? Yeah, sure. He was living in a fantasy world. They hadn't seen each other in nineteen years. It was inconceivable that she might still think about him. He was probably nothing more than the dimmest haze of a foggy memory.

Right?

He rolled onto his right side, away from the nightstand. Away from the phone. Away from temptation. His eyes remained open. Well, shit. This was futile. He knew he wouldn't fall asleep again until he checked. That was a good reason to check, wasn't it? So he could fall asleep again.

He rolled in the other direction and grabbed his phone. Opened the Facebook app. And stared for a long moment at what he was seeing. Could this be right?

Sylvia had accepted his friend request.

But there was more. Good God, there was more. He sat up straight as an arrow.

She'd sent him a message.

Marlin opened the garage door about two feet. The hinges on the left side of the door squealed, but just faintly. Not loudly enough to be a concern. Nobody inside the house could hear it.

He leaned forward to take a quick look to his left, and there it was, just as he expected. Bryce Cauley's truck—the blue Ford Ranger they'd been looking for earlier in the evening. The one Trevor Larkin had stolen after most likely killing Cauley. It was parked in the nearer bay. The gold Impala owned by Renee's grandmother was parked on the other side of the Ranger, on the west side of the garage.

Marlin could see everything inside the garage just fine, because the light he'd seen through the blinds wasn't coming from a battery charger or a lamp or a nightlight. It was an overhead light.

Maybe the light had been on when Trevor had parked the truck, and he'd left it that way in his haste to get inside with Caitlin.

Then Marlin noticed that there was also light inside the Impala. The dome light was on. But why? Had Trevor or Caitlin failed to close a door completely? Did it really matter at this point?

Marlin was about to pull back and exit the garage when he saw something that made him freeze.

Trevor stood as still as he possibly could. Holding his breath.

Thirty seconds earlier, he'd been sitting in the Impala, deciding what to do next, when he'd heard a voice. *Same here.* Male voice. Just barely audible. Who was it?

Trevor gently opened the car door, stepped out of the Impala, and eased the door shut—but not all the way. It would make a loud click if he closed it all the way.

Then he'd hustled to the garage door, hoping to reach it and lock it before—

Too late.

Somebody was turning the knob, and Trevor flattened himself against the wall behind the door. He had the gun raised in his right hand, pointing at the ceiling. Waiting to see. Was it Renee's dad? Who else would it be? A nosy neighbor?

Trevor realized he was scared, but also excited as hell. He would probably never have this chance again.

Then the door slowly swung open. Trevor began to lower the gun.

The rear window of the truck.

There was enough light in the garage that the glass reflected perfectly.

Marlin saw a figure in the glass—and it moved. Had to be Larkin.

Marlin didn't necessarily *decide* what to do next. Instead he reacted instinctively, on impulse, in a fraction of a second, without the benefit of weighing the pros and cons.

He swung the metal door open as fast and forcefully as he could, driving it with his shoulder and putting every ounce of his weight into it. Marlin felt the door collide with flesh and bone. He heard a loud grunt of pain and surprise.

Followed immediately by a gunshot, extremely loud in this closed space.

Marlin pulled the door back and prepared to slam it again, but Larkin lurched out from behind it and scurried past the rear of both vehicles, taking cover on the driver's side of the Impala.

Again, Marlin had little time to decide how to respond, and his emotions were running high, impairing his judgment. He should've ducked through the door he had just entered but instead he took three quick steps and crouched behind the Ranger's passenger-side front fender, using the engine for cover.

"State game warden! Drop the weapon!"

Marlin was looking through the sights of his M4, which was steadied on the hood of the truck. Larkin was out of sight.

By now, Bobby and Lauren would be headed in this direction, after hearing the shot. Marlin thumbed his microphone and said, "Shot fired by Larkin inside the garage. He is *not* inside the house. He is now on the west side of the garage, behind the Impala. Be advised that I am on the east side, behind the Ranger. I am not hit."

"Copy that," Garza said immediately.

Marlin had made an enormous error. A minute earlier, when Garza said he'd heard the female subject talking inside the house, Marlin had assumed Larkin was inside with her.

"I will be making contact with the girl shortly," Garza said.

"Copy," Lauren said.

Marlin spoke loudly. "Larkin, it's over. There's no getting out of here."

That was true for Marlin, too. He couldn't make a break for the door now without exposing himself. Again, Larkin didn't reply, but Marlin could hear heavy, shallow breathing.

"We've got half a dozen deputies here right now and a SWAT team is en route," Marlin said.

After a moment, Larkin said, "You're the guy from yesterday."

Yesterday? What was he talking about? Then Marlin realized Larkin was referencing the incident at Darren Meyer's ranch. Had that been just yesterday? It seemed like a week ago.

"You need to put your gun down and come out slowly," Marlin said.

"Yeah, right."

"Let me take you in, for your own safety," Marlin said.

Larkin had nothing to say.

"Why'd you point that rifle at me?" Marlin asked.

It would be good to keep Larkin talking until SWAT arrived.

"Sometimes I do things because I can't stop myself," Larkin said, and he laughed. He actually laughed.

"Like what?" Marlin asked, and at the same time, he leaned low, trying to look under the truck and see Larkin's legs on the other side of the Impala. But Larkin was wise enough to have set up behind one of the tires.

"All of this," Larkin said. "Right here, right now. And yesterday. All of it."

"Did you kill Bryce Cauley?" Marlin asked.

"Of course I did."

"Why? What did he do?"

"You'll figure all that out," Larkin said.

"But what if we don't? Tell me what happened."

"There's not enough time."

What did that mean? Was Larkin planning to act before the SWAT team arrived?

"Did you kill the man at Safari Adventure?"

"No. I don't even know who it is."

"Do you know who killed him?"

"How would I know that?"

"Do you know where Albert Cortez is?"

"No idea. Probably dead."

"Why do you say—"

Larkin suddenly raised the gun over the hood of the Impala and fired off a round, without aiming. Marlin felt the impact on the driver's side of the Ranger.

Caitlin was just about to pull her jeans down and pee right there in the closet when she heard a gunshot. It was from outside the house, but not far away. Really close, in fact. Not some deer hunter half a mile away. Plus, it sounded like a handgun, not a rifle. Caitlin had shot both enough to recognize the difference.

Her hopes soared. She didn't budge at all. Just listened. Who was it? Cops? Somebody else? Renee's dad? Or was it Trevor? Had he fired his gun for some reason? What if he'd shot himself? That was a possibility.

If it wasn't him and he was still inside the house, how would he react to the shot? Was he freaking out? She kept the shotgun leveled at the bedroom doorway, just in case he might rush back into the bedroom.

Deep. Slow. Breaths.

"Trevor?"

The house sounded empty. It *felt* empty. Trevor had probably gone outside. Unless she'd hit him and he died. She found herself hoping that was the case, and then she felt guilty about it.

But it wouldn't explain the shot from outside.

"Did you hear that?" she called.

A few minutes passed. Then she heard another shot. What in the world was going on?

Then she heard the front door opening again. Her hands were trembling.

Deep. Slow. Breaths.

"Caitlin?"

Oh, my God. It was a man's voice, but not Trevor.

"Yes! I'm back here!"

"This is Sheriff Bobby Garza. Can you hear me?"

"Yes!"

"Do not move, okay? Stay right where you are. Do you hear me?"

"Yes!"

"Is there anyone else inside the house with you?"

"I don't know where Trevor is."

"Is there anyone besides you and Trevor here?"

"No!"

"Who were you talking to earlier?"

"I thought Trevor was still here, but I don't know where he went. He might've gone outside."

"Are you armed?"

"Yes! I have a shotgun! I shot at him twice."

"I need you to put the shotgun down. Do you hear me?"

"Yes. I'm putting it down!"

42

Albert's finger hovered over the Messenger app icon for the longest moment, wanting to tap it, but afraid of what he might read. Finally he couldn't stand it any longer.

He tapped it, and he began to read, and then he began to smile.

Hi there, Chuck.

So good to hear from you. It's been a long time. Maybe you saw me on television recently and that's why you got in touch. Either way, I appreciate it. I'm hearing from a lot of people lately, and it makes me wish we had all been able to stay in touch better than we did. I wish I could get some of those years back. But it's not too late, right?

I remember you saying that sometimes we come to a crossroads in life and choices aren't easy—but if you listen to your heart, it will guide you. Do you remember saying that? I have an important meeting coming up soon—this Sunday at noon—and it's a bit of a crossroads for me. This time, I'm going to follow my heart, just as you suggested. I hope our paths might cross again sometime soon.

Yours,
Sylvia

He read it a second time, almost afraid the words would change, but they didn't. They stayed the same. And even though Sylvia had written her message knowing investigators might see it, he knew exactly what it meant.

A crossroads. Just like in the movie. A literal crossroads. She was saying she would meet him there.

The same intersection in the desolate Texas Panhandle where Chuck Noland met the woman in the Ford truck at the end of *Cast Away*. Chuck had driven out there to return the one package he'd left unopened on the island. The one with the wings logo on it. The same wings that inspired the design of the raft that saved him. He wanted to say thank you to the person who'd sent it. And when he met the woman—well, it was left unsaid, but good ol' Chuck's life had gone in a fresh new direction.

A crossroads. *The* crossroads. Sunday at noon.

Three days from now. Actually, two days and twelve hours.

The Texas Panhandle.

That wasn't far from here. Not far at all.

He slowly began to type a reply, choosing his words oh so carefully.

"See there?" Larkin said from behind the Impala, laughing. "I can't resist it."

Lauren's voice was in Marlin's earpiece immediately. "John?"

"All good," Marlin replied. "Subject fired again. Hit the truck."

"Where is he right now?"

"Same," Marlin said, trying to limit his answers so Larkin couldn't follow the conversation.

"Hiding behind the Impala?"

"Right."

"And the Impala is on the west side of the garage, facing due north, correct?"

"Affirmative."

"I don't want to wait for SWAT," Lauren said. "I want to get you out of there now. You up for that?"

Marlin knew it could be quite some time before SWAT arrived from Travis County. Did he really want to stay hunkered down behind this truck until they got here? And did he want to present a complication once they arrived?

"I could be persuaded," Marlin said, keeping his voice low.

"Is there anything between the garage door—meaning the overhead door—and the Impala? Shelving, cabinets, anything like that? Anything stored there after the Impala was parked?"

"Nothing at all," Marlin said. "All clear."

"How far would you say the driver's side of the Impala is from the west wall?"

"About six feet."

"Bobby, you on board with this?" Lauren asked.

A moment passed. Then Garza said, "Ten-four."

"John, sit tight," Lauren said. "I need to go get the SUV."

Marlin knew what Lauren was planning. She would park the SUV in front of the garage and use it for cover. Then she would hunker behind it, prop her M4 on the hood, and fire directly through the garage overhead door, estimating where Larkin was located. The bullets would cut through the aluminum garage door like paper. Lauren would lay down cover fire, giving Marlin time to exit safely. If Lauren happened to hit Trevor Larkin with the barrage, that would just be a bonus that would end the standoff.

A moment later, Garza said, "I've got the girl. No injuries. I've cleared the house. We're in the back bedroom, northeast corner, and will stay here until further notice. Be advised that she found a shotgun and fired twice at the male subject. She doesn't know if she hit him, but I haven't found any blood."

The lack of blood didn't necessarily mean anything.

"What kind of ammo?" Marlin asked.

"Double aught."

Could a gunshot wound explain Larkin's heavy breathing? Maybe, but Marlin wasn't going to make another mistake by jumping to conclusions.

Marlin wasn't sure if there was any value in engaging Larkin at this point, but there was still the possibility of extracting additional information, and now would be the time to do it, before Lauren returned.

"I'm not your enemy," Marlin said. "I have no interest in harming you. Nobody does."

"As long as I give up," Larkin said.

"At this point, why shouldn't you? We have Caitlin now. She's safe."

"She was always safe. I would never do anything to her."

Except force her to go along with your lunacy.

"But it's over now," Marlin said. "Time to face that fact. You don't have much time left."

"What does that mean?"

That the chief deputy is about to unleash holy hell on you.

"You're injured, right? Where did she hit you?"

"Doesn't matter."

That meant he'd been hit.

"You might be bleeding inside," Marlin said. "We need to get you to a hospital."

"No, thanks. Just tell Caril Ann I said goodbye."

Caril Ann? Who was he talking about?

Sylvia,

So nice to hear back from you. I did see you on the news, and I have to say you look fantastic! Still gorgeous! I swear you haven't aged at all. And your natural warmth, your intelligence, your ability to handle anything thrown your way—it all shone through and reminded me how much I miss you.

I never realized just how tumultuous your life was back then, but despite your regrets, it sounds as if you eventually straightened everything out. Good for you. We all have regrets, don't we? I know I do. Like you, I've decided it's time to set things right in my own life.

I'm surprised you remember my advice about hitting a crossroads in life, but it means a lot that you do. When you're standing at those crossroads on Sunday, about to make a decision, just remember that I'll be right there with you.

Always,
Chuck

Caril Ann. It was so familiar.

Charlie and Caril Ann.

A moment later, Marlin pieced it together. Charlie Starkweather and Caril Ann Fugate. When Bryce Cauley had said Larkin was obsessed with a killer named Charlie, it wasn't Manson, it was Starkweather.

"You mean Caitlin, right?" Marlin asked.

A moment passed before Larkin said, "Yeah. Caitlin."

"I'll tell her, but I have a question for you first."

Larkin said nothing.

"What would Charlie do?"

Still no reply.

Marlin heard an engine. Lauren had just coasted to a stop outside the garage. When the shooting began in a moment, Marlin wouldn't simply dash for the open door. He would first check to make sure the cover fire was working—that Larkin wasn't waiting to shoot Marlin as he tried to leave.

"I think I know what he'd do," Marlin said. "He'd give up. That's what he did at the end, wasn't it? He didn't fight it out until the end. He knew it was futile."

Lauren spoke through Marlin's earpiece. "In position. You ready?"

"One moment," Marlin replied quietly. Then, louder, he said, "How about it, Trevor? Why don't you put the gun down and we'll—"

Boom!

Marlin ducked as Larkin raised the pistol and fired another shot. This time, the bullet made it all the way through the Ranger's engine compartment and left a neat round hole in the fender about two feet from Marlin's shoulder. Marlin crouched even lower, his head just above the top of the tire.

"John?" Lauren said.

Boom!

Another shot slammed into the Ranger and now Marlin could hear coolant or some other fluid dripping to the concrete floor. There was no point in talking to Larkin any further. He'd made up his mind.

"Ready when you are," Marlin said.

"Five seconds," Lauren said.

"Copy," Marlin said.

Four.

Three.

Two.

One.

The shots began—enormously loud and deep and full—and they continued so rapidly that half a dozen rounds had been fired before Marlin peeked over the top of the Ranger. He was hoping Larkin would shout a surrender, but instead, Larkin reacted to the gunfire by moving to the front of the Impala and crouching low behind it, using the length of the vehicle as a shield against Lauren's withering assault.

And exposing himself to Marlin.

Lauren continued to fire.

For the third time, Marlin had very little time to weigh his options.

Hurry for the door? Larkin might see him and open fire.

That left one alternative. Marlin shouted, "Larkin! Drop your weapon!"

Even with the gunfire, Larkin heard him and swiveled in his direction.

Marlin had his M4 aimed squarely at Larkin's chest.

Don't do it. Don't be an idiot.

Larkin rose to his feet, grinning, and pointed the pistol.

Marlin fired two rounds at center mass and Larkin fell backward to the floor, where he lay unmoving.

43

"Red!"

That was followed a few seconds later by several thumps on Red's flimsy bedroom door.

"Red!"

"Uuuhhhh?" Red said, his face half-buried in a pillow. He opened one eye and saw that the clock on his nightstand read 4:14. He figured that was in the morning, not the afternoon, but he couldn't make any promises without looking out the window.

"They caught him!" Billy Don said.

"Go away," Red said, but it was kind of muffled.

"What the hell?" Mandy muttered, waking up next to him.

"They got Garrett!" Billy Don said. "Marlin caught him last night."

"I don't care," Red said. "Go away."

"Can I come in?"

"No," Red said.

"I'll kick your ass if you do," Mandy said.

"Oh, I forgot you was in there," Billy Don said. Then he giggled. "You nekkid?"

"Go away!" Red and Mandy said in unison.

But she *was* naked. She slept that way most of the time, unless it was real cold, and that's the way Red liked it.

"They shot the guy that took that girl from the Dairy Queen," Billy

Don said. "That's what everybody's saying. Marlin shot him."

Okay, that was reasonably interesting news, and it raised some questions.

"He dead?" Red asked.

"Don't know yet," Billy Don said.

"Why'd he take that girl?"

"Nobody knows that either."

"Y'all shut up," Mandy said. "Talk in the morning."

"It *is* the morning," Billy Don said.

"Where are you getting all this?" Red asked.

Mandy groaned, which meant *Why are you egging him on?*

"Facebook," Billy Don said.

"Pffftt," Red said. If it was on Facebook, it was probably all bullshit.

"Guess we'll find out soon enough," Billy Don said, and then Red felt the trailer vibrate as Billy Don retreated down the hallway.

Now Red was wide awake. That was the bad news. The good news was, he had a hot naked lady in bed with him.

"Can't believe he woke us up for that," Red said, to see if Mandy was going back to sleep or not.

She didn't say anything.

"Pain in the ass, huh?" Red said.

Mandy was breathing slowly and deeply.

Red casually reached over and placed a palm flat on her warm stomach. Rubbed it a little bit. Played with her bellybutton.

She still didn't say anything.

He slowly moved his hand upward and cupped her left boob.

"Go away," Mandy said.

Albert couldn't sleep for the rest of the night, of course, so as it got closer to dawn, he found himself peeking out the window every ten minutes, hoping to see Bob's truck parked outside the front office.

Finally, at 7:15, there it was. Albert hustled over there and walked inside, to find Bob seated behind the counter, reading a newspaper.

"Any chance we can speed 'em up?" Albert asked. "The documents, I mean. From your friend."

"He said it would take—"

"Can he have them ready by tomorrow?"

"I don't think that's—"

"I'll pay twice as much. Another thousand bucks."

Bob raised his hands in a calming gesture. "I'll talk to him, okay? That's all I can do."

"Thank you," Albert said.

"What's the rush? What happened?"

"I'm leaving town. Tomorrow. Noon at the latest."

"What happened?"

Albert could feel his face break into a smile. "I talked to her. Sylvia. We messaged."

"When was this?"

"Early this morning. We had to be very careful what we said. But we're going to meet up."

"Where?" Bob asked. "No, don't tell me. If I don't know, I won't have to lie about it later."

Albert estimated that the drive from Gallup to the crossroads in the Texas Panhandle was about eight hours. A straight shot on Interstate 40 most of the way. But maybe he should take back roads. Figure twelve hours, or maybe even more, just to be safe. Factor in a flat tire or a dead battery or whatever else might slow him down on the most important drive of his life. Today was Friday morning. He was supposed to be there on Sunday at noon. He should leave as early as possible tomorrow.

"How did you message her?" Bob asked.

"On Facebook," Albert said.

Now Bob got a funny expression on his face.

"What?" Albert asked.

"What if it wasn't her?"

"What?"

"What if the cops have control of her account? What if it's a trap?"

That possibility hit Albert hard. He took a few steps backward and sat in a chair next to a rack for sightseeing brochures. Thought about it for a long moment.

"No," he said. "She said things the cops couldn't know. She

wouldn't tell them."

"A lot can change in nineteen years," Bob said.

Albert remained quiet for a long moment.

"What're you gonna do?" Bob asked.

"I appreciate everything you've done for me, but I'm going anyway," Albert said. "No question. The message was from her. I'll leave tomorrow, with or without the documents."

Marlin and Lauren Gilchrist sat quietly in a small room and waited. A small monitor rested on a table in front of them. It was nearly eleven o'clock. The tremble in Marlin's hands had gone away.

He and Lauren and Bobby Garza had remained at the scene until dawn, and each had given a full statement to Brad Anderson, a Texas Ranger out of Llano who would now be investigating the shooting.

Then Marlin had gone home and slept for a couple of hours, but it was fitful sleep, punctuated by bad dreams that startled him awake several times. During one of those waking moments, he'd found Nicole standing in the bedroom doorway, watching him, with a concerned expression on her face. Then she'd come into the room and lay quietly with him on the bed, wrapping her arms around him tight.

Now this.

Bobby Garza was in the interview room next door, and Caitlin McGregor and her parents would be joining him shortly. Garza would interview Caitlin and get her full account of the abduction. Marlin and Lauren would be able to watch it on the monitor.

Marlin and Lauren were both on restricted duty after the shooting of Trevor Larkin—standard procedure—but that didn't preclude them from watching the interview.

Marlin had seen Caitlin briefly after the shooting and she was amazingly composed. Bobby Garza was preparing to take her to the office to get a full statement, but her parents had arrived and insisted on taking her home, at least until the morning. Marlin couldn't blame them for that. Give her some time to recover. They'd agreed to bring her in at 11:00.

Nicole, in her role as victim services coordinator, had visited the McGregor home in the morning to help them understand Caitlin's rights and what to expect in the weeks and months to come, should any of these events lead to a trial. Nicole had offered to accompany them home last night, but the McGregors had declined.

It was now 11:12. He hoped Caitlin's parents hadn't changed their minds about allowing her to give a statement.

Lauren, reading something on her phone, said, "We just got an ID on our victim at the zoo. Joseph Barella from Framingham, Massachusetts. Just as we guessed, he's part of Anthony Carducci's crew. No record at all, though. Never been busted. Never even a suspect in any specific case. He was a low-level guy."

Carducci had almost certainly sent Barella down to kill Albert Cortez, but unless Carducci had been very sloppy, he would likely be able to successfully deny any involvement. Marlin would bet that there were no emails, no texts, and no calls between Carducci and Barella. No record of any meeting. No witnesses who could or would testify about the attempted hit. Even if, say, Barella had told somebody that Carducci had asked him to kill Albert, that wouldn't be enough.

Had Albert killed Barella in self-defense? They might never know the answer to that question.

Marlin couldn't help feeling sorry for Albert. A fugitive for nearly twenty years, and now he was on the run again. He'd had to abandon everything he'd built here and start over. A man like Carducci would never let him rest.

"There they are," Lauren said, nodding toward the monitor.

In walked the McGregor family. Garza thanked them for coming, and they all sat around a small wooden table.

"She looks good," Lauren said.

She did, too. Strong young woman.

She proceeded to answer Garza's questions with confidence and no sign of trauma whatsoever. She recounted exactly what happened, starting when Trevor Larkin walked into the Dairy Queen, and up to the moment Garza entered the house.

Larkin had never laid a hand on her, and she said that if he'd tried, she would've been prepared to rip his eyes out. At one point, she'd gotten cold, and when she looked for a sweater in the bedroom closet, she found a shotgun leaning in the corner. She knew it might not be loaded, but eventually she decided it was a risk worth taking. She grabbed it and shot at him as he scrambled out of the room. Didn't know if she'd hit him or not.

Trevor talked to her from within house, and later tried to trick her into thinking he'd left. Then she fell asleep, and when she woke, she called out to him—trying to engage him in conversation, so she'd know where he was. That's what Garza had heard through the window. Not long after that, she heard two shots from the direction of the garage. Then Sheriff Garza came into the house and she knew she was finally safe. She was so relieved and happy. Then she heard more shots, and a few seconds later, somebody said something to Garza through his earpiece, and Caitlin knew it was finally over.

Garza asked some questions, but not many, because Caitlin had done such a good job covering everything in detail.

Then Caitlin said, "I need to tell you what Trevor told me right before I got the shotgun. I have no idea if it's true or not."

"What is it?" Garza asked.

Then the story took a turn nobody had seen coming.

44

Red heard a knock on his front door, which was weird, because he hadn't heard a vehicle coming up his long caliche driveway. It wasn't just weird, it was cause for alarm. People didn't just walk up and knock on his door. Billy Don was in town and Mandy was at work, so Red was home all alone.

He grabbed his .45 and had it in his hand when he peeked through a window. Well, hell. It was Garrett, just standing on the porch in his orange jacket like he had every right to be there.

Red swung the door open and leveled the .45 at his head.

"Whoa," Garrett said, holding his hands up at shoulder height. "Please don't shoot me. I'm not armed."

He had his backpack on his back, so even if the gun was in there, he wouldn't be able to get to it quickly.

"What are you doing here?" Red asked. "Why aren't you in jail?"

"I came to apologize," Garrett said.

"Gonna take more than an apology," Red said.

"I know," Garrett said. "I need to fix your truck. I'll pay for that."

"Damn right you will."

"I will. I promise."

"Gonna cost a lot."

"I'm sure it will. That was stupid of me. I lost my temper."

"Why aren't you in jail?" Red repeated.

"It's a long story, but you know that girl that was missing yesterday afternoon? I knew where the guy took her. So I told the cops, and we made a deal, and now I'm free."

"Wait a sec. They didn't charge you for shooting my truck?"

"I realize that probably makes you mad, but no, they didn't. That's why I'm here."

"How did you know where the girl was?" Red asked. He couldn't help being curious.

"The guy that took her picked me up hitchhiking the day before you did. He mentioned an empty house where I could stay if I wanted. I didn't stay there, but I figured there was a good chance that's where he went with her. And I was right. My arms are getting tired."

"That's tough," Red said, but the gun was getting heavy in his hands.

"Anyway," Garrett said. "I came back to say I'm sorry."

"You hitchhiked out here?"

"Actually, I walked, because I never got a ride."

Garrett had walked a damn long way to apologize. Red wasn't sure what to make of that.

He lowered the pistol and Garrett lowered his arms.

"Here's the thing," Garrett said. "I don't have a lot of money right now, so I can't pay yet, but I will."

"What about the life insurance?" Red said. No reason to hold back at this point.

"What?" Garrett said.

"I read that your dad had eight hundred thousand in life insurance and you get half."

"They haven't paid out yet," Garrett said. "They'll drag their feet as long as they can. The cops mentioned that to the press just to make me look bad. One of many things they did."

"No wonder you hate cops," Red said.

"Well, yeah, but maybe I need to work on that attitude. That guy Marlin was okay last night. He probably could've shot me and got away with it. He treated me, you know, like a real person."

Red nodded. "Marlin's okay."

"So what I want to do is send you the money later," Garrett said. "Just tell me how much and I'll send it. I can mail a check or Venmo it or whatever. Are you cool with that?"

"That's fine," Red said.

"And in the meantime..." Garrett reached into the right front pocket of his jeans. Red decided that he would shoot Garrett right between the eyes if he came out with a pocketknife. But it wasn't a knife. It was a diamond ring. The one he'd found on the side of the road. Only one diamond, but it was damn big. "You can have this," he said. "It's probably a fake, but if it's real, it's all yours, whatever it's worth. Sell it, keep it, whatever. Doesn't matter to me."

Garrett held it toward him. Red slowly put his hand out and Garrett dropped it into his palm.

Garrett grinned. "If it does turn out to be real, well, that can be just another one of the wild stories you two guys can tell. The tattooed pig, the Vegas trip, the chupacabra, and the crazy hitchhiker who gave you a diamond ring."

"What we need to do," Rory said, "is find someone to check the PO box for us. Some sucker who has no idea what we're doing and what's in the package."

"But then Carducci might kill *that* guy," Bryce said. "No way am I gonna be responsible for—"

"Hold on," Rory said. "You need to stop bashing my ideas right off the bat. If you don't like 'em, figure out a way to make 'em better. Don't just toss 'em out completely."

They sat quietly for a long moment.

"Okay," Bryce said. "I have an idea."

"What?"

"What if we rent a PO box, then forward the mail to another PO box? So then if someone is watching the first PO box, it won't matter, because we'll never go there. We'll only be going to the second box."

Rory took a moment to think about it. It had caught him by surprise, because it was actually kind of smart. "Can you even do that—forward mail from one PO box to another?"

"I don't know," Bryce said. "I mean, why couldn't you?"

Rory googled with his phone. "I don't see anything saying you can't. In fact, yeah, you can."

"Okay, then, what do you think? Will that work?"

Rory mulled it over for a minute. "I can see only one possible problem, but it's such a long shot, I don't even know if we should worry about it."

"Huh?"

"If Carducci does send some thug down here, I'm wondering if he might threaten a post office employee for the name of the person who rented the PO box. Like, follow the employee home and put a gun to his head. Make him go to work the next day and get the name."

"Hmm," Bryce said.

"I'd say that's pretty unlikely," Rory said.

"Yeah, but what if he does?"

"That would be pretty extreme."

"He might do it, though."

Rory was wishing he hadn't brought it up. He kept thinking. They were almost there. It just needed one more little tweak. Then he had it.

"What we do is tell Carducci we're paying some total stranger to rent the box for us, and that stranger won't be able to tell him who we are."

Bryce said, "What?"

"If his thug threatens a post office employee for the name, it won't do any good, because the employee would name the stranger, and the stranger wouldn't be able to tell him who we are."

"Oh," Bryce said. "So how do we find a stranger?"

"That's the thing—it doesn't *have* to be a stranger. As long as Carducci thinks we got a stranger, that's all that matters."

"I'm confused," Bryce said.

"Here's how we do it. We get someone to rent a PO box for us. Doesn't have to be a stranger. Then we forward that PO box to a second PO box. And then, as an added layer of security, we have that same person pick up the package for us."

"Oh, okay," Bryce said. "I get it. I like it."

Finally, Rory thought. "We just need to find someone to do it. We'll probably have to offer some pretty good money. Can you think of anyone? Someone who won't ask a lot of questions?"

Five minutes passed.

"Actually, I can," Bryce said.

"He was talking about Trevor," Caitlin said. "Bryce invited him to go shoot guns on his uncle's ranch, like they were buddies, and when they were out there, that's when Bryce asked him. That was early last week, I think. Trevor told me he wondered if the package was going to contain drugs or something else illegal, but he didn't really care. He thought Bryce and him were becoming friends, and that's the kind of thing you do for a friend. He didn't even want any money for it."

Caitlin stopped for a moment to take a drink of water. The room was otherwise quiet.

"So Trevor rented a PO box in San Antonio, but then the package never showed up. They had signed up to get an email if anything was delivered to the PO box, but nothing ever was. So Bryce finally tells Trevor not to worry about it anymore, because the package got cancelled."

Marlin was spellbound. Everything was finally falling into place.

"At this point, though, Trevor didn't know the full story. He only knew that Bryce had asked him to rent a PO box, and that the package never came. But then they were out at the ranch again this past Tuesday night, and they were smoking pot, and Bryce told him everything I just told you—which includes all that stuff about Albert, and the guy he killed a long time ago, and how Bryce and Rory were trying to get some money from the Mafia guy." She paused for a second and looked at Garza. "Does any of this sound true?"

"We'll have to look into it," Garza said, "but I can tell you it's very helpful, so please go on."

"I thought maybe he'd made it all up in his head."

"What happened after that?" Garza asked.

"Okay, well, Trevor was seriously pissed off—sorry, Mom—because now he knows he'd been in some serious danger, and so they argued about it, and Trevor starts to realize Bryce had just been using him all along. They weren't really friends. It was kind of sad the way Trevor talked about that. If he'd had just one friend, maybe none of this would've ever happened."

She continued with her story and all the facts fit neatly into place. After they argued, Bryce drove away, leaving Trevor at the ranch without a vehicle. Trevor didn't care. They had gone inside the house earlier, and the door was still unlocked, so Trevor went inside and waited for Bryce to come back. Eventually he fell asleep.

He woke up the next morning and Bryce still hadn't returned. Screw him. Trevor poked around and found the keys to Bryce's uncle's truck, so he knew he could drive that to town if he needed to. Or just walk. It wasn't that far. But he had the day off, so he decided to go deer hunting first. He was walking around the ranch with the rifle when he spotted an axis deer, so he shot it.

"And just a few minutes later, the game warden showed up," Caitlin said. "Trevor's first thought was that Bryce had told on him. He figured Bryce had said he was trespassing or something, so Trevor got pissed again—sorry, Mom—and just, like, instinctively pointed the rifle at the game warden. He knew how stupid that was, so right after that, he ran back to the house and took the truck, and as he was leaving, the game warden pointed a gun at him, so Trevor drove right past him and then plowed through the gate."

45

Albert was sitting on the edge of his motel bed, bag packed, when Bob knocked on his door. It was 11:36.

Bob stepped into the room and closed the door behind him. He handed Albert a manila envelope and grinned. "Just in time."

Albert pulled the contents out: a Social Security card, an electric bill, and an auto insurance card. It all looked completely genuine. He checked the name on the documents.

"Clarence Maxwell?" he said.

Bob shrugged.

"That's not exactly a Hispanic name," Albert said.

"Maybe you were adopted," Bob said.

"Good point. That would work."

"If anybody ever asks."

Bob reached into his pocket, came out with a key, and said, "Take this, too."

"What is it?" Albert asked, taking the key.

"My truck."

"What? You're kidding. I can't take your truck."

"You can't be driving that rental car."

"But I can't take—"

"Maybe you park it somewhere later and tell me where it is. Or you don't. Either way, it's okay."

"What're you going to drive?"

"I'll buy another truck. I have plenty of money."

"What will you do with the rental car?"

"I'll just park it somewhere. But not at a Denny's, because there might be cameras."

Albert laughed, but then his eyes started to well up. "I just don't know what I would've done..." he said.

Bob shook his head. *It wasn't anything, really.*

Albert stepped forward and gave the old man a hug.

"He took off down 281, but the truck overheated and died on him," Caitlin said.

"What did he do then?" Bobby Garza asked.

"He took off through the woods and walked back to Blanco, to Bryce's apartment complex, where his SUV was parked, because they'd ridden to the ranch in Bryce's truck. Then he drove home, and he expected to see a bunch of cops waiting for him, but nobody was there. That's when he saw the news about the body at the zoo, and Albert was missing, and all that. He figured the Mafia guy had somehow figured out where Albert was, so he'd sent somebody down to kill him, and now it was just a matter of time before the cops figured out that Trevor and Bryce and Rory were involved, too. Now he was seriously pissed—sorry, Mom—at Bryce and Rory for getting him involved in all this mess."

Marlin was making a mental note that they would need to get cell phone records for all three men. At a minimum, perhaps the location data would confirm that Bryce and Trevor had been at the ranch together on Tuesday evening.

Caitlin continued. "So Trevor starts texting and calling Bryce, but Bryce is totally ghosting him. Trevor sits at home all night, freaking out, and still waiting for the cops to show up, but they never do. Then, the next morning, Trevor was trying to decide whether he should go to work and act like nothing happened or get in his SUV and just take off, and that's when Bryce showed up at his house."

Even better if the cell phone records would back that up, too.

"Bryce said the game warden had come to talk to him about what had happened on the ranch the day before, so Bryce told Trevor that they all needed to keep their mouths shut about everything, including Albert and the PO box and all that stuff. That's when Trevor lost his temper and shot Bryce. He just grabbed his rifle and shot him."

She stopped talking then. For the first time, she was getting emotional. Her mother squeezed her hand. Garza waited patiently.

"He took off in Bryce's truck, and then later, he came to the Dairy Queen. You know how it went from there."

Garza spent the next twenty minutes asking questions, but he learned nothing valuable beyond what Caitlin had already shared.

Then Garza said, "Caitlin, I know it wasn't easy to come in and tell me everything that happened, but I want you to know how much I appreciate it, and everybody working on this case appreciates it. We might have some more questions in the coming days, but we'll try not to bother you too much."

"Whatever you need," Caitlin said. "But I have a question."

"Yes."

"Do you think you'll be able to charge Rory with anything?"

"I'll be honest—I just don't know at this point. We still have some work to do."

"But I might need to testify against him, right?"

"That's a possibility."

"It seems like he started all of this. Maybe Trevor and Bryce and that guy at the zoo would still be alive if it wasn't for Rory. He's dead, right? I mean Trevor. That's what they said on the news."

"That is correct. I'm sorry to tell you that."

"I can't help feeling a little sorry for him. He was just so...lost."

"Wow," Lauren said softly in the room next door. "That right there is an amazing girl."

They watched as the McGregors left the interview room, followed by Garza.

"I can think of two big questions," Lauren said. "First, how did Anthony Carducci figure out Albert's whereabouts if Bryce and Rory never told him?"

"If Rory Grafmiller doesn't talk—and I can guarantee his mother won't let him—we may never know. Sounds like he was the ringleader, and I doubt he was stupid enough to use his own cell phone to contact

Carducci. I'd guess they used a burner and he destroyed it several days ago."

"Yeah," Lauren said. "I'm sure Carducci used a burner, too. And he'll blame everything on Joseph Barella. He'll say Barella came up with the idea all on his own. Which brings up the other question."

"Who killed him."

"Right."

"It would be easy to assume it was Albert, but he would've gone on the run regardless, just because Carducci knew where he was."

"If it wasn't Albert, it was your man Garrett Becker," Lauren said. "One or the other. No way was it random. And there isn't anyone else it could be."

"I agree," Marlin said.

"Oh, there is one other question," Lauren said.

"Which is?"

"When are you taking me to lunch?"

Marlin smiled, but there wasn't much to it.

"You okay?" Lauren asked.

"Yeah," he said. "A little shaken up, but I'll be all right."

He'd been here before—dealing with the aftermath of killing a man. He knew from experience that your mind replays the incident again and again. What could he have done differently? Had he missed an opportunity to resolve the situation without firing a shot? Probably. If he had never entered the garage…

Lauren leaned forward and looked him square in the eye. "You go home and talk to that smart wife of yours, okay? Don't keep it all bottled in. You hear me?"

He nodded. "Thanks for getting me out of there," he said.

"We've got each other's backs," she said. "Always will."

46

Albert was parked on the shoulder in the southeast corner of the intersection, facing west. Toward Amarillo. Weird being in a place he'd seen so many times without ever actually being here.

He'd arrived a full two hours early. He couldn't help it. He'd been so anxious about being late, he'd padded his schedule, and now here he sat in Bob's truck, parked at the famous intersection, feeling conspicuous. Fortunately, only one vehicle had passed in the first hour. They hadn't paid him any mind at all.

On the drive, Albert had had plenty of time to think, and he'd come to the conclusion that maybe, someday, he might call the Blanco County sheriff, Bobby Garza, and tell him exactly what had happened at the zoo. No, scratch that. He'd call John Marlin, the game warden. Marlin had saved his animals, so Albert owed him one.

So maybe Albert would call Marlin and walk him through it, from start to finish.

The note. *Zoos are prissons.* Postmarked from Dallas.

The young man on the tour, solo, in a Dallas Cowboys hat.

Albert's alarm bells going off, but still not understanding exactly why the kid was here.

Then Albert, being an idiot, patrolling the zoo grounds off and on all night, wondering if the kid was going to show up and try to turn all the animals loose. Why else had he paid so much attention to the gates and the fences and the grounds in general? He wanted to release the animals from prison.

Albert's thoughts were interrupted by a vehicle on the horizon, coming this way. Could it be Sylvia, also arriving early? He was so damn nervous, he couldn't sit still. His mouth was parched. What would he say to her? What if it was awkward. What if they both knew in the first few minutes that their reunion simply wasn't meant to be?

What if she didn't show at all? That could happen. He knew that. No sense in pretending that possibility wasn't looming out there, bigger than a water buffalo and twice as ugly.

But this vehicle coming now—it could be her.

Now he could tell that it was an SUV of some kind, which could certainly be a rental. He figured she would have flown into Amarillo, and four major car-rental companies operated out of that airport. It wasn't like it was some little rinky-dink outfit, so she could've—

The SUV took a left and kept going.

A minute passed.

Albert's thoughts returned to that night at the zoo. He had gone out at midnight and all was quiet. The gates were closed and chained. No sign of any problem whatsoever. The animals were calm.

He had fallen asleep after that, but woke at 2:35. He walked the grounds again, and as he neared the main entry gates, he heard something. Metal on metal. A chain rattling? Somebody attempting to enter? Then he was pretty sure he heard someone running away. Was it a person, or an animal trotting along the fence line? It could even be a wild deer outside the fence. He shined a powerful flashlight in that direction, but he saw nothing unusual. He waited for a full fifteen minutes, but he heard nothing more that concerned him.

Back inside, he dozed, but didn't really sleep.

He decided to make another round at 6:00. Surely if the kid from Dallas had planned some sort of vandalism, he would've tried it already. The sun would rise in an hour, but at the moment, it was dark outside. The three-quarter moon was obscured by a heavy blanket of clouds.

He went straight toward the entry gates. The flashlight was in his hands, but he didn't have it turned on. Didn't need it. He could walk these grounds blindfolded.

Then he saw it. There was somebody out there, using a small light as he fooled around with the inner gate. He had already made his way through the outer gate.

Albert should have turned around and called 911. Or he should've shouted from here to scare the person away. But that's not what he did.

He turned his flashlight on and jogged forward, yelling, "What are you doing? Get away from there!"

As he got within thirty feet, he could see that it was in fact the kid from that afternoon. The Dallas Cowboys fan. The kid raised his own flashlight—and a gun in his other hand. He immediately fired a shot and Albert instinctively hit the ground, covering his head. His flashlight hit the ground and went out.

He remembered screaming, "Don't shoot me!" and it made sense at the time. The kid wasn't here to kill anybody, was he? Albert hadn't recognized the truth yet. He thought the kid might just run away, given a chance.

But there was another shot. And another. Albert could feel the impact of one of the bullets in the ground very near his head.

And then somebody yelled, "Stop!"

It was confusing out there in the darkness, but Albert realized that a third person was present. After that, it all happened fast. The Dallas kid wheeled around and fired again, but the other person shot back. Just once, but it was enough. The kid from Dallas collapsed, and now it was hard to see anything at all.

It was hazy after that. Memories muddied by adrenaline.

Albert remembered picking up his flashlight and confirming that the kid was dead—but he wasn't from Dallas after all. The ID in his wallet said Framingham, and then Albert realized the truth. Carducci had sent him. But how? How had he discovered where Albert was? It didn't really matter, did it?

Albert had to act fast. There wasn't time to weigh his options. And what options could there possibly be?

Albert took the kid's wallet. Took the gun—a revolver. And now he saw a car parked on the shoulder of the highway. Not right outside the gate, but twenty yards south. A neon-green Ford Fiesta. Hard to miss.

Albert hurried back to his house and grabbed his getaway bag. Never thought he'd need it, but he was so glad he'd kept it ready all these years.

He stopped at his truck, but if he drove that, they'd know what to look for. So he went to the Fiesta and saw the keys in the ignition. He got in and just drove south. Maybe he'd change his mind later and decide it was time to stop running, but for now, he just drove. He just wanted some time to think.

He'd closed the outer gate behind him, but he couldn't lock it closed, because the chain had been cut. One of the animals must've nudged it open later. After that, the grass eaters among them were happy to find fresh grazing on the side of the highway, and the rest of them had probably followed out of curiosity.

It took a good thirty minutes for Albert's heart to stop racing. What now? Where would he go? Was there any hope at all?

Who the hell was that person who had saved him? After firing the shot, the person had simply stood there for a long moment, as if pondering what he had done—and what he should do next. Then he had turned and sprinted into the night.

But right before he had run, for a brief moment, the clouds had opened and the moonlight shone through. Albert saw a face, but shadows were cast across it, and he couldn't make out any features. A young man? Maybe. Difficult to tell.

He was wearing an orange jacket and carrying a backpack. That much Albert knew. But nothing else.

Maybe he'd share these details, sparse as they were, with John Marlin someday, or maybe he—

Another vehicle, this one coming from the west. The right direction, if it was Sylvia coming from Amarillo.

Albert took a deep breath.

The vehicle was closer now, and Albert saw that it was a larger luxury car. Maybe a Chrysler or a Cadillac. That was more Sylvia's style. Black car. Four doors. Definitely did not fit in with the flat, dusty landscape. Yes, a Chrysler.

The car slowed and stopped at the intersection, facing him. No blinker. Now just twenty yards away. Albert couldn't see the driver through the glare on the windshield.

Could the driver see him?

The Chrysler sat there for a long moment, then moved forward slowly.

Albert was holding his breath.

Then the Chrysler eased off the side of the road, toward Albert, and came to a stop in front of the truck.

He could see her now. He could see Sylvia. She was smiling, and maybe crying a little, too.

This was really happening.

They opened their doors at the same time.

47

Eight days after Caitlin McGregor's interview, on a Saturday, John Marlin was having a cup of coffee in a booth at the Kountry Kitchen at ten in the morning. Just a little quiet time before he got back out there. There were some hunting camps he wanted to check. It was always nice to get back to his regular routine—at least for a while.

Things hadn't concluded quite the way he'd hoped, but there were some bright spots.

Rodney Bauer was out of the hospital and healing just fine. The newspaper had run an article about him and his heroic behavior at the Blanco Dairy Queen. The girl who had called 911 and been grazed by a bullet had chosen to keep a low profile and had so far remained unnamed in the media.

Caitlin McGregor was doing well. Nicole had connected her with a therapist, but she didn't seem to need it. For now, it didn't appear that Caitlin would need to testify about anything, because the sheriff's office hadn't been able to build a case against Rory Grafmiller. They'd pulled some texts from his phone—including texts to and from Bryce Cauley—but none of them had anything to do with Albert Cortez or Anthony Carducci or Trevor Larkin. Rory's mother, the attorney, was refusing all requests for an interview. So there was no solid evidence to implicate Rory in anything.

That left Albert. Where was he right now? Nobody knew. Marlin was okay with that. Technically, Albert was a free man and could go wherever he wanted. The manslaughter charges from Massachusetts nineteen years earlier had long since reached the statute of limitations, and down here, there was no probable cause to arrest him. He was a person of interest in the shooting of Joseph Barella, but whoever had done it, it was likely an act of self-defense.

What would happen to the zoo? So far, Tracy Lavelle and the rest of the employees, minus Rory Grafmiller, had been taking care of the animals, but something would need to be done for the long term. There would be nothing to stop Albert from selling the place, if he wanted to. The only thing Albert had to worry about was Anthony Carducci. That might never change.

Carducci, like Rory Grafmiller, was facing no charges. There was absolutely no evidence he had talked to Joseph Barella about anything, much less attempting a hit on Albert. Carducci was a savvy criminal and had played his cards just right, building a wall of deniability for himself.

Meanwhile, just outside the plate-glass windows of the restaurant, traffic was flowing on Highway 281 and the sun was shining.

Marlin was about to leave when Red O'Brien's old Ford truck pulled into the lot and O'Brien stepped out. The front and rear glass still had not been repaired.

O'Brien came into the restaurant, looked around, spotted Marlin, and sat down across from him uninvited.

"You got a minute?" he asked.

"What's up?" Marlin asked.

"I've been thinking about something."

Marlin waited.

"Garrett came to see me before he left town," Red said. "He had this ring he found on the side of the road somewhere, and he gave it to me—to cover fixing my truck, or not, if it was fake."

Marlin was about to say that a lost item like that should've been reported to the police by Garrett when he'd first found it, and that O'Brien couldn't just take possession of the ring and do whatever he wanted with it, but quite frankly, Marlin didn't know if it was worth the battle.

"What kind of ring?" he asked.

"Diamond ring. Like an engagement ring. Just one big diamond. I took it to a jeweler in Austin and it turns out it isn't fake. It's real. And real valuable."

"Oh, yeah?" Marlin said.

O'Brien leaned in close and kept his voice low. "The guy said it was worth seven thousand bucks—at a minimum. Maybe up to eight or nine."

Now, however, Marlin would have to burst his bubble.

But before Marlin could say anything, O'Brien added, "Yeah, yeah, I know. I can't just keep it. Obviously somebody lost it, or it got stolen, or something, and now we gotta look for the righteous owner. That's why I'm talking to you. I'm hoping you can tell me what I need to do next."

"Just take it over to the sheriff's office and fill out a found-property form. Give as many details as you can. They'll explain everything."

"I have to leave it with them?"

"Yeah, you do."

"But if they don't find the owner, then it's all mine, right?"

"That's generally how it works. Some diamonds nowadays have tiny numbers etched on them, so they can be identified."

"Yeah, the guy in Austin said this one didn't have that."

"Did Garrett say where he found it?"

"Nope. I don't think he even remembers. Does that make it more likely I'd get it back?"

"I can't make any promises either way," Marlin said.

"Yeah, okay."

Marlin couldn't help but be curious. "If you get it back, what are you planning to do with it?" he asked.

"Well," Red said, "Nothing right away. I'll just hold on to it. Stick it in my safe. But then we'll see after that. I been seeing Mandy for a while, so...well...I don't know. Maybe I'll give it to her someday."

Marlin grinned at him. He had met Mandy and she was perfect for Red.

O'Brien looked a little alarmed and quickly said, "Don't say nothin' to nobody, okay?"

"Of course not," Marlin said.

"I might not even do that," O'Brien said. "I'm just thinking out loud."

"I understand."

"Hell, she might not even want it. You know how women are. Plus, she's way outta my league."

"I won't argue about that," Marlin said.

"Nice-looking lady, don't you think?" O'Brien asked.

"She's very pretty," Marlin said.

"And that rack," O'Brien said.

Marlin figured it was best to let that one go. "I hope it all works out for you," he said.

"Appreciate it," O'Brien said, sliding out from the booth. "You doin' all right otherwise?"

Marlin knew what O'Brien was asking. How was Marlin doing since the shooting?

"I'm doing just fine," Marlin said, "but thanks for asking. That means a lot."

O'Brien nodded and said, "I'll see ya later."

Marlin drained the last of his coffee, then checked his phone and saw that he'd missed a call earlier. It came from an unknown number, but the caller had left a voicemail.

Marlin put the phone up to his ear and listened.

Hey, John Marlin. This is Albert Cortez. I figured I'd better let somebody know that I'm alive and well, and that somebody is you. Don't you feel lucky? I also wanted to say thank you for saving my animals. I saw it on the news and you handled it great. I can't tell you how happy I was to see that. I'm planning to deed the place over to Tracy. She'll take good care of everything. But that's not why I called...I want to tell you what happened the night Joseph Barella was killed, and what happened before that. I hope you're comfortable, because this is going to take a few minutes...

Want to know when Ben Rehder's next novel will be released?

Subscribe to his email list at www.benrehder.com.

Have you discovered Ben Rehder's Roy Ballard Mysteries?

Turn the page for an excerpt from

GONE THE NEXT

GONE THE NEXT

1

The woman he was watching this time was in her early thirties. Thirty-five at the oldest. White. Well dressed. Upper middle class. Reasonably attractive. Probably drove a nice car, like a Lexus or a BMW. She was shopping at Nordstrom in Barton Creek Square mall. Her daughter — Alexis, if he'd overheard the name correctly — appeared to be about seven years old. Brown hair, like her mother's. The same cute nose. They were in the women's clothing department, looking at swimsuits. Alexis was bored. Fidgety. Ready to go to McDonald's, like Mom had promised. Amazing what you can hear if you keep your ears open.

He was across the aisle, in the men's department, looking at Hawaiian shirts. They were all ugly, and he had no intention of buying one. He stood on the far side of the rack and held up a green shirt with palm trees on it. But he was really looking past it, at the woman, who had several one-piece swimsuits draped over her arm. Not bikinis, though she still had the figure for it. Maybe she had stretch marks, or the beginnings of a belly.

He replaced the green shirt and grabbed a blue one covered with coconuts. Just browsing, like a regular shopper might do.

Mom was walking over to a changing room now. Alexis followed, walking stiff-legged, maybe pretending she was a monster. A zombie. Amusing herself.

He moved closer, to a table piled high with neatly folded cargo shorts. He pretended to look for a pair in his size. But he was watching in his peripheral vision.

"Wait right here," Mom said. She didn't look around. She was oblivious to his presence. He might as well have been a mannequin.

Alexis said something in reply, but he couldn't make it out.

"There isn't room, Lexy. I'll just be a minute."

And she shut the door, leaving Alexis all by herself.

~ ~ ~

When he first began his research, he'd been surprised by what *he'd found. He had expected the average parent to be watchful. Wary. Downright suspicious. That's how he would be if he had a child. A little girl. He'd guard her like a priceless treasure. Every minute of the day. But his assumptions were wrong. Parents were sloppy. Careless. Just plain stupid.*

He knew that now, because he'd watched hundreds of them. And their children. In restaurants. In shopping centers. Supermarkets. Playgrounds and parks. For three months he'd watched. Reconnaissance missions, like this one right now, with Alexis and her mom. Preparing. What he'd observed was encouraging. It wouldn't be as difficult as he'd assumed. When the time came.

But he had to use his head. Plan it out. Use what he'd learned. Doing it in a public place, especially a retail establishment, would be risky, because there were video surveillance systems everywhere nowadays. Some places, like this mall, even had security guards. Daycare centers were often fenced, and the front doors were locked. Schools were always on the lookout for strangers who —

"*You need help with anything?*"

He jumped, ever so slightly.

A salesgirl had come up behind him. Wanting to be helpful. Calling attention to him. Ruining the moment.

That was a good lesson to remember. Just because he was watching, that didn't mean he wasn't being watched, too.

2

The first time I ever heard the name Tracy Turner — on a hot, cloudless Tuesday in June — I was tailing an obese, pyorrheic degenerate named Wally Crouch. I was fairly certain about the "degenerate" part, because Crouch had visited two adult bookstores and three strip clubs since noon. Not that there's anything wrong with a little mature entertainment, but there's a point when it goes from bawdy boys-will-be-boys recreation to creepy pathological fixation. The pyorrhea was pure conjecture on my part, based solely on the number of Twinkie wrappers Crouch had tossed out the window during his travels.

Crouch was a driver for UPS and, according to my biggest client, he was also a fraud who was riding the workers' comp gravy train. In the course of a routine delivery seven weeks prior, Crouch had allegedly injured his lower back. A ruptured disk, the doctor said. Limited mobility and a twelve to sixteen-week recovery period. In the meantime, Crouch couldn't lift more than ten pounds without searing pain shooting up his spinal cord. But this particular quack had a checkered past filled with questionable diagnoses and reprimands from the medical board. My job was fairly simple, at least on paper: Follow Crouch discreetly until he proved himself a liar. Catch it on video. Testify, if necessary. Earn a nice paycheck. Continue to finance my sumptuous, razor's-edge lifestyle.

~ ~ ~

You'd think Crouch, having a choice in the matter, would've avoided rush-hour traffic and had a few more beers instead, but he left Sugar's Uptown Cabaret at ten after five and squeezed his way onto the interstate heading south. I followed in my seven-year-old Dodge Caravan. Beige. Try to find a vehicle less likely to catch someone's eye. The windows are deeply tinted and a scanner antenna is mounted on the roof, which are the only clues that the driver isn't a soccer mom toting her brats to practice.

Anyone whose vehicle doubles as a second home recognizes the value of a decent sound system. I'd installed a Blaupunkt, with Bose speakers front and rear. Total system set me back about two grand. Seems like overkill for talk radio, but that's what I was listening to when I heard the familiar alarm signal of the Emergency Alert System. I'd never known the system to be used for anything other than weather warnings, but not this time. It was an Amber Alert. A local girl had gone missing from her affluent West Austin neighborhood. Tracy Turner: six years old, blond hair, green eyes, three feet tall, forty-five pounds, wearing denim shorts and a pink shirt. My palms went sweaty just thinking about it. Then I heard she might be in the company of Howard Turner — her non-custodial father, a resident of Los Angeles — and I breathed a small sigh of relief. Listeners, they said, should keep an eye out for a green Honda with California plates.

Easy to read between the lines. Tracy's parents were divorced, and dad had decided he wanted to spend more time with his daughter, despite how the courts had ruled. Sad, but much better than a random abduction.

The announcer was repeating the message when my cell phone rang. I turned the radio volume down, answered, and my client — a senior claims adjuster at a big insurance company — said, "You nail him yet?"

"Christ, Heidi, it's only the third day."

"I thought you were good."

"That's a vicious rumor."

"Yeah, and I think you started it yourself. I'm starting to think you get by on your looks alone."

"That remark borders on sexual harassment, and you know how I feel about that."

"You're all for it."

"Exactly. Anyway, relax, okay? I'm on him twenty-four seven." Crouch had taken the Manor Road exit, and now he turned into his apartment complex, so I drove past, calling it a day. I didn't like lying to Heidi, but I had a meeting with a man named Harvey Blaylock in thirty minutes.

"Well, you'd better get something soon, because I've got another one waiting," Heidi said.

I didn't say anything, because a jerk in an F-150 was edging over into my lane.

"Roy?" she said.

"Yeah."

"I have another one for you."

"Have scientists come up with that device yet?"

"What device?"

"The one that allows you to be in two places at the same time."

"You really crack you up."

"Let me get this one squared away, then we'll talk, okay?"

"The quicker the better. Where are you? Has Crouch even left the house?"

"Oh, yeah. Been wandering all afternoon."

"Where to?"

"Uh, let's just say he seems to have an inordinate appreciation for the female form."

"Which means?"

"He's been visiting gentlemen's clubs."

A pause. "You mean tittie bars?"

"That's such a crass term. Oh, by the way, the Yellow Rose is looking for dancers. In case you decide to — "

She hung up on me.

~ ~ ~

I had the phone in my hands, so I went ahead and called my best friend Mia Madison, who works at an establishment I used to do business with on occasion. She tends bar at a tavern on North Lamar.

Boiling it down to one sentence, Mia is smart, funny, optimistic, and easy on the eyes. Expanding on the last part, because it's relevant, Mia stands about five ten and has long red hair that she likes to wear in a ponytail. Prominent cheekbones, with dimples beneath. The toned legs of a runner, though she doesn't run, but must walk ten miles a day during an eight-hour shift. When Mia gets dolled up — what she calls "bringing it" — she goes from being an attractive woman you'd certainly notice to a world-class head turner.

On one occasion, she revealed that she has a tattoo. Wouldn't show it to me, but she said — joking, I'm sure — that if I could guess what it was, and where it was, she'd let me have a look. Nearly a year later, I still hadn't given up.

"Is it Muttley?" I asked when she answered.

"Muttley? Who the hell is Muttley?"

"You know, that cartoon dog with the sarcastic laugh."

"You mean Scooby Doo?"

"No, the other one. Hangs with Dick Dastardly."

"I have no idea what you're talking about."

"Before your time, I guess. Are you at work?"

"Not till six. Just got out of the shower. I'm drying off."

"Need any help?"

"I think I can handle it," she said.

"Okay, next question. Want to earn a hundred bucks the easy way?" I said.

"Love to," she said. "When and where?"

3

Harvey Blaylock was maybe sixty, medium height, with neatly trimmed gray hair, black-framed glasses, a white short-sleeved shirt, and tan gabardine slacks. He looked like the kind of man who, if things had taken a slightly different turn, might've wound up as a forklift salesman, or, best case, a high-school principal in a small agrarian town.

In reality, however, Harvey Blaylock was a man who held tremendous sway over my future, near- and long-term. I intended to remain respectful and deferential.

Blaylock's necktie — green, with bucking horses printed on it — rested on his paunch as he leaned back in his chair, scanning the contents of a manila folder. I knew it was my file, because it said ROY W. BALLARD on the outside, typed neatly on a rectangular label. I'm quick to notice things like that.

Five minutes went by. His office smelled like cigarettes and Old Spice. Rays of sun slanted in through horizontal blinds on the windows facing west. As far as I could tell, we were the only people left in the building.

"I really appreciate you staying late for this," I said. "Would've been tough for me to make it earlier."

He grunted and continued reading, one hand drumming slowly on his metal desk. The digital clock on the wall above him read 6:03. On the bookshelf, tucked among a row of wire-bound notebooks, was a framed photo of a young boy holding up a small fish on a line.

"Boy, was I surprised to hear that Joyce retired," I said. "She seemed too young for that. So spry and youthful." Joyce being Blaylock's predecessor. My previous probation officer. A true bitch on wheels. Condescending. Domineering. No sense of humor. "I'll have to send her a card," I said, hoping it didn't sound sarcastic.

Blaylock didn't answer.

I was starting to wonder if he had a reading disability. I'm no angel — I wouldn't have been in this predicament if I were — but my file couldn't have been more than half a dozen pages long. I was surprised that a man in his position, with several hundred probationers in his charge, would spend more than thirty seconds on each.

Finally, Blaylock, still looking at the file, said, "Roy Wilson Ballard. Thirty-six years old. Divorced. Says you used to work as a news cameraman." He had a thick piney-woods accent. Pure east Texas. He peered up at me, without moving his head. Apparently, it was my turn to talk.

"Yes, sir. Until about three years ago."

"When you got fired."

"My boss and I had a personality conflict," I said, wondering how detailed my file was.

"Ernie Crenshaw."

"That's him."

"You broke his nose with a microphone stand."

Fairly detailed, apparently.

"Well, yeah, he, uh — "

"You got an attitude problem, Ballard?"

"No, sir."

"Temper?"

I started to lie, but decided against it. "Occasionally."

"That what happened in this instance? Temper got the best of you?"

"He was rude to one of the reporters. He called her a name."

"What name was that?"

"I'd rather not repeat it."

"I'm asking you to."

"Okay, then. He called her Doris. Her real name is Anne."

His expression remained frozen. Tough crowd.

I said, "Okay. He called her a cunt."

Blaylock's expression still didn't change. "To her face?"

"Behind her back. He was a coward. And she didn't deserve it. This guy was a world-class jerk. Little weasel."

"You heard him say it?"

"I was the one he was talking to. It set me off."

"So you busted his nose."

"I did, sir, yes."

Perhaps it was my imagination, but I thought Harvey Blaylock gave a nearly imperceptible nod of approval. He looked back at the file. "Now you're self-employed. A legal videographer. What is that exactly?"

"Well, uh, that means I record depositions, wills, scenes of accidents. Things like that. But proof of insurance fraud is my specialty. The majority of my business. Turns out I'm really good at it."

"Describe it for me."

"Sir?"

"Give me a typical day."

I recited my standard courtroom answer. "Basically, I keep a subject under surveillance and hope to videotape him engaging in an activity that's beyond his alleged physical limitations." Then I added, "Maybe lifting weights, or dancing. Playing golf. Doing the hokey-pokey."

No smile.

"Not a nine-to-five routine, then."

"No, sir. More like five to nine."

Blaylock mulled that over for a few seconds. "So you're out there, working long hours, sometimes through the night, and you start taking pills to keep up with the pace. That how it went?"

Until you've been there, you have no idea how powerless and naked you feel when someone like Harvey Blaylock is authorized to dig through your personal failings with a salad fork.

"That sums it up pretty well," I said.

"Did it work?"

"What, the pills?"

He nodded.

"Well, yeah. But coffee works pretty well, too."

"You were also drinking. That's why you got pulled over in the first place, and how they ended up finding the pills on you. You got a drinking problem?"

I thought of an old joke. *Yeah, I got a drinking problem. Can't pay my bar tab.* "I hope not," I said, which is about as honest as it gets. "At one point maybe I did, but I don't know for sure. Probably not. But that's what you'd expect someone with a drinking problem to say, right?"

"Had a drink since your court date?"

"No, sir. I'm not allowed to. Even though the Breathalyzer said I was legal."

"Not even one drink?"

"Not a drop. Joyce, gave me a piss te — I mean a urine test, last month, and three in the past year. I passed them all. That should be in the file."

"You miss it?" Blaylock asked. "The booze?"

I honestly thought about it for a moment.

"Sometimes, yeah," I said. "More than I would've guessed, but not enough to freak me out or anything. Sometimes, you know, I just crave a cold beer. Or three. But if I had to quit eating Mexican food, I'd miss that, too. Maybe more than beer."

Blaylock slowly sat forward in his chair and dropped my file, closed, on his desk. "Here's the deal, son. Ninety-five percent of the people I deal with are shitbags who think the world is their personal litter box. I can't do them any good, and they don't want me to. Most of 'em are locked up again within a year, and all I can say is good riddance. Then I see guys like you who make a stupid mistake and get caught up in the system. You probably have a decent life ahead of you, but you don't need me to tell you that, and it really doesn't matter what I think anyway. So I'll just say this: Follow the rules and you can put all this behind you. If you need any help, I'll do what I can. I really will. But if you fuck up just one time, it's like tipping over a row of dominoes. Then it's out of your control, and mine, too. You follow me?"

~ ~ ~

After the meeting, I swung by a Jack-In-The-Box, then sat outside Wally Crouch's place for a few hours, just in case. He stayed put.

I got home just as the ten o'clock news was coming on. Howard Turner had been located in a motel in Yuma City, Arizona, there on business. Police had verified his alibi. He had been nowhere near Texas, and the cops had no reason to believe he was involved.

So Tracy Turner was still missing, and that fact created a void in my chest that I hadn't felt in years.

ABOUT THE AUTHOR

Ben Rehder lives with his wife near Austin, Texas, where he was born and raised. His novels have made best-of-the-year lists in *Publishers Weekly, Library Journal, Kirkus Reviews,* and *Field & Stream. Buck Fever* was a finalist for the Edgar Award, and *Get Busy Dying* was a finalist for the Shamus Award. For more information, visit www.benrehder.com.

OTHER NOVELS BY BEN REHDER

Buck Fever
Bone Dry
Flat Crazy
Guilt Trip
Gun Shy
Holy Moly
The Chicken Hanger
The Driving Lesson
Gone The Next
Hog Heaven
Get Busy Dying
Stag Party
Bum Steer
If I Had A Nickel
Point Taken
Now You See Him
Last Laugh
A Tooth For A Tooth
Lefty Loosey
Shake And Bake

For more information, visit www.benrehder.com.

Made in the USA
Monee, IL
04 March 2021